Soup

in the

CITY

To Matt
Breath -
I hope you enjoy!
Best wishes,
Kelly

Soup

in the

CITY

KELLY HOLLINGSWORTH

Soup in the City. Copyright © 2009 by Kelly Hollingsworth. All rights reserved.
Printed in the United States of America. No part of this book may be used or reproduced
in any manner without written permission, except in the case of brief quotations
embodied in critical articles or reviews. For information, contact Margate Media
Group, LLC, 9129 West Driftwood Drive, Coeur d'Alene, Idaho, 83814.

ISBN-13:   978-0-9816958-0-8
ISBN-10:   0-9816958-0-9

First Edition: January 2009

10 9 8 7 6 5 4 3 2 1

CONTENTS

CHAPTER 1:

Thanksgiving Hangover

- - - - - - -

MONDAY, NOVEMBER 26, 2007

Monday morning. My eyes are cemented shut. I'm sure this has something to do with all the frosting I ate this weekend. I pry my lids open, roll out of bed and assess my ability to bend. It's not good. My lower back feels tighter than a tourniquet. Tighter than my jeans, if that's even possible. My hamstrings, which actually resemble ham hocks, are even tighter.

I resolve to commence a disciplined study of some exotic form of yoga as I strain to pluck my cold, wrinkled jeans off the floor. They've been crumpled in the same spot for days, a reproachful pile of denim reminding me I'd better get myself together at some point soon.

I shake out the jeans and step into them slowly, one foot at a time, saying a silent prayer that goes unheeded. The size gods are oblivious to me this morning and the fabric's slow ascent halts abruptly at mid-thigh. At some point during my two-day binge, my saddlebags became a formidable enemy set on destroying my life.

I take a deep breath and grunt as I wrestle the fabric upward. It doesn't move, so I thrust my body forward in a series of leaping pelvic tucks as I jerk on the belt loops. After many of these frog-leaps, the jeans are on.

If I had more time, I would patent this process. Make a video of it and sell it on Amazon.com for $19.95 to slothful, gluttonous girls just like me. But of course there's no time for such entrepreneurial endeavors, because I still have to find a way to zip these unyielding jeans.

Now I'm sweating, which is unfortunate because damp denim is not fat-friendly. I grasp the waistband, hold my breath and wriggle, tugging and pulling and straining against the fabric until my offending flesh is as tightly packed as I can get it. Then I fall back on the bed, inhale and zip the jeans like a corset.

At this point, fastening the button isn't difficult, but the end result is bad. The snap digs into my flesh in a way I know will leave a very significant dent, possibly even a bruise.

I head to the bathroom to get a visual, but my steps are impeded by the thick seam at my crotch, the place where five or six layers of fabric come together. It cuts me in two like a ripcord. Straddling a tightrope naked would be more pleasant. I slow down and take mincing, stiff steps the rest of the way.

In the unflattering overhead light of my small bathroom, things look worse than I anticipated. My over-processed bangs are frizzy from sweat and exertion and my face is red and puffy. I stand on tiptoes to check out the jeans. From every angle, the fabric pulls and strains.

I look like a linebacker in drag.

This is ridiculous. I look ridiculous. I resolve to eat nothing but eggs when I meet Courtney for breakfast. I'm not hungry anyway. As I peel off the jeans, I decide I can have half-and-half in my coffee because there's no carbs in it. That's it. I resolve to eat nothing but carbs until my birthday. I mean, nothing but protein. And vegetables. But no starchy ones.

I abandon the jeans on the bathroom floor.

Although I can move freely now, I continue to walk as if I'm wearing snowshoes to avoid the disturbing feeling of my thighs rubbing together. I go to my dresser and yank a drawer open. Stacks of identical black exercise pants wait at the ready for just this sort of emergency, which frankly occurs all too often these days.

I grab a pair from the top of the stack and pull them on with relative ease. No muss, no fuss. Whatever this miracle fabric is forgives all the garbage I shoveled in my mouth this weekend. Still, the pants feel a little tighter than they did last week.

Courtney will think I'm on my way to the gym. She'll be jealous because she has to go to the office. Or at least she'll pretend to be.

The truth is, though, I'm not a member of any gym. In Manhattan, it's just too damn expensive. And I mean this in every possible respect. Emotionally, psychologically, spiritually, financially. Any way you slice it, I can't afford it.

I spend the next thirty-five minutes applying invisible makeup. When I'm finished, the tell-tale signs of my two-day binge barely show. Only a tiny double chin gives me away, and if I wear my hair down Courtney won't be able to see it.

I grab my keys and slide my Dolce & Gabbana sunglasses on as I walk to the elevator. I practice stepping in a bouncy sort of way, as if I have all the energy in the world.

"Acting as if" is my new thing. I read about it in a fashion magazine I used to subscribe to but which I no longer buy, because every issue included some stupid, depressing article about teenage sex slaves in Darfur or wherever.

Anyway, the point is that however you want your life to be, you just act as if it's that way already. Eventually, the acting becomes reality. I've been at it for a few weeks now and I'm finally starting to get the hang of it.

For example, this morning when I meet Courtney I will not tell her I spent the entire Thanksgiving weekend on my couch with my remote and a jilted wedding cake I bought on clearance from the bakery around the corner. All Courtney needs to know is that I'm hung over, which is certainly true enough. Maybe she'll think I was actually invited to go somewhere. And if Courtney starts to see me as someone who gets invited places on the weekends, eventually she will invite me to go some places with her. On the weekends, I mean. I see plenty of Courtney during the week, when her rich, handsome boyfriend is hard at work managing his zillion dollar hedge fund.

This is the theory, anyway. To work out the kinks in the practical application, I've invented a boyfriend named Simon Montrose, who serves as the perfect fictitious companion on my imaginary outings.

Although Simon Montrose exists only in my mind, the image is quite vivid. Of course he's very tall, and since there's nothing worse than a weak chin he has a strong, well-sculpted face. He has brown hair, blue eyes and manages a phantom hedge fund from his hypothetical home in London. He plays squash every Wednesday and drinks Grey Goose martinis, except on Sunday mornings when, being English, he drinks Pims with enormous garnishes that look like a huge salad.

My relationship with Simon Montrose is going pretty well, at least for now. He's there when I need him and happily ensconced in London when I don't. But I'm anticipating trouble because I've never been to London, and at some point someone is going to expect me to answer questions about it. In other words, eventually my lack of foresight in setting the location of Simon's fictitious residence could bite me in the butt.

I try not to think about this as I walk into the diner.

Courtney is sitting at our regular table. She is beautifully dressed in a miniscule Armani suit that looks slightly too big on her tiny frame.

"So," she says, stirring cream into her coffee with a twist of her bony little wrist. "What's Simon going to get you for your birthday?"

Courtney and I have known each other since college. Our birthdays are two days apart. Hers is coming up on Thursday and mine is on Saturday. We'll celebrate on Friday, the day in between, like we always do. Anyway, whatever Richard is getting for her, I want to top.

I lean forward conspiratorially. "Don't tell anyone." I dart my eyes from side to side, as if there's a danger anyone in the restaurant is listening, while my brain frantically races for a gift more extravagant than whatever Courtney is likely to get.

She leans forward. "Tell me."

I click my tongue against the back of my teeth, raise my eyebrows and smile. "I think it's a sable coat."

Her eyes open wide. "Are you kidding me?" Her voice is low, uncharacteristically low for Courtney.

I sit up and shrug. "I know. Crazy, isn't it?"

She shakes her head. Her mouth is sort of open, like she's watching a train wreck in slow motion. "And you just met this guy. I can't believe it."

I take a sip of my coffee, set my cup down and shake my hair back. Then I remember the burgeoning layer of fat under my chin. I duck my head and take a sip of my water, which conveniently puts my double chin back under the protective cover of my hair, and look at Courtney over the edge of my water glass. "What do you think Richard is going to get you?"

She sighs. "We're going to St. Maarten for a week."

Courtney is one of those girls men love to whisk away to the islands, which is mainly because she has the body of an adolescent male that is oddly accessorized with alarmingly voluminous breasts. She pretends she doesn't like it but I know she does because she works harder at bikini-line maintenance than any girl I know. Not that I actually know any other girls, but you get the idea.

"That sounds nice," I say. "Don't you think that's nice?"

"I guess so. I just wish he would give me something a little more . . . tangible."

She's jealous of my fictitious coat. I can tell. I feel bad for lying to her. "Well," I say. "It will serve as a nice distraction from the size of my ass. The truth is any girl who looks good in a bathing suit doesn't need a sable."

Courtney sips her coffee and pushes her long, curly red hair behind her ear. "Why are you so sure it's a sable? Isn't that a very expensive gift?"

For a second, I can't believe she could be this hostile after the compliment I just gave her. But she's been my friend for a long time so I shrug it off.

"Oh," I say, trying to be breezy while I scan the menu. "I may have seen the receipt or something. What are you going to have?"

Just then the waiter approaches. He's in tight black slacks and a white apron, which also is pretty darn tight.

"You look exactly like Nicole Kidman," he says to Courtney. "Did anyone ever tell you that?"

Courtney laughs. "Once in a while. I'll have oatmeal with extra brown sugar." She closes her menu and hands it to the waiter, who is clearly smitten with her in spite of his flaming homosexuality. "And a side of bacon," she says.

He turns to me. I wait for him to ask if people often tell me I look like Roseanne Barr. Mercifully, he refrains.

I'm about to order a Denver omelet with no toast and no hash browns, but suddenly my high-protein order seems too pathetically Atkins, too retro, too loserville for words.

I look at Courtney, who sits in blissful ignorance of the staggering amount of carbs in her order. Then I look back at the waiter, who is staring at Courtney again. "I'll have the same." I shove the menu into the waiter's unsuspecting hands, which he correctly interprets as his signal to leave.

Now Courtney is looking at me with an amused expression. "You never eat oatmeal."

"Really," I say. "That's funny. I thought I did."

I want to change the subject but I can't think of anything else to say because I'm amazed anyone could eat so many carbs and stay so skinny. Maybe what I'll do is just start eating everything Courtney eats. She's impervious to sugar and any fat she consumes goes straight to her chest. "What did you eat yesterday?"

My tone is so demanding her answer comes right out, like a belch that follows a quick punch in the stomach.

"A pint of Häagen-Dazs and three vodka cranberries."

"That's it?"

"Well, that and a few French fries at dinner."

I hate Courtney. But since she's my only girlfriend in New York, I keep this to myself.

The waiter returns with our oatmeal. Courtney dumps both containers of brown sugar into her bowl and adds several glugs of half-and-half and a few pats of butter.

I do the same.

She stirs, I stir.

When the oatmeal looks like cookie batter, we eat.

It tastes better than I deserve. Although I'm not remotely hungry, I eat bite after bite. When it gets too sweet, I take a few bites of bacon to refresh my palate and forge ahead.

Courtney, however, is distracted with texting her boyfriend. When she's finished, she glances at her mostly untouched plate and then looks at me. My food is gone, of course, but she pretends not to notice.

"He's started calling me bunny lately," she says. "Do you think I should be offended?"

I pause from licking brown sugar off my spoon and think about this. "Absolutely. Anytime a rich, handsome, successful hedge fund manager calls me bunny, I kick him to the curb without hesitation."

She laughs and looks at her watch. "I have to get to the office. What are you doing today?"

"Oh, you know," I say. "The usual."

"Must be nice," she says. "Maybe I'll get there someday."

Like me, Courtney raises money for hedge funds. But my efforts are almost purely theoretical because the only money I ever raised was eighty million dollars from a bank that was misguided enough to invest in a hedge fund I recommended, which happens to be managed by Courtney's boyfriend.

As a one-hit wonder in hedge funds, I make about twenty-five grand a month, for which I do absolutely nothing.

Because Courtney works full-time, she thinks I'm successful. But I know better.

The waiter sets our check between us. Without looking at it, each of us flicks a twenty-dollar bill in its vicinity. The Manhattan single. I go through them faster than breath mints.

"I want to see your coat when you get it," she says. We stand and give each other air kisses. "Can you meet for a drink on Friday?"

"A drink?" I'm surprised. We always have our birthday dinner together.

She turns and walks out of the restaurant. I follow. "Well," she says. "It's just that Richard wants to take me out after."

"Oh," I say. "Of course. Just let me know where and when."

"I'll text you," she says. More air kisses. I watch her as she walks up Madison Avenue toward her office on her enviably long legs. They're too skinny, if you ask me.

But no one ever does.

After my breakfast with Courtney, I walk toward the park, pull out my cell phone and dial my friend Fig. His real name is Anton but I like to call him Fig in honor of Anton Fig, who evidently is a famous drummer or musician or something.

Fig comes from old tobacco money and has one of those apartments overlooking Central Park that only exist in movies. I have rollerbladed around his terrace more times than I can count just to prove it's large enough to do so. Once I even did it sober.

Fig has never had a job but he does spend a few hours a week giving his family's money away, which eases everyone's guilt about where it all came from. His career as a philanthropist leaves him plenty of time to date athletic adolescents who would never think to wear makeup because they just don't need any. This explains why things between Fig and me have never gotten more physical than a few bouts of drunken rollerblading.

Also, Fig thinks I'm a pathetic drama queen. Unfortunately, I play into this illusion more regularly than I care to admit.

Also, Fig's nickname for me is Figlet. I try to interpret this affectionately but I am not unaware of its darker implications.

Fig answers his phone right away. "Hello," he says. He always says it the same way, with a cheery upturn at the end. I secretly believe he doesn't answer the phone this way for anyone but me.

"It's Figlet," I say. "What are you doing?"

"I'm on my way to a knife-skills class at the Culinary Institute. What are you doing?"

Fig likes to cook. His girlfriends like him to cook. The knife-skills class was a gift from his latest girlfriend, whose name is something like

Ashley Nicole or Nicole Ashley. I can't really remember the details, but suffice it to say that it's two first names strung together in a way that's supposed to convey she's actually a real person and not merely a caricature of a person with perfect ringlets and a tiny ass.

For a second I wonder if I should tell the truth. "If you must know, I'm going for a walk in the park."

He pauses. "I thought you were going to work today." His tone is a little more disgusted than I would like it to be.

I hate Fig. This is suddenly very clear to me. But I don't want to hurt his feelings so I say nothing.

"Did you think I wouldn't remember?" he demands.

"I can't work today," I say. "I have to walk at least four hours."

This tells him I binged.

"How bad was it?" he asks.

"Two days."

We no longer catalog the binges in terms of food items consumed. Now, the binge diary is a chronicle of the length of each binge. I used to report in hours. Lately, it's days.

"Do you think you should get gastric bypass?" he asks.

"You have to be obese for that." I look both ways as I cross Fifth against the light. "Anyway, those people all wind up raging alcoholics."

"At this point that would be an improvement," he says. "You can't keep doing this to yourself."

"I know, I know." Mentally, I wave him away. I'm in the park now and eager to start walking. I just want to forget about everything I ate in the last two days and move forward with damage control. I will walk a minimum of four hours and will stop only when my feet literally have no walking left in them. Hopefully by then I'll feel some circulation moving into the slabs of fat cemented to my butt and thighs. This daily dislodging effort, coupled with a diet of nothing but steamed shrimp, raw broccoli and espresso, should have me back in my jeans in a week.

"Avery, I'm serious. We have to figure out what's going on with you."

"Well," I say. "I think I was upset."

He pauses again, but this time I don't think he's disgusted. "What were you upset about?"

"I think The Tool is using me for sex."

The Tool is the guy I've been seeing, the real guy, as opposed to my imaginary boyfriend Simon. I call him The Tool because it's so appropriate it would be crazy to call him anything else. Well, maybe The Knob also would work now that I think about it. In any case, I've suspected he's been using me for sex since our first date. But given certain recent events, I must conclude this suspicion is actually more like a bona fide fact, or maybe even a universal law of nature.

"Now we're getting somewhere," Fig says. "What finally clued you in?"

"Well," I say. I pause because I'm walking pretty fast now and I have to gasp for air.

"Slow down and tell me."

"It's like this. I was at his place on Friday . . ."

"He ordered in again?"

"Right."

Fig is silent for a minute. "Did you pay?"

I take a few gulps of air and ignore the question. "Anyway, I reminded him my birthday was this weekend and he said he wanted to take me to a museum."

"A museum." Fig's voice is completely flat.

"On Saturday afternoon." I'm wheezing now and my stomach hurts.

"Oh, Jesus," Fig says.

I exhale loudly. "I know. It's really bad, isn't it?"

"It ain't good," Fig says. "Did you know he was seeing someone else?"

"Not officially." I struggle to stand upright in spite of the slicing pain in my side. I think I'm moving at lightning speed until an old lady passes me. I look away from her so I can focus on my conversation with Fig. "But I guess it's obvious now, right?"

At this point, I have to pull the phone away from my head because the sound of Fig pounding his phone into a hard surface is extremely painful to my over-caffeinated ears. After several whacks, he comes back on the line. He doesn't say anything but I can hear him breathing—snorting, actually—in an angry and frustrated sort of way.

"Okay," I say. "I guess it's been obvious all along. What do I do?"

"Avery, you're done with this guy. You have to dump him. You know this."

I sigh. "I know. I just get so confused."

"What is there to be confused about?" Fig is yelling now, something he almost never does.

"Well, he says he wants to date me."

"Avery, men don't pick up the phone and threaten to date women they're interested in. They just date them. That guy is a sociopath."

"He's not a sociopath." I speak with great certainty but eventually I crumple under the weight of the truth. I clutch the phone to my head and plod along looking at the ground. "Okay," I say. "So how do we know he's a sociopath?"

"Imagine you're deaf," Fig says. "Imagine you've never heard a word he's said to you. Just from looking at his actions, is there any way the things he's said could possibly be construed as true?"

I have nothing to say to this. Fig is such a know-it-all sometimes. Plus crazy. If I never heard The Tool's bullshit, how could I possibly assess whether it was true or not?

"We're done here," Fig says. "I've done all I can do for you on this topic." His voice is tight and clipped in the way it always is when he's had it with me.

"I know," I say. "It's a bad situation." My voice trails off. "I'll work it out somehow."

I brighten when I consider that maybe The Tool will hear about my hypothetical boyfriend Simon Montrose, the hedge fund manager who showers me with extravagant gifts, and will be whipped into an insane, jealous frenzy that will cause him to fall madly in love with me. Then Fig will have to eat his cruel words. Without jelly.

"Call me later," Fig says. "And stay the hell away from the donuts."

I hang up but dial back just a few seconds later. "What does a sable coat cost these days?"

"Hold on." I listen to him clicking on his keyboard for a few minutes. Fig is great at almost any kind of research because he has so much spare time. Philanthropy is a very easy profession.

"You can't afford it," he concludes.

"How much?"

"The cheapest one I found is almost two hundred grand."

"That must be new," I say. "I think I could get a used one for less." Gently used, of course. I keep walking while I do some mental math.

"Avery, you can't afford it. Put the credit cards down and back away before someone gets hurt."

"Okay," I say. I hang up, silence my phone, zip it back into my pocket and commence walking in earnest. Fig just has no idea what it takes to get anywhere these days.

When I return to my apartment, I have an e-mail from The Tool. There's no message in the message. Just a link I'm supposed to click on.

I click. A website with unflattering photos of Jennifer Love Hewitt in a bikini appears on my screen.

She looks much better in a bathing suit than I ever would, if I were misguided enough to put one on, that is.

Right then and there, I decide The Tool is a giant asshole. I daintily click the screen closed and resolve never to take his calls again. Or for at least a week, at which point my jeans should fit again and everyone will be sorry. The Tool most of all.

I just hope by then he's realized I'm not speaking to him.

Fig calls me later that night as I'm soaking my aching feet. "How do you feel?"

I take a sip of seltzer, which is calorie-free and is supposed to settle my bloated stomach, and lay back on the couch. "As well as can be expected," I say. "You?"

"We're going for a drink. Want to come?"

"You and Ashley?"

"Nicole," he says.

"Okay," I say. "Once and for all. Her first name is Nicole and her last name is Ashley?"

"That's right," he says. "Nicole Ashley."

"Surely you realize I'm far too fat to have drinks with such a person."

"Avery, we're talking about fifteen or twenty pounds here. Do you really think that warrants solitary confinement?"

Fig has never understood the reverse-magnifier effect of Manhattan, which basically slashes acceptable weight tolerances by at least 15 percent. In other words, a body that is socially acceptable, or maybe even hot, anywhere else in the country is completely disgusting in New York.

Anyway, Fig calls me voluptuous, but he's insane because voluptuous implies a buxom shapeliness that I just don't have. With me, all the extra weight is concentrated on my butt, hips and thighs. It's as if I came equipped with my own airbags in the event of a crash landing.

In any case, I don't bother to scold him, because he might be on to something. Self-imposed seclusion is a tactic that never even occurred to me, but now that he's brought it up I can totally see the wisdom. With no social pressure to eat, I'll easily shed my ugly outer layer. Also, in protective isolation I won't have to worry about releasing the silent but deadly gas currently afflicting me thanks to my shrimp and broccoli regimen. And when I emerge from my cozy cocoon, I'll be a glamorous, gorgeous butterfly flitting about the city in the teensiest clothes imaginable. "You know," I say. "I actually think a few weeks of solitary could work."

"Oh, God," he says. "Forgive me for fanning the flames of this madness. I'll call you tomorrow. Do you think you might be sane by then?"

I take another sip of seltzer as I consider the question. "I wouldn't count on it."

CHAPTER 2:

The Last Gasp of November

- - - - - - -

NOVEMBER 27 – 30, 2007

On Tuesday morning, I spend an hour getting ready for another day of walking around the park. This process is pretty involved because any good purge, walking included, necessarily involves some wear and tear, and you just won't get the most out of it unless you take sufficient precautionary measures.

For example, when walking is your purge of choice, the standard pedicure where they file the toenails straight across simply won't do. You have to clip the corners of the nails so they don't cut into the sides of your toes when your arches give out and your feet start rolling inward. Also, a pre-treatment of Icy Hot on your hip flexors is usually required after the first day of a serious walking purge, because they just can't take the pressure like the rest of the body can. Last, you have to stop by the athletic store and buy a bunch of those ultra-padded, extra-wicking socks used by marathon runners because eventually the weave in lesser-grade socks digs into your feet like grains of uncooked rice.

I buy ten pairs. This sets me back a hundred and twenty bucks, but I don't have a choice. My old socks have lost a lot of their cushioning and some even have holes and blood stains.

Once I've paid for the socks, I go to a bench in the store's shoe department and change into a fresh pair. They feel so good I'm optimistic I can walk for most of the day. Or at least six hours, anyway.

On my way to the park, I pull out my cell phone and put in a call to Providence Securities.

Providence Securities is the firm where I hang my securities license. Although I do absolutely nothing professionally, or even professional, for that matter, I'm required to maintain my status as a general securities representative so I can receive my big fat referral fee each month. The hedge fund pays the entire fee to Providence. Providence cashes the check, keeps 10 percent for the trouble of dealing with me and cuts a check to me for the rest, usually around twenty-five grand. This is my paycheck, and in spite of its size, it never lasts until the next one comes around.

Rob, the owner of the firm, answers the phone. Providence is a very small shop.

"Avery St. George," he says. "To what do I owe this pleasure?"

"It's that time of the month again. I just wanted to let you know I'll be by later to pick up my check."

I can hear him sorting through papers. "As much as we'd love to see you, Avery, the referral fee has not arrived yet."

"Oh, come on, Rob. You know they're good for it. Can't you just advance me my share?"

He hesitates, but only for a second. The sad truth is I'm the biggest salesperson he has. Poor bastard.

"Okay, Avery. I guess I can do that. When should I expect you?"

"Around noon, give or take. I'll swing by on my way through the park."

"Do you want to have lunch?"

I hesitate. "Okay. Maybe we can come up with something for me to work on."

"Maybe," he says. "But I won't hold my breath."

I wish Rob would make more of an effort to conceal the fact that he thinks I'm a giant fuck-up. But I decide not to tell him this until I get my advance. I'm going to ask for two months, which will give me just enough to buy the gently used sable I found on eBay last night. I'll have to live on credit cards for a while after that, but whatever. I consider it an investment in my future.

If I hustle, I'll take delivery of The Coat just in time to have drinks with Courtney, at which point I'll be the girl who inspires sable birthday presents.

I can only imagine what great things will happen to me once everyone sees that.

When I'm finished walking that afternoon, I stop at the bank to deposit my big fat check.

The teller hands me a deposit slip. "There's a hold on the funds," she says. "You can't draw on them for five business days."

"This is my paycheck," I say. "They usually let me have the money right away."

She leaves to go talk to someone and comes back with permission to lift the hold, which means I now have fifty thousand dollars at my immediate disposal. When I return home, I'm somewhat giddy but the feeling quickly subsides as I pick up the phone and order yet another meal of shrimp and broccoli from the take-out place down the street.

When I'm finished eating, I spend the rest of the evening fighting with myself about whether to buy The Coat.

Later that night, I'm lying in bed pondering the issue when it occurs to me that being a girl in Manhattan is sort of like being a chicken. I know because my grandmother used to keep a chicken coop when I was young.

There was one chicken, Chicken George, who was pecked by all the other chickens. He was too small, so they didn't like him. And they wouldn't let him near the food, which only made things worse.

Every day, I took Chicken George out of the coop and let him run around in the grass and eat bugs. When he was big enough, the other chickens forgot they didn't like him and started letting him belly up to the food dish.

This experience serves as the theoretical underpinning for my newly-formulated rule of dating and social life, which I refer to as the Jackie Kennedy Concept.

Here's how it works: Once a woman is pursued by a highly regarded man, she becomes attractive to other highly regarded men. And then she becomes interesting to the women of their flock, who want to know what makes her so successful with the men.

It's like my friend Courtney. Once I introduced her to Richard and they started dating, all kinds of men found her fascinating. And she was invited to lots of interesting places, by women and men, with or without Richard.

Like chickens in a coop, people started to smell something on Courtney. Something good.

In playing my little "as if" games, I don't feel like I'm lying as much as I'm trying to get some of that good smelling stuff to rub off on me.

And where's the harm in that? I slide out of bed, walk to my computer and open it. The blue light illuminates my dark bedroom. I smile a slow smile as I enter the eBay site and type in "Russian Sable."

The Coat appears. It's perfect and I do not hesitate, in spite of the very reliable mink already hanging in my closet.

No one ever talks about this, but the truth is mink is on the low end of the food chain because any idiot with a credit card can have one. I bought my mink at an end-of-season sale for a measly five thousand bucks. It should last twenty years, so the cost per year, even when you add in storage and cleaning, is probably less than five hundred dollars.

In other words, when you crunch the numbers, mink is a very frugal purchase. It's serviceable and practical in a way that almost nothing else is.

Better still, you can use a reasonably good mink to cover your behemoth backside in the same boring black dress at dinner after dinner, at least for a few years. By now, though, I need something new. I've worn my mink so many times I'm sure people are starting to get the idea it's nothing more than camouflage for my oddly misshapen lower-half.

Sable, on the other hand, is never subterfuge, because a sable kind of woman is never afflicted by cellulite, extra pounds or the insecurities that go with them. Women who wear sable do not apologize. For anything.

Also, sable is never serviceable or boring. It's pure, show-stopping drama and shines on its wearer accordingly. Even in jaded Manhattan, people take notice, which means sable is the blunt instrument that bludgeons all other competitors in the violent social battlefield that is Manhattan.

In a sable, I definitely will seem like the kind of woman who wouldn't dream of buying her own furs.

As I mull this over, my mind begins to purr. For a mere fifty thousand dollars, I can buy that life. I can become that woman. I have the ability, the desire and the technology. More importantly, I have the cash. With a quick click of the "Buy it Now" button, I'm on my way.

I feel no remorse. A deep sense of calm envelopes me as I shift into the pristine state of awareness that comes from recognizing one's true purpose in life. As I stare my destiny squarely in the face, I realize that everything else in my life is just details, which are no match for an enterprising New York woman with an Internet connection and a PayPal account.

I arrange for The Coat's shipping and pay extra for express delivery.

On Friday morning, I awaken with an extraordinary sense of possibility. Anything can happen, and because today is Coat day, I'm fairly vibrating with the idea that it will.

I intend to take extra care with my appearance but by the time I've showered and applied twenty minutes' worth of makeup, I'm starving. My hair is a mess so I decide my brand of glamour involves lots of hats because I need food. Now.

The thing no one ever tells you about hats, and diamonds, for that matter, is that one should deliberately buy them too large, thereby making one's ass appear tiny in contrast. In fact, since we're on the subject, the whole goal with diamonds is to have people walk away muttering, "She's really much too thin and those diamonds are *way* too big."

But getting back to hats. The right hat hides bad hair as well as any indication that one actually lives in the same world afflicted by wrinkles, acne and body odor.

I have one good hat. It lives in a lovely brown-and-white-striped hat box on the top of my hall closet. I used to regret the hat's purchase, which occurred during a mad spending spree at Henri Bendel that followed too closely on the heels of a *Breakfast at Tiffany's* marathon. Now, however, I can see the accessory gods were smiling upon me that day. I silently rejoice.

Today marks the beginning of my new life, so I decide it's time to begin using my Hermés bag—a deep ruby, ostrich-skin Birkin that set me back almost nineteen grand because I refused to languish on the waiting list for three years. I empty the contents of my dumpy Coach purse into the Birkin and fold my mink over the crook of my arm. I walk down the hall, drop the offending Coach into the incinerator and resolve never to think of it again.

On my way out, I tell the doorman I am expecting an important package and ask him to call me when it arrives. He scribbles down my cell phone number and promises that he will.

My mission this morning is to find a dress worthy of The Coat. This sort of reconnaissance requires an open mind, a sense of adventure and, above all, a sense of humor. With this firmly in mind, I put on my sunglasses, exit my building and quickly encounter a woman wiping her poodle's bottom with a tissue.

For once, I'm no longer sorry I live on the East Side. I really couldn't have designed a better neighborhood as a backdrop for The Coat.

I stop at the diner and eat a dainty breakfast of poached eggs and steamed spinach. Then I pay the check and hop in a cab. "Saks, please," I tell the driver. Barneys is closer, but I really like the raisin bread at Saks.

I mean, I *used* to really like their raisin bread.

Because the day is truly magical, I find the dress right away. It's long, emerald velvet with a high slit on one side and thick straps that cross in the back. It's perfect. The dress against which all other dresses would be judged and found lacking.

Unfortunately, it doesn't fit. And when I say doesn't fit, what I mean is it looks like a very thick belt because none of the fabric can get past my well-girded hips to cover my bottom half.

I get dressed and wait on a chair in the outer dressing room, insulated from life's cruelties in my mink, while the saleswoman goes in search of another size. A larger size, actually, but of course she is too discreet to say that.

She comes back, clicks her tongue against her teeth and shakes her head. I sigh and crumple in defeat. "I really wanted that dress."

"I know, I know." She nods in understanding. "Was it for a special occasion?"

At this point, I'm so upset I start telling big fibs to the saleswoman before I even know what I'm saying. "It's for work, actually. I'm a jazz singer." I warm to the idea and brighten like a freshly-watered orchid. "And I really need to get this weight off because I must have that dress for a special performance."

"Of course you must," she says. "Why don't we wrap it up for you? You'll be back down to size in no time."

Yes, why not. I pay for the dress and leave the store with it and what remains of my ego.

As I walk home, I fall into a deep depression bordering on clinical. I'm certain there's nothing worse than plunking down seventeen hundred dollars for a dress that doesn't fit after brazenly lying about your profession. Well, actually perhaps what's worse is to return to your apartment building painfully cloaked in the realization that, although it's not Halloween, you've been running amok in New York City in a Holly Golightly costume.

All afternoon. In broad daylight. On Fifth Avenue.

But then I realize there is something much worse, which is the feeling you get when your doorman hands you a package you ordered in your most excruciating moment of utter insanity and the cost of that package exceeds the price of a decent new Lexus. I sign on the dotted line and schlep away to the elevator with my jazz-singer dress in one hand and The Coat in the other.

Once inside the apartment, I drop everything at the door and go straight for the kitchen in search of carbohydrates. After a few cold toaster pastries, I'm calm enough to pace around the apartment. Eventually I find myself in the bedroom, where I unwrap myself from my wrap dress, put on my exercise clothes and lay on the bed with a pillow on my face. Everything in my world is sick and wrong.

I remain there for at least ten minutes. When the pain of the day's failures loses its edge, I go to the kitchen for more toaster pastry. This round is a little less frantic, so I'm able to hold off long enough to toast the next four pieces. I nibble on potato chips until the toaster makes that delightful pop-up sound, at which point I enjoy the contrasting sensations of alternating bites of sweet and bites of salty. After a while, my double chin begins to feel heavier and droopier. I hold my elbows up from my sides so I can't feel the growing layer of flesh over my hips. I scarf and scarf, bite after bite, until I begin to feel my pudgy cheeks wobbling with each chew and swallow.

Is a sable face mask next?

Disgusted, I abandon the empty chip bag, go into the living room and flop down on the couch. I briefly consider going to the park to burn off a few hours' worth of calories, but the way my thighs rub together is so disheartening I decide it's better not to move at all.

I pick up the phone and dial Courtney. "What are you wearing tonight?"

"Oh, I don't know," she says. "Probably just jeans."

"Great," I say. "I'll see you at six." I hang up the phone and silently curse her and all other members of the exclusive society of women who look good in jeans. They totter around on their stilettos in their teeny-tiny jeans with that elegant space between their thighs, secretly ruling the world because they have so much time on their hands. They pair their jeans with Chanel jackets, old T-shirts, whatever. It doesn't matter. They look good regardless. Their wardrobe planning is easy, casual and the bane of my existence.

I wallow in this until it's time to begin the arduous process of getting ready to meet Courtney and her microscopic jeans and her rich boyfriend.

In spite of my broccoli and shrimp protocol this week, my jeans still don't fit so I have to wear one of my stretchy wrap dresses. I spend a couple hours doing glamour-girl pin curls and take extra care with my makeup because obviously a sable coat calls for everything to be just so. When I'm finished, I look a little too painted, but I decide it's just the bathroom light. In a dark bar, I'll look smoky and mysterious.

Unfortunately, I don't feel that way when I get there. I feel over-dressed and old and the pin curls are ridiculous. Mrs. Robinson gets a new perm and goes out on the town.

Richard and Courtney are sitting at a table in the bar with a couple I've never met. Stuart, a chubby blond guy who's a client of Richard's, and Stuart's Australian supermodel girlfriend. I don't catch her name but I know I saw her in last month's Vogue. Her hair is long and breezy and her face is completely bare. Courtney's is too, although she really doesn't have the features to carry it off.

My own face suddenly feels like it's covered in a spackle of clown paint.

"Are you from the South?" the model wants to know. Her nose is running profusely and she keeps wiping it with bar napkins.

I lick my dark matte lipstick, which is all wrong, and take a sip of wine. "No." I smile brightly to reveal my freshly-bleached teeth but close my mouth when I realize they're not as bright as hers. "Why do you ask?"

She looks at me with a dreamy expression. "Oh, I don't know," she says. "Maybe your hair?" She reaches up with her long, elegant fingers and tosses my curls like wilted lettuce. "It doesn't look like it would move. But I guess it does now that I touch it." She pats my hair back into place. "Sorry," she says.

"Not at all," I reply.

Courtney, who is already drunk, starts to giggle. The supermodel is not trying to be a bitch. Courtney, on the other hand, is doing so effortlessly.

"So tell us about this boyfriend," the model says. "The one who bought you this beautiful coat." She takes a sip of her drink and I see that her straw is shaped like a penis.

Courtney keeps giggling but I can't tell if it's about the straw or something else.

I shrug and pull The Coat closer around my bloated body. "There's not much to tell," I say. "We only just started dating a few weeks ago."

"Well, it's a pretty extravagant gift," Courtney sneers. "I think he's overcompensating."

Courtney is very unattractive when she's pie-eyed and it's worse when she's jealous.

I look around. "I can't imagine what you're talking about."

"It's too expensive," Courtney says. "He's clearly trying to hide something."

I look meaningfully at Courtney, who has complained about Richard's lack of endowment one too many times. "Like maybe he has a little dick or something?" I ask. I'm not trying to be mean. I only say it because I want her to shut up.

Courtney shrugs. "I don't know. Maybe he's married or something."

The model strokes The Coat with the back of her hand. "Well, anyway, it's a gorgeous coat."

This is the thing about extraordinarily beautiful women. They can afford to be classy and generous all the time.

The model picks up a napkin and wipes her nose. Then she sets her drink down, stands up and announces, "I have to pee."

I am so jealous of this woman I can't stand it. Even with the runny nose, she seems classy. And I could never get away with using the word pee in mixed company. I don't even say it when I'm alone. But when she says it, it's charming.

Everyone at the table watches in awed silence as she glides away toward the bathroom. Three seconds later, Stuart excuses himself and follows her. He's not five feet from the table when Courtney leans in and hisses at me. "What are you doing?"

I glance over in Stuart's direction just in time to see him follow his girlfriend into a single, unisex bathroom. Then I turn back to Courtney. "I'm having a drink with you and your coked-out friends. What are you doing?"

She rolls her eyes. "Those are clients, Avery. You can't use the word *dick* in front of them. What's the matter with you?"

"Courtney, she's drinking out of a straw shaped like a penis. Do you really think she's going to mind?"

Courtney opens her mouth to say something but Richard puts his hand on her arm and shushes her. "Avery," he says. "I realize this is a social outing but I need to take a few minutes and talk to you about something."

"Okay," I say. "What is it?"

"Well, your client filed a redemption notice. We sent them their money today."

"Really." I feel the bottom of my universe fall away, like I've read about when divers swim over the edge of that underwater cliff in the Caymans. I feel dizzy and disoriented and sick.

I look at Courtney but she's looking at the floor. Her lips are pressed tightly together, like she's trying not to smile. I look back at Richard. "How long have you known about this?"

"Since late October," he says. "I didn't say anything, because I assumed the bank copied you on the redemption request."

My mind races to explain this occurrence in a manner that doesn't involve the end of my income stream. I feel like I'm running through a dark hallway yanking on doors but nothing gives.

The bottom line is the bank pulled the money, which means I'm in lockdown.

I look at Richard and try not to cry. "I didn't know anything about it."

He pats my forearm. "I figured as much when Providence called looking for the referral fee. I'm sorry, Avery."

I almost nod at him but stop when I realize the gesture could cause the tears welling in my eyes to seep out onto my face and make my clown paint run down my chubby cheeks in big black streaks. I press my fingers hard against my mouth to keep my lips from wobbling.

Richard puts his arm around my shoulders and rests his other hand on my knee. "Are you going to be okay?"

"Sure," I say. "But I think I'm going to go now. Thanks for the drink." I pat his hand and bend to pick up my purse, which is resting on the floor near my feet. Emotion and my support garment suffocate me. I sit upright and clutch my Birkin to my soft underbelly while I try to catch my breath.

"You sure you're all right?" He hugs my shoulders and looks deeply concerned. He looks at Courtney and then back at me. I can tell he thinks he should do something, like maybe ask me to go to dinner with them.

Courtney glares at him. "Of course she's all right. You're all right, aren't you, Avery?"

"I'm fine." I stand and put my purse over my arm. "I'll see you later. Thanks." I stumble out of the bar without a backward glance.

On my way home, my purse starts ringing. It's The Tool.

I answer the phone but don't say anything.

"Avery?"

I speak quietly, as if I'm in a fancy restaurant that doesn't allow cell phones. "Yes?"

"I'm just calling to wish you happy birthday."

"Oh, yes," I say. "You, too."

"It's not my birthday," he says. "Where are you?"

I look around. I'm at the corner of Fifty-Sixth and Eighth. "Manhattan."

"Where in Manhattan?"

"The best part."

"Is something wrong?"

Of course it would be a huge mistake to tell The Tool I no longer have an income. "No," I say. "Nothing is wrong." I also want to tell him I hate him, but I manage to keep this part to myself as well.

"Listen," he says. "I know it's your birthday and all, but I just couldn't get out of this thing tonight." I can hear a party in the background. Probably Courtney's birthday party. "Anyway, I don't think you should be alone tonight."

I'm tempted to tell him my birthday is actually tomorrow, but somehow I don't think this would matter so I remain silent.

"Hang on a sec." He puts me on hold. For some reason, I stop walking. Probably because I'm on the West Side, which is where The Tool lives, and I think he's going to change his mind and spend the evening with me. It's snowing lightly as I stand on the street corner and wait for him to come back on the line.

After five minutes, I hang up and resume walking.

Quite a while later, somewhere around Madison and Sixty-Fifth, he calls back.

"Listen," he says. "My buddy just got in from Chicago. He's at my apartment."

I scrunch up my face and try to process this information.

"Avery?"

"What?"

"Did you hear me?"

"Yes."

"Okay," he says. "So why don't you go over to my place and have a birthday drink with him?"

"What are you talking about?" What I mean is I hope I have no idea what you're talking about.

"I just think you two would get along. You know what I mean?"

Of course I do. I'm crying now, but trying to do so silently. I swallow hard to hide any emotion. "I think so." My voice sounds watery, like I have a mouthful of slush. I swallow again.

At this point, I finally get what Fig has been saying all this time. The Tool is a sociopath. I count five steps before I speak. "I'm going to get off the phone now."

"What?" he asks. Then he's quiet for a second. "Come on, Avery. I think it would be good for you. Expand your horizons a little."

I don't remember hanging up, but when I get back to my apartment the phone is turned off and has tumbled down to the bottom of my purse.

I find it when I dig through my bag for my keys. I'm tempted to turn it back on so The Tool can call and apologize for the misunderstanding in which I thought he asked me to have sex with his buddy from Chicago. Also, so Courtney can call and apologize for giggling as I was made aware that I no longer have an income. Also, so Fig can call and apologize for being so goddamn right all the time.

But I drop the phone back in my purse when I realize the only person who's sorry is me.

One good thing, though. At least I'm too upset to eat, which almost never happens. I take a sleeping pill and go to bed.

CHAPTER 3:

Happy Freaking Birthday

- - - - - - -

DECEMBER 1 - 2, 2007

I am awakened on my birthday by the phone exploding next to my head.

It's my doorman. "Uh, yes," he says. "A person named Fig is here to see you."

"Fig?" I ask. I clear my throat. "Are you quite certain this person is called Fig?"

"Yes, ma'am, I am." My doorman sounds tired. Or maybe he hates me.

"Very well, then. Please send him up."

I live in a decent apartment on the Upper East Side. I'd love to live on the West Side like Fig because the East Side is a little stuffy these days, but I can't afford it. My rent is $3950 a month as it is.

I get out of bed to open the door for Fig. I'm wearing an oversized rugby shirt that has Yale printed on the front. My alma mater. At some point in the distant past, I was smart and this shirt reminds me of that. But the best thing about the shirt is that both the fabric and the cut are thick, making me appear less so.

Fig has a cup of coffee in his hand, not Starbucks but some kind of bitter swill he buys from a stand at the entrance to the park. He also has a New York Times tucked under his arm.

"Get dressed," he says. "We're going to breakfast."

"Is alcohol involved?"

"It's your birthday isn't it? Plus, I think you're going to need it." He pats his newspaper meaningfully.

If things can get worse, I don't want to know. I roll my eyes and lumber towards my bedroom. When I realize Fig can see the backs of my knees, which are more than a little lumpy these days, I scamper into the room and close the door almost all the way. I throw on a somewhat clean and very stretchy outfit.

I'm digging through the bottom of my closet when he yells through my door. "I hate to do this on your birthday. But your largest client, I mean, your *only* client, just wrote down three billion in bad loans."

I'm barely listening. I can't find a pair of socks to save my soul. I poke my head out of the bedroom and look around the living room. My dirty socks from yesterday will have to do.

"It's the subprime mortgage crisis," he says. "Did you happen to hear about that?"

Now he's just being insulting. I pick up a paper every once in a while and he knows it. I flop down on the couch and shove my feet into my dirty socks. "Oh, that," I say. "I think the press is exaggerating."

He takes a gulp of his bad coffee and smacks his lips like it's the best stuff in the world. "Avery, there are places in this country where almost half of new mortgages are in foreclosure."

I sigh as I pull on my boots. "Well, I just don't get it. My rent certainly hasn't gone down."

"The Manhattan market is seemingly unaffected. But your client is not."

Fig shoves the paper at me as I walk past him into the kitchen. I ignore him and pick up my toothbrush, which is conveniently perched on the edge of the sink next to my toothpaste, and brush vigorously.

"This could be very bad for you," he says.

I spit into the sink. "It already is. The redemption check was cut yesterday."

I run some water into my cupped hands, swish it around in my mouth and spit again. I'm thankful I don't have to admit to Fig that my client pulled out without telling me. My relationship with the bank was just that tenuous. Frankly, I can't believe I made money on it for so long.

"I'm sorry," Fig says. "You must really be freaking out."

"What's there to freak out about?" I grab a dishtowel and wipe my mouth. "It is what it is. I'll just have to find something else to do."

"Will you stay in sales?" He follows me out of the apartment, so upset he doesn't even notice the rather noteworthy garment I've just thrown over my shoulders.

We walk down the hall. "You ask that like I've ever been in sales. We both know I just got lucky." I punch the down button with conviction because that's clearly the direction I'm headed.

We stand in the elevator side by side and stare at the door on the way to the lobby. "Better lucky than good," Fig says.

I don't respond.

He looks sideways at me to see if I'm even listening. I'm not.

Then he plucks at the hair on the arm of my sable. "What the hell are you wearing?"

"Don't get all upset," I say. "It's a cost-savings measure."

"In crazy world, maybe. It's sable, isn't it?"

"It might be," I say mysteriously.

His jaw falls open in a mouth-breather sort of way and he covers his right eye with his hand like he's just been shot. He is suddenly shorter, as if the stupidity of my purchase has weakened him somehow.

"Don't get freaked out." I walk out of the elevator and put on my Dior sunglasses. "My clothes are too tight right now. I can wear this over my suits when I look for a job."

"You can't show up for job interviews in a sable coat."

I stride up Madison Avenue as if I don't have a care in the world. He skips a few times to catch up with me.

"No one will hire you," he says. "They'll think you don't need the job."

"That's the only way to get hired? You have to actually need a job to get one?"

He hesitates a minute and then nods. "Yes," he says. "That's exactly how it works."

I turn and look over my sunglasses at him in my favorite gesture of disdain. "Coming from a guy who's never actually had a job, I'm not quite sure you're the authority. Anyway, Jackie Kennedy got a job in publishing."

I pull my collar tight around my neck. I can feel people staring at me as we walk up the street. I know they're wondering who that glamorous, mysterious woman in The Coat is.

"Figlet," he says. His voice has a cautionary tone.

I hold up my hand before he can ruin my good time. "Stop," I say. "Just stop talking before you say something you'll regret."

"Like what?" he asks.

"Like, you, madam, are no Jackie Kennedy." I push open the door to the diner and wait for him to enter. Then I whisper harshly at the back of his head as I follow him to a table. "We just don't need that kind of negativity at a time like this."

He ducks into a booth and I slump into the seat across from him. We're both exhausted. Neither of us is particularly healthy. He smokes, which happens to be the only vice I don't have. Together, we have every-thing covered.

I pull my arms out of The Coat's sleeves and sit with it resting around my shoulders. I feel very fragile and troubled.

A waitress appears. "Coffee?"

Fig turns his cup over and she pours. I rest my forearms against the edge of the table and stare at Fig. "Can we go to Starbucks later?"

"Yes," Fig says. "But this is the last time. You can't afford Starbucks anymore."

"I still have eighty dollars on my card thingy. I can afford it until that's gone."

"That won't cover you for a week," he says. "You're going to have to get a job."

I have no response. The truth is my espresso habit would make the lease payment on a new Jag and Fig knows it. Thank God I live in the city so I don't need a car. I briefly wonder if crack would be cheaper.

The waitress returns and we order. Eggs Benedict for Fig, French toast for me. At the last minute, I order hash browns, too. "We can share them," I say.

He barely nods. He's heard this nonsense many times before. He slides a section of the newspaper over to me. "Here are the jobs. I circled some for you."

The thing about Fig is he has a one-track mind. As I scan the circled ads, I realize he's also cruel and sadistic in a way I never imagined before.

He's circled ad after ad for accountants. It seems the entire hedge fund world is desperate for them.

I put the paper down in disgust. "You're kidding, right?"

"You are an accountant, aren't you?"

I cross my arms and look at a spot across the room. "Now you're just being vicious." I look back at Fig. "Do I look like an accountant?" The answer to this question is so self-evident I can't believe I even have to ask.

"Forgive me, Avery. But do you not hold a master's degree in accounting from an Ivy League university?"

I clench my jaw and allow my nostrils to flare as I exhale loudly. "That's just because my scholarship money was running out. I had to major in something."

"And you chose accounting because?"

I pick up the salt shaker and turn it over to see if it works.

"Avery?" He ducks his head to look into my face. "Why did you major in accounting?"

I shake salt at him and set the shaker back on the table with a thud. "Because I couldn't figure out what else to study. And it's a safety net."

"I rest my case."

"Fine," I say. "You win. But I'm not doing it. The only reason I went to law school is so I wouldn't have to be an accountant." I shrug one shoulder and raise my right eyebrow. "Maybe I could do something in law."

Fig shakes his head. "Those law firms are funny, Avery. They all seem to want someone who actually finished law school. Five semesters doesn't quite cut it, which I believe I mentioned before you dropped out."

I lean back against the booth. I would glare at him if I had the energy. "You're enjoying this, aren't you?"

"Not so much," he says. "I'm leaving in less than a week and you're a mess."

Fig goes to New Zealand for the worst of the winter each year. He doesn't return until June when it's time to open his summer house in the Hamptons.

"Well, you better start being a little sweeter or I'm not going to water your plants."

"Kill my plants, you mean."

I stop slathering butter across my freshly-delivered French toast and point my knife in the vicinity of his throat. "There was absolutely no evidence that thing was a cactus. You should leave better instructions and crap like that wouldn't happen."

He laughs. His teeth are blinding white in spite of daily indulgence in tobacco, whiskey and bad coffee. "Okay," he says. "Please water my plants." He cuts into his Eggs Benedict. "And I'm going to stop worrying so much. I'm sure you'll land on your feet."

I douse my food in syrup and shovel in the first glorious bite. As I chew and swallow, I look around the diner. God bless Fig. He's too trusting to grasp the hard truth, which is that any poor sot whose destiny lies entirely in my hands is in a very precarious position.

And I'm not just talking about the plants.

After breakfast, Fig and I go to Starbucks. I get five shots of espresso with steamed whole milk. I silently rue the day Starbucks adopted 2 percent as its standard because now I have to specially order the full-fat stuff, which is embarrassing among all the skinny lattes out there.

I add two packets of blue death to my six-dollar beverage and we're out the door. We spend the morning bombing around the city, which means stopping at various dive bars and chatting with the bartenders, all of whom Fig knows well. I alternate beer with my coffee, which grows progressively colder throughout the morning.

When we've finished our drinking adventure, I return to my apartment and change into my walking shoes. Since it's cold today, I decide my new sable needs to go out for a walk as well.

I leave my purse at home but take my phone with me. Maybe The Tool will call. I hope he does so I can feel smug when I don't answer.

But the only person I hear from is Courtney. This is odd because I never hear from her on weekends, which means The Coat must be working. She's obviously calling to apologize for being such an asshole last night.

"Hello?" My voice is too bright because I'm kind of excited.

"It's me," she says flatly.

"How are you?" I put the emphasis on the "are" like I'm a movie star or something.

She sighs. It sounds like a hiss. "Well, I was wondering if you'd mind telling me exactly what you were doing last night."

I pull the phone away from my head and stare into the tiny speaker that's channeling Courtney's voice. This is not what I expected at all. "Excuse me?"

"Don't play dumb with me, Avery."

I look at my watch. I've only walked ninety minutes and the beer is making me sleepy in spite of the espresso chaser. "I don't have the energy to play dumb, Courtney. What do you want?"

"I want to know why you feel the need to flirt with every man in sight."

I look around. The park is empty. "What are you talking about?"

"Your little crying jag. It was all Richard could talk about. All night. You ruined my birthday flirting with my boyfriend like that. Not that he's my boyfriend anymore, thanks to you."

I push my bangs out of my face and keep trudging. In spite of my fancy socks, my feet are killing me. "Let me get this straight. Richard broke up with you and it's my fault?"

"God," she says. "I hate it when you turn things around like that."

At times like these, I'm grateful I was born a woman so I don't have to date them. I look up at the clouds and mouth my thanks to the heavens.

"You should be ashamed of yourself," she says.

I return my attention to earthly matters and continue walking. "Look, Courtney. I'm sorry to hear about your boyfriend. Why don't you give The Tool a call? He has a friend in town who sounds interesting."

Then I snap my phone shut, turn it off and slide it into my pocket. Aside from Fig, I am officially friendless.

I don't even know if this bothers me. Maybe it's just a relief to finally admit it.

When I return home that evening, I'm ragged from exhaustion, dehydration and irritation. I pull a half-empty bottle of Chardonnay from the fridge, pour myself an oversized glass and chuck the bottle into my brushed stainless-steel waste can that cost two hundred dollars not counting the delivery fee. The bottle makes a satisfying thunk at the bottom of the can.

Then I call the diner and order my birthday dinner. This year it's a bacon double cheese, fries and a side of cherry pie. I used to ask for the pie à la mode but not anymore. Now I just keep a half-gallon of French vanilla Häagen-Dazs in my freezer at all times.

I take my wine into the living room and flick on the TV while I wait for the food. Although I pay for over a hundred channels on cable, including the premium movie channels, all I ever watch is *Sex and the City*. I own all six seasons on DVD and cycle through them again and again.

Tonight, I'm watching the episode where Carrie is strung out on credit cards and her date, a handsome French architect, mistakes her for a prostitute. He leaves a thousand dollars by the bed before he skulks out of the hotel room.

Although no one in this show ever really suffers from financial woes, there is another episode in which Carrie attempts to balance her budget by writing articles for Vogue at four bucks a word.

So these are the options for Manhattan's broke but fabulous single girl. Fashion writer or unwitting call girl.

This analysis doesn't help me at all as I have no discernable skills in either area.

I slide off the couch to answer the phone. It's the doorman summoning me to the lobby to fetch my food. Since the occurrence of certain notable terrorist events, delivery people are no longer allowed past the lobbies of Manhattan's less accommodating buildings.

I wrap The Coat over my exercise clothes and head for the elevator. As I descend to street level, I lament the decline of civilization in the post-September 11th environment.

The delivery man is standing alone in the center of my marble-coated lobby. He holds a plastic bag of Styrofoam, the contents of which are readily identifiable by the glorious smell of grease wafting through the lobby. I slip some money into his hand and slink away with the bag. The transaction feels somewhat shameful. Like a drug deal.

The scent of char-grilled cholesterol follows me into the elevator. Just before the doors shut, a fresh-smelling couple enters. They are slim and beautiful. Their hair is shiny, their skin is polished and their clothes are Italian and impeccably ironed.

The Coat seems huge and ridiculous in their presence.

She sniffs and tilts her head toward him. "Shall we have Japanese?"

He is too well-mannered to do anything but look at the floor and nod. But I know they're both wondering if the effects of my food pollution will hang on them as they proceed through their otherwise brilliant evening.

I hope so.

I get off the elevator first, which makes sense because it's the law in Manhattan that the beautiful people always get off on the higher floors. This keeps the hierarchy clear to everyone, just in case someone was briefly deluded enough to forget their place in the natural order of things.

Of course, such a transgression would only be temporary, because it's impossible to forget for very long. This thought looms large as I bask in the blue light of my beloved *Sex and the City* episodes.

I daintily dab a spot of ketchup on each fry without taking my eyes from the screen. When the fries are gone, I tackle the burger, which is warm and gooey and savory and delightful. Then I pause my DVD player, go to the kitchen and scoop a large hunk of ice cream onto a dinner plate.

I return to the living room, dump the pie onto the plate alongside the ice cream and resume watching my TV friends conduct their amazing existences.

When the food is gone, I shove my Styrofoam containers aside. Tonight was a minor transgression. I'm confident that tomorrow I will find the strength to consume only those foods that will make my skin glow with vibrant good health.

I contemplate my next move as I draw a bath and extravagantly dump the last third of a fifty-dollar bottle of bubbles into the tub. This grand gesture makes me feel fantastic. If I believe life holds more good things in store for me, they will come. Squirreling my luxuries away would be extremely counterproductive at this point.

As I sink into the tub, I close my eyes and decide my current situation is a blessing. If I had actually finished law school or had a real job or some prospects for reasonable employment, I would be locked in a golden cage from which no responsible person could ever escape.

Who needs benefits when the cafeteria plan called New York, New York is right outside your door?

The city is my smorgasbord. This thought pleases me enormously. Since I'm not locked on a nine-to-five, wage-slave treadmill, I am free to consider all possibilities and their impact on my objectives in life, the most notable of which is how to chink out a toehold in this city's slippery social terrain.

I start by clicking through the professional options as presented by Carrie Bradshaw & Company. There's art, public relations, seedy journalism and law. Since the lawyer is the least popular of the bunch, I no longer feel any regret about that incomplete law degree I've been dragging around behind me.

This leaves PR and the arts. PR is out because popularity is a prerequisite. Since it's also my goal, I'm left in a chicken-and-egg quandary that makes my head hurt.

At which point it becomes clear that a career in the arts offers my only graceful means of penetrating New York's unforgiving outer shell.

I have no particular bent toward any particular aspect of the arts. But this, too, in its own strange way, gives me nothing but options. I can simply decide what I'd like to do best and then do it. And I already have the dress to become a jazz singer.

I can see myself, luxuriating across a black concert grand in its rich velvet glory, singing soulful songs in a way that makes people ache with sadness.

The only trouble is I'm not remotely artistic. In any way.

This thought is discouraging, until I remember reading somewhere that Michael Jordan was cut from his high school basketball team. I decide not to do anything that might bring the accuracy of this rumor into question. At this point, I really have nothing else to hang onto.

I get out of the tub, go to bed and contemplate my new career as a jazz singer and all of its attendant implications.

First, I will be extremely pale. I will wear sunglasses with no makeup other than red lipstick and false eyelashes. My brows will be dramatically arched. I'll sleep until noon, have espresso for lunch and three bites of juicy steak for dinner. I will eat tiny salads with gobs of blue cheese dressing.

I'll wear mysterious perfume and vintage cocktail dresses during the daytime. On stage, I'll wear nothing but Valentino red. I will not wear jewelry, so when a rich and handsome investment banker proposes to me, the rock will be all the more conspicuous.

My non-performing hours will be occupied with appointments. I'll see my voice coach at least three times a week and observe a regular daily maintenance schedule of Pilates, yoga, manicure/pedicure, facial and massage.

I will not own a laptop, Blackberry or cell phone. I'll go on dates with men who drink scotch, open doors and pay the tab with Black American Express cards.

I pull my covers up around my neck and sleep with the quiet confidence that only comes from having a solid plan of action.

The next morning, though, my musical path to success doesn't seem quite so easy. In fact, in the harsh light of a cold day, I can barely drag my dimpled ass to the bathroom, much less out into the city for voice lessons from some judgmental opera has-been.

As I stand on the scale, it occurs to me that the only part of me that is naturally thin is my voice, at which point I know my singing career is over.

I go to Starbucks and spend five dollars on as many shots of espresso. Since I'm economizing now, I don't ask for milk, which means I save a little. Once the transaction is complete, I ask for a copy of the Sunday Times.

The clerk or barista or whatever she is glares at me as she runs my Starbucks card through the money-deducting machine again.

I ignore her, pick up my Times and wait for my espresso. The people around me are dressed in Sunday workout-wear casual, which on them somehow seems sporty and stylish. On me, it just seems invisible and sad.

This is exactly the frame of mind you want to be in as you look through the paper to find a job. As the minutes tick by, my paranoid anxiety is heightened to a fever-pitch by uncut caffeine. Eventually, I'm in a twitchy, gritchy and bitchy state that can only be alleviated by two cinnamon-chip scones and a Vanilla Bean Frappuccino.

When I'm bleary-eyed and bloated from coffee and carbs, I leave Starbucks and head to the park to walk around in circles for another four hours. It's goddamn exhausting being me, let me tell you. I have no idea how I could possibly add "working stiff" to my existing list of daily responsibilities so I toss the jobs section into a trash can on my way to the park.

I spend Sunday evening eating microwaved chocolate cupcakes slathered in butter and dodging phone calls from Rob, who I'm sure is freaking out about the fifty grand.

I brush my teeth until my gums bleed and go to bed. Maybe I'll feel better tomorrow, but I doubt it.

40

CHAPTER 4:

If Only It Were That Easy

DECEMBER 3 - 7, 2007

I awaken Monday morning on my side in a fetal position. The flesh on my abdomen is quite sore from being stretched and pulled by its own weight during the night.

This has never happened before. Things are changing, and not for the better.

I am alarmed. I wrestle myself into a pair of Spanx Power Panties, that miracle support garment every woman should own in triplicate, and sit on the edge of my bed and call Fig.

"I'm in trouble," I say.

"I know," he says. "I'm coming over."

He arrives in less than five minutes. I'm dressed and brushing my teeth when I open the door.

"At least you still have the presence of mind to observe good oral hygiene."

I run to the sink, spit and rinse. When I look up, Fig is dropping a bag of fresh croissants, a yellow legal pad and a pen on the table. "We need a plan of attack."

I dab at my mouth with a dishtowel. "A brainstorming session?"

He nods, pushes past me and starts poking around in my kitchen cabinets.

"I'll do better with caffeine," I say. "Let's go to Starbucks."

"I brought you some tea bags. I just need to find a pan to boil some water."

Now this is just too much. "Are we also going to have lunch at a soup kitchen?"

He looks up from his crouched position in front of my never-used oven. "Don't joke about that, Avery. Soup is all some people get to eat in a day."

One thing I've noticed about rich people is that their level of sanctimony tends to increase with the zeros on their balance sheet.

I turn on my bare, cracked heel, walk to the kitchen table and sit down. My posture is extremely bad as I watch Fig rummage around in my cupboards. And then my sinuses start to feel hot, like I've just inhaled a big whiff of horseradish.

I sit up and reach for the croissants. They're still warm. I tear one apart and shove a hunk in my mouth. The taste is rich and buttery and wonderful.

Fig finds a pan, fills it with water and turns on the gas. "I brought marmalade, too." He grabs two plates and two knives, sits at the table beside me and opens the jar.

God bless Fig. I slather marmalade on my croissant as he picks up his pen.

"Okay," he says. "First we need to determine where you stand financially."

I look up and freeze, mid-slather. I'd rather stand naked on a digital scale on Park Avenue. The kind that projects your body fat percentage and weight onto the wall in big red numbers.

Fig, oblivious to the baked goods before us, stares at me. "Avery, we can't begin to solve the problem until we know how bad it is. How much money is in your possession right now?"

"You mean actual cash?" My voice is a little squeaky and my hands are shaky. I resume slathering, which calms me somewhat.

He puffs up his cheeks with air and expels it loudly. "Yes," he says. "Cash money. I know you have nothing in your wallet so let's start with your checking account."

I have not balanced my checking account in months. But I do have the receipt from my last deposit. I jump up, rummage through my purse and find it crumpled up in a ball. I smooth it out on the table and subtract the fifty grand I spent on The Coat. "According to the bank, I have $2,351.67."

He writes this down on the first line of his legal pad. "Do you have any other assets?"

I stare at Fig as I press my lips together and release them, making a loud smacking sound. Then I shake my head.

"What about credit cards?"

I nod several times. "Oh, yes. I have lots of those."

"No," he says. "I mean, how much do you owe on credit cards?"

I wipe the sleep out of my eyes and inspect it closely. "Why didn't you tell me I had splooge on my face?"

"I didn't notice." Fig scrapes his chair back and goes into the kitchen to make tea. "Go get your credit card statements. We'll add it up."

I am riveted to my chair.

"I'm not kidding, Avery. I will withhold caffeine until I get them."

I slide off my chair and open the kitchen drawer nearest my front door. It's jammed full of mail and take-out menus.

Fig peers over my shoulder. "Oh, God," he says. "Just go sit down."

He pulls the drawer out and brings it over to the table. "Sort through this stuff," he says. "Do you want sugar in your tea?"

"What do you think?" I reach into the drawer and carefully grasp the corner of an envelope between my thumb and index finger, making sure not to touch any of the nasty little past-due stamps. I lift it as if it's covered in excrement and fling it, stamp-side down, onto the table before Fig sees.

He returns with two steaming cups of tea. "Avery, you're not going to get out of this mess without getting your hands dirty." He reaches in and grabs a handful of mail.

I feel almost violated. And definitely nauseous. I hold onto the table for support while Fig rips open envelopes and tallies the damage. When he's finished, he slides the calculator in front of me like he's one of those jewelry salesmen who have been trained never to say the number out loud.

I peek at the calculator. My total credit card debt is somewhere north of forty-three thousand dollars. I say somewhere because I know there have been substantial charges since these statements were mailed, but I have no idea how much.

I do not mention this to Fig.

"Hmm," I say.

To add insult to injury, Fig then grabs his handy-dandy calculator, presses a few more buttons and announces that the minimum monthly payments exceed the amount of cash in my checking account.

I study Fig carefully. "Are you sure you're not an accountant?"

"I'm sure," he says. "But don't think we won't bring one in if we need to. How much is your rent?"

"Three thousand and change."

"How much change?"

"Four thousand." I sip tea as the bleakness of my situation washes over me like a thin film of stinky green mucous.

Fig tosses the pen onto the table and slumps back in his chair. "You spent fifty grand on a coat and you don't have money to pay your rent?"

I blink several times. I really can't believe it either. "I honestly have no idea how this happened."

"What were you thinking?"

"I guess I was thinking I'd get an advance on my credit cards for a few months. It didn't seem like a big deal."

"When you were pulling in three hundred grand a year it wasn't."

We gaze at the table, too shell-shocked to speak. I can't find the heart to tell him about the fifty thousand I owe Providence.

"Want to go to a movie?" I ask.

Fig spreads his hands on the table and counts his fingers, like there's a chance one got sucked into the financial black hole that is my balance sheet. "I guess so," he says. "I think I could use a break."

His sudden shift from "we" to "I" does not go unnoticed. But it doesn't bother me, because I never expected him to bail me, anyway.

Later that night, I sit alone at the kitchen table and fold the yellow sheet containing Fig's scribbles over the top of the notepad. I tap the pen on the fresh page and decide there's no need to panic. I just need to put one foot in front of the other. This is, after all, New York City. The opportunities are endless.

 46

I just have to keep my eye on the ball and take care of first things first. The most important thing is staying up with my rent. All of my credit cards are maxed out save one, which has a limit of fifteen thousand dollars. This should cover me for almost four months while I figure the rest out. I'm tempted to get an advance on the card tomorrow, but then I realize it's only the first week of December. I imagine the money sitting in my checking account, vulnerable and exposed, for almost a month until the rent is due. I decide to wait a while before I get the advance.

I write this down at the bottom of the page, reserving the space above for all the things I must do between now and then. If things go well, maybe I won't even need the advance.

Clearly, the big thing I have to do is find a job. I decide to break the task into ten parts so it doesn't seem quite so daunting. I write the numbers one through ten along the left side of the page, sit back and close my eyes. In a few minutes, I pick up the pen and write the first task.

Find a suitable interview outfit.

I stare at the words and try to imagine where I might locate such a thing.

Obviously, the frugal thing to do would be to find this outfit somewhere in my own overstuffed closet. I put down the pen, go into the kitchen and open a bottle of cabernet. I pour myself half a glass and proceed to my bedroom to commence shopping.

Three hours and twenty minutes later, I'm drunk and clothes are scattered around my room as if I've been bombed with a decade's worth of refuse from *What Not to Wear*.

Even if the clothes weren't horribly dated, which they are (I mean, there are shoulder pads in here, for God's sake), none of them fit. Each garment was purchased with the certain but deluded conviction that I would soon be alarmingly thin. The blouses don't button. The pants are too short. Since I have not grown any taller, this is a sure sign my thighs are completely out of control, a troubling fact that is further confirmed by the dresses, which cling to the rolls between my ribcage and kneecaps like sausage casings.

Worst of all, I have the upper arms of a Russian potato farmer.

I slump down on my bed, pass out and dream I am embalmed in fat and buried in a tomb of bad clothes.

The next morning, I'm lying in bed trying to recover from my hangover when it occurs to me that looking for a job in December is entirely out of the question.

It's the holidays, after all, and no one in hedge funds does anything during the holidays. They're all skiing in Jackson Hole in trim, zippy little outfits.

I would look like a complete idiot if I tried to get a job right now, especially if I showed up in my dated, ill-fitting suits. They'd smell my desperation. When the interview was over, they'd just roll their eyes at each other and toss my resume without another word.

Besides, first I have to think what kinds of jobs I should look for.

Fig is right. I am an accountant. At least on paper. But I've never practiced accounting in my life so I have absolutely no experience.

In the spirit of living as if, I wonder if I shouldn't just invent some, until it occurs to me that only the biggest loser imaginable would lie to create the impression she is an accountant.

Since I'm in a horrible mood anyway, I decide I might as well face the music with Providence Securities. I pick up the phone and dial Rob's direct number.

"She lives and breathes," he says.

"Hi, Rob."

"I was thinking you fell off the face of the earth."

"Not exactly," I say. "How about I come in and see you about the advance?" This is good. Maybe he'll be less testy if I take the bull by the horns.

"Are you bringing your checkbook?"

As if. I say nothing.

He waits for a minute. Even the silence is testy.

"Is a couple of hours okay?" I ask.

"Hang on." He puts me on hold for several minutes. When he comes back on the line, he says, "Do whatever you want, Avery. I can't see what difference it makes at this point."

"Look," I say. "I'm sorry. I want to come in and find a way to make this right."

"Then you need to go to your bank. They're the ones you left holding the bag."

My heart stops. "What are you talking about?"

"I put a stop payment on your advance as soon as Richard told me about the redemption. I just spoke to my bank, which confirmed for the umpteenth time that the advance check you weaseled out of me bounced, which means this is your problem now."

My mouth begins watering profusely. The saliva is slimy and cold and there's way too much of it. Without thinking, I spit the excess into my hand. I'm a little surprised by this, but not too much because I'll generally do anything to avoid throwing up. Such as walking around in Central Park for four hours every day.

When I can finally speak, my voice is quiet. Humble, even. "Why didn't you tell me?"

"God, you're a piece of work. In spite of the fact that you tried to screw me, I've been calling you every day for a week to give you the head's up. I hope for your sake you didn't spend that money, Avery. But I'm sure you did, in which case, good fucking luck."

He hangs up. I feel life's cameras zooming in on me and I'm momentarily forced to focus on what's really happening.

At which point I can't fight it anymore. I go to the bathroom and throw up in spite of my best efforts otherwise.

When the world stops spinning, I brush my teeth and leave the apartment with every intention of going straight to the bank. But instead I make a quick stop at Starbucks for a chai tea latte to mask the lingering taste of vomit. The first one doesn't quite do the trick so I order another for the road.

When I get to the bank, I'm high on caffeine, sugar and adrenalin, which is unfortunate because the thing about banks is you really just have to leave your bullshit at the door. There's no room for it inside a bank, particularly if your account is overdrawn by $48,973 and you are inside a tiny room with a tall, skinny, balding bank manager and a short, dumpy woman who is somehow involved in the bank's fraud department.

The fraud woman is wearing a bad polyester suit that clings to her substantial thighs in a most unflattering way. I hate the way she looks. I also hate that I am forced to acknowledge her as one of my own kind. I actually think my thighs are bigger.

For a second, I feel sorry for her. That is, I would feel sorry for her if she had any likable characteristics whatsoever.

But she doesn't. They are playing good cop, bad cop with me. She is the bad cop.

So of course it goes without saying that I hate her.

She hates me, too, because I am wearing a sable coat worth more than her measly salary.

I am only wearing it to show that I am a woman of means in a temporary credit crunch. Surely the bank will understand and sympathize with my situation, given how crunched banks are these days, what with all those bad mortgages out there.

Unfortunately, my strategy seems to be biting me in the ass.

"Ms. St. George," she says. She's said my name so many times it's clear she must think I'm in danger of forgetting it. "Your account is underwater by a very significant amount. Yet you seem completely unable to grasp the seriousness of your situation. Perhaps we should go over it again."

I am leaning back in my chair. This has been going on for hours. Or at least thirty minutes. She keeps saying the same stupid things over and over again, as if that will somehow make money miraculously appear.

Her voice is humming around my head like a bumble bee that won't stop buzzing no matter what I do. Eventually I snap. I explode into an upright position and look at the bank manager. "Is there something about me that makes you think I'm unable to grasp simple concepts?"

He opens his mouth to speak but the dumpy fraud woman beats him to it.

"Besides the fact that you're overdrawn by $48,973?" she asks.

I keep my gaze fixed on the bank manager. This fraud woman does not exist for me. "Is that kind of sarcasm really necessary?"

"Not at all, Ms. St. George," he says. "We're simply trying to find the most expeditious manner to resolve this situation."

"Actually," I say. "I don't think that's what you're trying to do at all." I look around to make sure they're both listening. "In fact, I think what you're doing is browbeating me with the threat of criminal prosecution in your efforts to settle a civil matter, which I happen to know is illegal."

At least, I think it's illegal. I sit back and wait for a response.

They just look at me and say nothing.

"Fine." I wish I felt as confident as I sound, but this seems to be working so I forge ahead. "The bottom line is you want your money. I understand that. But you need to give me a little time."

"Ms. St. George," the fraud woman says. I rest my elbows on my knees and put my hands over my ears. I am absolutely unable to bear the sound of her stupid voice repeating my name one more time.

When she stops talking, I look up and point at her. "Look," I say. "If your paycheck bounced, how much time would you need to clean up the mess?"

This shuts her up for a second and I turn to the bank manager. "I will take care of this somehow. Calling the police and having me thrown in jail will do nothing but divert my attention and my remaining funds, which obviously won't do you any good at all."

His eyes dart around the room as he mulls this over. Then he crosses his arms and shakes his head. "We're going to need something today, Ms. St. George. We can't just let you walk out of here owing us such a substantial amount."

"I can get a cash advance." I pull out my last usable credit card. "How's ten thousand sound?"

He plucks the card from my fingers and smiles ruefully. "You already owe this particular bank almost forty-nine thousand dollars. Surely you realize this card doesn't work anymore."

"I guess you'll just have to wait then. All I have left is the coat on my back."

At which point the nasty, polyester-clad woman standing before me holds out her stubby little hand. "Which we happen to know was purchased with our money. We'll just hold that in our vault as collateral until such time as this loan is paid in full."

"You can't do that," I say. "You don't have any authority to do that."

"Not yet," the manager says. He opens a file and pushes it toward me.

I eye the documents in the file as if he's just revealed a big, stinking turd. "What is this?"

"These are loan documents, Ms. St. George, for the amount of your overdraft. You'll see on page two that your coat is pledged as collateral."

I clutch The Coat around me. "That's ridiculous. You can't seize someone's coat in the middle of winter."

"Now Ms. St. George." The bank manager is speaking to me in soothing tones, as if I've been recently lobotomized. "By your own admission, you have no income. And this bank does not extend unsecured credit to people with no income. So I'm sure you can see that you don't qualify for an unsecured loan in the amount necessary to cover this overdraft. Ordinarily, we wouldn't even accept clothing as collateral but under the circumstances, we're willing to make an exception because it's your only asset."

"This isn't exactly clothing," I say. "It's a sable."

"Right," the fraud woman says. "And we didn't exactly extend this credit to you. So it's either this or we go back to talking about criminal liability."

I look at the file again. As stinky as it is, it seems to be my only exit strategy. "What's the interest rate?"

"Eighteen percent," the manager says. He hands me a disposable pen with the bank's name printed on it.

"That's egregious." I raise my eyebrow and stare into his watery blue eyes. "Usurious, even." All that law school is finally paying off. I sign the documents with a flourish. "You should be ashamed of yourselves."

"That's funny, Ms. St. George. We've been thinking the same thing about you."

I pretend I don't even hear this. I slide out of The Coat, drop it into the arms of the fraud woman and glide noiselessly and gracefully through the office door as if I'm stepping onto a red carpet.

The second I'm past the threshold, though, I veer off the imaginary red carpet and scurry a few feet to the right before proceeding across the lobby. That way, they won't be able to see my back fat as I exit the bank.

As I stand on the frigid sidewalk outside the bank, I am amazed at how easily I am able to find ways to pretend the bad things aren't really happening.

First, I jog home in my T-shirt and running pants so no one is able to discern that my creditors have literally stripped me of my outer garments. Since they don't know, I don't really have to acknowledge it, either.

Also, this makes me look really athletic and hard-core because it's freezing outside.

Next, I call my credit card companies and request increases in my lines of credit. They will not accommodate me, which is total crap because I pay more interest than anyone in America. I'm hanging up on the last credit card company when The Tool calls.

I'm so upset and dejected I agree to have dinner with him. Also, saying yes somehow allows me to avoid acknowledging his demonstrated propensity to pass me out among his friends like floss.

On my way to the restaurant, it occurs to me that a good diet plan might be to consume only those food items purchased for me by other people. But then I remember The Tool rarely pays, so this plan could obviously use some work.

I enter the restaurant and slide into the booth across from him.

"You look terrific," he says. And he's right. I've applied forty minutes' worth of makeup and spent much time on my hair. The platinum highlights look pretty amazing against my dark mink.

Because I am not naturally blonde, I have my roots touched up every three weeks at a cost of four hundred and fifty dollars per session not including tip. I briefly wonder how I will continue to maintain my hair. Then I realize I'm frowning. Since I can no longer afford Botox, I decide to stop thinking about any of this.

The Tool reaches for my hand. "I missed you."

I look at his hand wrapped around mine and am repulsed by his touch, which surprises me a little. I don't know what to do about this so I do nothing.

"So how have you been?" he asks.

I smile a fake, glassy smile that probably makes me look like I'm being zapped with a cattle prod.

He pulls his hand away and takes a drink of his beer. "You're a little bitchy tonight."

"Am I?" My voice is distant and disconnected. "I didn't realize." As I look at him, it occurs to me that his facial features, mainly his ears and his nose, are a little too pointy. He looks like one of those evil troll dolls but without the blue hair.

I wonder why I've never noticed this before. I can't look at him anymore. I pick up my menu and peruse it carefully.

"God, Avery. Lighten up a little. I only asked you here tonight to figure out what's going on with Richard."

The Tool is the broker for Richard's fund, which means every time Richard puts on a trade, The Tool makes a commission. This is a state of affairs that may have been helped along by me at some point before I knew The Tool's true nature as a sociopath.

I look at The Tool, but not his face. I keep my eyes focused on his neck, which is too beefy. Also, the skin is wrinkled and loose from too much time basking in the sun with bimbos on his big, stupid boat. Everything about The Tool disgusts me.

"I don't know," I say. "What's going on with Richard?"

"He closed his account. That's what."

I press my lips together and nod as I realize this result was inevitable. When my client pulled out of Richard's fund, Richard was no longer beholden to observe my brokerage suggestions. And The Tool lost the business as a result. "Hmmm," I say. "That's too bad."

The Tool raises his eyebrows and looks away like I'm an idiot.

I take a sip of my water. "Do you think I'm somehow responsible for this?"

"Of course not," he says, reaching for my hand again. "How could you be responsible? I just thought maybe you'd like to try to make me feel a little better."

I nod again. And smile. I feel dazed from binging and exercising. I could sleep for a hundred years.

"Why don't we get out of here?" he asks. "We can go to my place. I'll order sushi in later."

"When?" I ask. "Two minutes later?" In spite of his former career as a professional athlete, The Tool is not exactly known for his stamina.

I look at The Tool's evil face. He is speechless.

"Well," I say. "Maybe your friend from Chicago is still here. Do you think he might have a little more staying power than you?"

It's a moot question anyway, because the fact is I'm far too pudgy to get naked in front of anyone right now, even people from Chicago who might be a little more tolerant and accepting of the effects of an eating disorder run amok. I stand up and walk out of the restaurant.

I feel positively triumphant until I get home, at which point all I feel is lonely and sad.

I take a pill and sleep straight through until morning. Well, not exactly straight through. But each time my eyes open, I stay awake only long enough to take another pill.

When I awaken on Wednesday, I'm groggy and nauseous and sad. I get up, open my blinds and rest my forehead against the glass. After a few minutes, I decide I'm terribly bored with my drama and depression. Watching all the poor slobs scurrying around on the sidewalk below my building gives me some hope for the future. I will put one foot in front of the other, just like they do.

I take a shower, get dressed and go to my laptop to write a resume.

The education part is easy. Master of Science in Accounting, Yale University, 2000. I type in Magna Cum Laude. Then delete it. Then type it in again.

This goes on for a while until I finally type it in and leave it there. It is true, after all, even if it doesn't feel that way.

I decide to leave off the part about my five semesters of law school at NYU. It might not look good, missing that last semester for reasons that entirely escape me now.

Once my education is laid out for the world to see, I'm stuck. How to describe what I've been doing since then is impossible. I call Fig. "How would you describe me?"

"Full-bodied, yet bubbly. With a lingering finish."

"How can I have a lingering finish? I never finish anything."

"Oh," he says. "Dwindling?"

I don't say anything.

"Okay, so that sounded terrible. I'm sorry." He's silent for a minute. Then his voice brightens. "What's this for, anyway?"

"My resume. I'm trying to describe my professional experience. But I have none."

"Avery, there is a name for what you do. It's called capital introduction and it's perfectly respectable. Why is it so hard for you to grasp this?"

For some reason, Fig never believes me when I assure him my success was entirely a fluke. "I can't do that now. Those cap intro jobs never pay until you actually sell something. I need to earn a salary right out of the gate."

"Bullshit," he says. "You should be able to pull a six-figure salary at a hedge fund plus bonus with your asset-raising experience. If you hold out for the right offer you should get your old income back. Maybe more."

"How would you know?" My voice is shrill.

"My cousin told me." He sounds a little meek, because I've caught him pretending to be an expert when he isn't. But then I feel bad because I do remember Fig saying his cousin works in hedge funds.

"Anyway," he says. "You raised eighty million dollars from one notoriously conservative client on your first attempt. Most people would find some confidence in success like that."

"Maybe," I say. "If we had any reason to believe I could do it again."

"Everyone thinks you can do it again but you."

"I'm too fat right now. It's important to look good at the meetings when you're in sales."

"Did it ever occur to you that anorexia is not the solution to every problem?"

At times like this, I think Fig is truly out of his mind. "I don't know," I say. "Let me think about it and call you back."

I hang up. Fig is flying to New Zealand today, so I decide to let things cool off and not speak to him until he returns in June. But he's a persistent little devil, so I'm not surprised when an e-mail from him arrives twenty minutes later.

He has sent me a link to a saved search of hedge fund jobs on Monster.com. I click on the link and scan through the jobs. Most of the listings are posted by hedge fund head-hunters who all want to sink their teeth into people who know how to raise money.

I click back to my e-mail and read the text of Fig's message, which he's typed in capitalized, bold letters. **"CALL ALL THESE HEAD-HUNTERS. DO IT NOW. TIME IS OF THE ESSENCE. FIG."**

But I don't even have a resume yet, which is obviously the first thing any headhunter is going to ask for.

Fig is no help at all sometimes.

I return my attention to my resume, or rather, the gaping hole that appears immediately below my name, contact information and stellar education. After that, there's nothing. On the page or otherwise. I get up, walk around the room and shake out my shoulders.

Fig is right. I did raise that money. That sort of thing doesn't happen by accident.

Does it?

I sit at the computer and type out a deal sheet. I'm not exactly sure what a deal sheet is, but everyone on Monster.com seems to want one. Although I'm wholly unfamiliar with deal sheets, I'm quite certain it would be a mistake to create a deal sheet with only one deal on it, so I list my deal statistics instead. Average sale: eighty million; Average length of investment: sixty months. And so on. I keep going until the page is almost full of tasty little deal tidbits and I can't think of anything else.

When I'm finished, my deal sheet looks pretty damn impressive. And unless someone thinks to ask, they'll never know there was only one deal.

I e-mail the resume to all the headhunters on Fig's list.

Confident that calls for interviews will soon pour in, I take the rest of the day off and go to the movies. I silence my phone, stuff it into my purse and buy a feedbag of trans-fatted popcorn and a swimming pool of Diet Coke to sustain me during the triple feature.

I did, after all, miss lunch I was working so hard.

When I come out of the theater, it's dark and cold outside. I check my phone. I've missed ten calls, all from Manhattan phone numbers I don't recognize. The headhunters are after me.

I don't know what I was so afraid of before. I raise money in eighty-million-dollar chunks, for God's sake. Everyone is going to want me.

I decide to treat myself to sushi on the way home. I'm not hungry but it feels really healthy to eat all that seaweed and raw fish and soy and wasabi. And of course my health is really important now that I'm going to be working.

I feel a slight twinge when I pay the tab, which is almost a hundred dollars. To make matters worse, I have a hard time walking when I leave the restaurant because my stomach is stretched tight as a drum. Maybe I'll save a few bucks and not eat at all tomorrow.

I return home and check my many messages. Nine are from head-hunters. I would be excited about this if it weren't for the final, disturbing message from my landlord.

"Ms. St. George," he says. "Your rent check bounced. You have five days to come up with the money."

There are several features about this message that tell me this guy isn't messing around. First, the way he phrases things. People who are messing around talk about rectifying situations and resolving issues, phrases that are obviously not in this guy's vernacular. Second, his voice is deep and gravely, like the pit he's going to dump my sorry carcass in if I don't come up with the money.

More important, there's only one message. People who are messing around leave lots of messages because there's nothing else they can do to get their money. With this guy, however, I know there will be no additional voice mail messages. The next communication will be much scarier and probably in person. The reason I know this is because I'm not dealing with the kind of guy who troubles himself about due process requirements typically observed by landlords with deadbeat tenants.

In other words, this is a guy who sort of operates outside of those rules.

This didn't bother me on the front end, when I was renting the apartment. There was no credit check and no income verification. Also, unlike the poor saps who rent Manhattan apartments through legitimate channels, I didn't have to pay a broker ten or fifteen thousand dollars to find the apartment for me.

I listen to the message one more time and then delete it. When the scary voice has been exorcised from my existence, I close my phone and look around my apartment. As much as I love it, it's probably time to vacate.

This is unfortunate because being homeless is really going to set me back in my efforts to find a job.

At this point I enter a brief period I think of as my grocery cart phase, which is basically the scary time when you look around your apartment and assess how much of its contents can be carried with you as you schlep around on the street in your new life as a homeless person.

This is not a comfortable state of mind, as I'm sure you can imagine. I take a pill, go to bed and dream I'm sleeping in a beach house with a radio playing near my head. In my dream, I'm jolted out of bed by a news flash that vicious American Gladiators are approaching by sea and will storm the beach in fifteen minutes. My dream-self leaps out of bed and frantically tries to stuff my belongings into the teensy trunk of a leased Mercedes convertible.

In the morning, I sit up and look around my apartment. I contemplate getting up and racing around like a nitwit, as I did in my dream, but I really don't have the energy for it. Also, it's obvious where I'm going, which makes packing for the trip much easier.

I lug my big suitcase out from under my rejected interview outfits and haul it into the bathroom with me. As I shower and apply makeup, I put each item I touch into the bag. I'll clearly need this stuff because there's no way Fig has duplicates or even reasonable replacements that will do in a pinch.

Besides, this isn't exactly a pinch I'm packing for. Fig will be gone for six months. I figure I'll need a good chunk of that time to get back on my feet.

When I'm finished in the bathroom, I pack only the items in my wardrobe that fit me. This includes exactly two wrap dresses, three pairs of Spanx, most of my exercise clothes and a small assortment of socks and underwear. The jazz-singer dress makes the cut only because the tags are still on it and maybe I can take it back. I also pack any shoes that might have resale value on eBay, including all the Stuart Weitzmans. Then I throw my laptop and a tangle of electrical cords into the bag.

At this point, I'm almost done packing because the bag is almost full.

I give myself a fifteen-minute reprieve before the landing of the American Gladiators and walk around the apartment looking for things I can't live without. There isn't much, which strikes me as odd because all this crap seemed so important when I was flush and trying to impress people. I add to the bag only three items: my *Sex and the City* DVDs, my last bottle of wine and the tea bags Fig brought over in those lighthearted days when a little belt-tightening was all that seemed necessary.

Then I pick up my purse, put on my mink and leave the apartment with my suitcase, knowing but strangely not caring that I will never see the rest of my things again.

As I pull my belongings across Central Park, I wait for something dramatic to happen. Perhaps it will start raining and my bag will lose a wheel and I'll be forced to abandon my last remaining possessions in the mud, but of course not until I drag them far enough to first ruin my mink.

Perhaps I'll be mugged and raped and become so upset I'll be unable to eat for at least three weeks, the cruel irony being that my abandoned clothes would then fit me but I wouldn't have them anymore.

SOUP IN THE CITY

But there is no drama to becoming homeless in the high-rent district. There's just me wheeling a bag across Central Park to Fig's building and his doorman helping me take it up to the apartment.

Fortunately, I don't have to tip him. That's all taken care of by the owner of the apartment at Christmastime.

The doorman pulls my bag into the foyer of Fig's apartment, which is larger than the living room of my old apartment, and drags it across the black-and-white tiles to the wide staircase that winds up to the second floor.

"Would you like me to take it up for you?" he asks. Fig must have tipped very well this year.

"No, thank you. I can do it." The doorman leaves. For a second, I hesitate in the foyer. I can't say it feels wrong to crash at Fig's without asking, but it definitely feels funny. I think about calling him to ask if it's okay but the possibility that he might say no is so scary I decide I can't risk it.

So I proceed into Fig's and yank my bag up the stairs, pausing every two or three feet to catch my breath. My head is pounding like someone smacked me between the eyes with a croquet mallet because I'm woefully lacking in caffeine. Also, for the second day in a row, I've somehow managed to forget to eat for a few hours.

This is the only trend in my current situation that I hope continues.

Halfway up the stairs, the headache is so bad I'm forced to abandon my bag and leave Fig's building for an infusion of espresso. Once that's taken care of, I feel a little hungry so I decide I need some sushi. I'm not at all worried about the expense. Other than the minor problem of the stairs, the move went off without a hitch so I can get right back to looking for work.

When I'm finished eating, I sit in the empty restaurant and return the headhunters' calls. I set up back-to-back meetings for Monday, which will give me a few days to find an appropriate interview outfit.

Then I return to Fig's apartment. Properly fortified, I'm able to drag my bag to the top of the stairs and into Fig's cavernous bathroom. I put Fig's stuff in a laundry basket and stow it in an empty bedroom. When all evidence of Fig has been removed, I find a pair of rubber gloves and some fancy cleaning products and scrub the bathroom. It already looks clean but for some reason I feel the need to put some distance between Fig's stuff and mine. When I'm finished, the room smells of lavender and lemon verbena. I unpack and arrange my own bathroom accessories on the counters and shelves and stand back and admire my handiwork.

I quickly add my sparse wardrobe to the clothes in Fig's closet. Then I change the sheets on Fig's bed, crawl under the covers and sleep for several hours.

I awaken after midnight, lumber into Fig's bathroom and flip on the light. I turn on the shower and undress. On my way into the shower, I catch a glimpse of myself in Fig's floor-to-ceiling mirrors. What I see stops me cold. I am nothing short of aghast.

My body is grotesque. Beyond grotesque. Revolting. Repugnant. Repulsive. All of the above.

I forget the shower and square off with the mirror. Other than chunky little globules of fat that have escaped from my underarms and are clinging to the front of my torso like they're afraid to jump, my upper body looks fairly normal. Below the waist, however, it's a different story altogether. My hips are so round it looks like my ass is trying to overtake the front of my body.

From the rearview, things are even worse. I'm not even going to describe the cottage cheese mess that has attached itself to the backs of my thighs.

I guess everyone has their moment of truth. And this is mine. I have a serious problem. I wish I could take a knife and slice away my excess flesh like so much meat off one of those gyro spindles at the Greek diner.

No longer can I delude myself with notions that I am merely chubby, pudgy or afflicted with "a few extra pounds," as they say in Internet dating.

I am deformed.

My status as the elephant man of Manhattan consumes my thoughts as I shop for an interview dress the next morning. My other afflictions, including broke, homeless and friendless, pale against this backdrop.

I stop in a petite boutique on Madison Avenue to see if they have anything A-line that might work. As I flip through the racks, a salesgirl approaches me.

"May I help you?" She speaks in the elegant, refined way of the naturally thin.

"Yes." I continue flipping through the racks. "I'm looking for an interview outfit. It's in finance, so I'll need something appropriate but not too boring."

"Hmmm," she says. "What size?"

She's speaking in such a breathy voice it's not out of the question for me to ignore the question, which is obviously my preference because my size is one number I try never to say out loud.

I take a dress off the rack and inspect it closely.

She clears her throat. "Ma'am?"

I continue to pretend I'm suddenly deaf and that the plain black dress in my hands is intensely fascinating.

She leans over. "Ma'am, I asked what size."

Now this is just way too loud, so I have no choice but to look at her. Her hands are curled into claws around the rack and she's staring at me expectantly. I roll my eyes, put the dress back on the rack and start flipping through clothes again. "I think a twelve would work."

"Oh," she says. "I see." She pauses for a second to twirl her hair around her finger.

At which point I'm more than a little sick of this girl staring at me. "Is there a problem?"

"Well, it's just that we don't have big girls' sizes in this store."

Last time I checked, twelve wasn't exactly a big girls' size. But then I remember I'm in Manhattan, in which case it's obese. Still, I think I have a right to be in this store . . . barely.

I look around and locate a size-twelve divider on the rack of clothes behind me. "What about this?"

Now she's eyeing me with unabashed disdain. Or maybe it's just disbelief. Finally, she speaks. "But this is petites."

I stop flipping and look at her. My hands are frozen on the clothes. "Yes," I say. "Last time I checked, I was under 5'4" and I don't believe I'm any taller today."

She raises her eyebrows and glares at me. Then she rearranges her features in an effort at composure and sighs heavily. "I'm sorry. I just don't think there's anything for you in this store."

I purse my lips together until I realize it probably makes my cheeks look fatter. "Oh," I say dully. "You think I'm bigger than a size twelve." There is no interrogative inflection in my voice at all. I'm speaking in the flat tones of someone who has heard and absorbed a horrifying truth.

"Aren't you? I mean, what I mean to say is, are you sure?"

"I don't know." My voice comes out in a whisper and I realize I'm staring at the floor. I look up at her. "Do you think I could just try something on and see?"

She shakes her head. "I'm sorry, but I just don't think that would work. There might be a petite section for bigger girls at Lord & Taylor. Would you like me to call them for you?"

"No, thank you. The bigger girl is leaving." I back away from her and weave my way blindly through the racks.

When I burst out of the store onto the sidewalk, I realize I've been holding my breath. I gasp for air and listen to it wheeze through my lungs as I stumble across Madison. When I reach Fifth, I pause and try to get myself together. After a while, I notice a crowd of insipid Asian girls making their way up Fifth, at which point all I can think about is how their arms look too skinny and useless to support the weight of their knock-off Louis Vuitton handbags.

My pity party thus ended, I wipe my eyes and walk down Fifth to Lord & Taylor. Once inside, I adopt a "don't ask, don't tell" policy with regard to the name of the department in which I'm shopping. I buy the first black dress that isn't painfully tight.

I am now properly equipped to take on the hedge fund universe.

I return to Fig's building with my shopping bag. A tall, elegant woman with thick, prematurely silver hair follows me onto the elevator. She briefly smiles at me and then thanks the elevator man when he presses the button for her floor.

The woman is wearing a camel-hair coat tied firmly around her wispy waist. It could be brand-new or thirty years old. Much like its wearer, the coat's quality is so high its true age will never show.

I know I've seen her before and I think it was somewhere other than in this building. I conjure up her past as we ride the car upward. She's probably a Broadway actress or something like that. Her posture is impeccable, so maybe she's a prima ballerina for the New York City Ballet.

She's carrying a bag from Barneys. I surmise she just had lunch at Fred's, which is the restaurant on the ninth floor of that store. The ladies who shop go there to get re-caffeinated and pretend to have lunch. A bowl of chicken soup at Fred's costs ten dollars and contains about four bites of actual chicken. The rest is just broth and celery. Of course, noodles are conspicuously absent from this picture. Add iced tea and a tip and you're looking at twenty bucks for around two hundred calories.

The women at Fred's have real money. Real friends. Real lives. They wear cashmere twin sets with stove-pipe jeans and Christian Louboutin heels. Their feet never hurt and their diamonds look like flashbulbs set in platinum. Their hair is blown out every morning by men named Andre and Philippe. They have houses in the country where they once in a while allow themselves to wear something from the Gap, but only as long as everyone knows it's a whimsical, Sharon-Stone-on-the-red-carpet kind of experiment and not at all a part of their serious wardrobe. They exercise in silk T-shirts that have to be dry-cleaned.

They have bi-monthly bikini waxes at J. Sisters. Their hair is thick and glossy and so are their perfectly lined eyelashes. They are never tired or bloated.

I enter Fig's apartment and flop down on the couch. I spent the last five years and the better part of a million dollars trying to become them.

The sad thing is I'm not even close. The clothes I bought were wrong. The restaurants I went to were unwelcoming. The velvet ropes around the clubs and parties may as well have been iron curtains.

I never got in. My name was never on the list. And the price of my failed admission ticket was my financial security. I have no idea where my money went. All I know is it's gone and I have nothing to show for it but a dismal credit rating and a few fancy shoe boxes.

I get up and pace around Fig's wickedly expensive apartment feeling cheated and misled. I don't know what to do with myself. I am uncomfortable and out of sorts.

And hungry.

I rifle through Fig's kitchen for take-out menus and order some sushi and green tea ice cream from the nearest Japanese restaurant. It arrives in less than fifteen minutes. This being a civilized building, the doorman brings it right to my door.

I put my ice cream in the freezer and take the sushi into the den, where I put a disc into Fig's DVD player and flick on the TV. The theme of *Sex and the City* fills the room as I rip open my chopsticks and pound the wasabi into a small bowl of soy sauce.

Unfortunately, my enjoyment of the food is disrupted by my dismay at the garbage spewing at me from the TV. I set my plate aside and flick through episode after episode but I can't watch any of them. I'm feeling nothing for these girls. Frankly, I just can't take their bullshit anymore.

I click off the TV in disgust. Carrie Bradshaw writes a weekly column for a second-rate newspaper but she religiously wears five-hundred-dollar shoes. Her clothes cost even more. A single Dior dress she flaunts in one thirty-second scene easily costs over three thousand dollars. She occasionally bitches about not having enough money, but the money problems evaporate by the next episode, when we see her at Prada or Bergdorf's buying yet another bag of haute couture.

This kind of fairy tale just can't exist. As far as I know, Carrie's column isn't even in syndication. She couldn't make more than a hundred and fifty grand a year.

Six figures may seem like a lot, and outside Manhattan, it is. But in the city, money evaporates before your very eyes. Federal, state and city taxes eat up about 50 percent, so Ms. Bradshaw's maximum monthly take-home pay would be a little over six thousand dollars. At least half of this would go to rent. The *Sex and the City* writers love to mention Carrie's rent-controlled apartment, but from what I've seen of rent control on the Upper East Side, you basically get a rat hole with an efficiency kitchen, which in Manhattan means a hot plate perched on the back of the toilet. The accommodations would be on par with the twenty-something apartment Carrie flees when she sobers up after a night of drunken sex with its twenty-something inhabitant.

Having lived on Carrie's side of the park for five years, I feel quite confident in my assessment that an apartment like Carrie's would easily run over three thousand a month.

This means Carrie's rent and one of her flippy little sundresses would consume everything she makes in a month. Yet she's inexplicably able to eat every meal in disdainful restaurants, take cabs to clubs, parties and bars, give expensive gifts to her wealthy friends and continually feed a clothing habit more expensive than the worst cocaine addiction I've ever heard of.

The whole thing is a big fat lie. And I've been living it.

I'm so upset I can't finish my sushi and I forget all about the green tea ice cream stashed in the freezer.

CHAPTER 5:

Credit Crunched

- - - - - - -

DECEMBER 8 - 15, 2007

The next morning, I get up and head out for my hair appointment. I keep a standing appointment at my salon, every third Saturday at eleven, to have my roots touched up. My hair is naturally quite dark so the process is lengthy, tricky and expensive. At times I wonder if drinking bleach might be easier.

I could go to the salon during the week, but I like to go on the weekends when everyone else is there. It's my only real contact with the popular girls. For a few hours and several hundred dollars, I get to feel like I'm part of something.

I always stop at Starbucks before my appointment. Although I fear credit is getting tight, I see no reason to abandon this ritual on such an important weekend. I am, after all, preparing for the interviews of my life. I spend the remaining balance on my Starbucks card and am completely whacked out on caffeine when I get to the salon. Also, my empty stomach is churning from all the espresso. I hope I don't have to go to the bathroom during the appointment because that would be completely uncool.

My colorist's name is Frederick. He's gay of course, and more bitchy and sensitive than any woman I know. Frederick is pencil thin and talks about nothing but food. He's as obsessed about food and eating as I am, so I know his anorexia requires a significant and admirable amount of discipline. At any given moment, he's either smoking or chewing nicotine gum. He doesn't like black but it's all he wears because it's so slimming.

He is happy to see me. I sit in the chair and he musses my hair with his fingers. We're both staring at me in the mirror.

"So how are things going?" He speaks in a melodious way, which calms me to the point that I actually consider telling him about my recent troubles. But that would violate the unspoken covenant between us. Because I am fortunate enough to be his client, I am obligated to take my wonderful hair out into the world and use it to create an amazing life. And I'm further obligated to return to his chair and feed him stories of my amusing and successful antics in the city, which are largely thanks to my fantastic hair.

"Still seeing the football player?"

I sigh. "I'm tired of him." I stare at my expensive, white-blonde hair. "I think I need a change."

He purses his lips. "Are we talking about a new guy or new hair?"

I hesitate for just a second. "Both." I glance from my reflection to Frederick's. His expression is troubled.

He puts his hands on my cloaked shoulders, as if he's bracing both of us. "I don't think so, honey. We've finally gotten this color just where it needs to be. It's perfect with your complexion."

It really isn't. The truth is my blonde hair requires Herculean make-up efforts so I don't look washed out, exhausted and old. But I don't admit this because it would make me appear weak and lazy.

"I was thinking about glossy brown," I say. "Like Elizabeth Taylor before the freakazoid highlights."

"Really," he says. I may as well have told him I intend to invent a process that would cause the cellulite on my ass to reproduce and spread across my body quicker than the Ebola virus.

"Humor me," I say. "I'm thinking of going back to work and I'll need more serious hair."

His expression looks pained. I try to laugh. "Oh, come on," I say. "Keep an open mind. How bad could it be?"

When he speaks, his voice is barely audible and his eyes are on the floor. "Just a second." He turns and walks away.

A few minutes later, one of his minions is standing next to me. "So Frederick is saying you want to go dark." His lisp is so pronounced I wonder if he's doing it on purpose. But he just stares at me, waiting for an answer, so I guess he's not trying to be funny.

I look around the salon. "Where is he?"

"He had some things to do."

"He left?"

The minion glares at me with wide eyes and then busies himself straightening bottles on the counter in front of me. "You booked a three-hour appointment. If you're not going to use your time, Frederick has better things to do."

I pause to take this in. I've just been rejected by a man I've tipped a hundred and fifty dollars every three weeks for the last two years. "So you're going to color my hair?"

"I'm going to try. But frankly, I don't think dark brown will work on you at all."

"How can it not work?" I ask. "It's my natural color."

He shifts his inconsiderable weight and sticks his hip out. "Do you want to do it or not?"

What I want is to stab him with a pair of scissors but instead I count to five because I definitely can't afford to get arrested in this fancy salon. "I don't know. Do you have any experience at this?"

"No," he says, rolling his eyes. "They just grabbed me off the street and instructed me to make women look as ordinary as I possibly can."

I look at my reflection. My roots are totally out of control so I don't really have a choice. "Okay. Go ahead."

"I'll go mix your color." He leaves for a few minutes and returns with a bowl in his hand. I close my eyes so I don't have to look at him not looking at me. I can smell his peppermint-scented breath as he works on my hair. Actually, it's not peppermint. It's something more sophisticated than that. Probably a unique spearmint-rosemary-lemon combo found only in designer appetite-suppressing gum for the rich and bitchy.

I hate this guy. And when it's over, I hate myself. I look in the mirror and inspect my newly-brown hair.

As promised, I am ordinary. Completely ordinary.

The minion snaps his fingers and a shampoo girl comes and leads me away. Shrouded in the white cape, I look bigger than I actually am, which means I am invisible. In this salon, no one exists except the properly emaciated.

I tip the shampoo girl my last ten dollars and she leads me to another chair for my blow-out. This chair is manned by a thin person who might be a man and might be a woman but who is definitely the most bored person I've ever met. When s/he is finished, I get up and walk to the counter to pay.

The girl who collects the money glances at me and looks down at the register. "It's nice," she mumbles.

"Right," I say. "Thanks." I click my credit card against the granite counter.

"It comes to three hundred dollars. How much tip do you want to leave?"

"Oh," I say. "No, thank you."

For the first time, she looks me square in the face. She is so beautiful I can't believe she's an actual human being. "You're saying 'no, thank you' to a tip?"

"That's right," I say. "No tip." I'm surprised how this sounds when it comes out. With one decision, with four words, I'm somehow transformed into a sensible, fat Midwestern housewife in elastic-waist pants. I am now the kind of woman who would never get an appointment in a salon like this. I may as well be wearing those white, foam-soled sandals old ladies wear over their reinforced-toe nylons.

The money girl studiously avoids looking at me as she runs the card. I pick up a pen, rest my elbow on the counter and wait to sign the credit slip.

She sighs. "Your card was declined."

I swallow and speak quietly. "Can you run it again? Maybe there's a mistake."

72

She runs the card again. "Declined," she says, louder this time. She looks around for someone to kill me. Finding no one, she looks back at me with an annoyed expression. "Do you have another card?"

I open my wallet and put another card on the counter. "Why don't you try two hundred on this card and a hundred on the other one?"

"You must be joking."

I glance over my shoulder. A line of busy, glamorous people is forming behind me. I scratch my temple and feel my body temperature rise. I can smell my own sick sweat. I wonder if I forgot deodorant. I wonder if I can still afford deodorant.

"Could you please just do it?" I ask. "I don't know what's wrong but I've been coming to this salon for two years."

She picks up the new card and runs it through her little machine. I am thankful and amazed when it spits out a paper for me to sign. She puts it in front of me. "That's the whole three hundred."

I sign the slip and slide it across the counter to her. My hand is shaking. She gives me my credit cards. I'm sure they're both useless now but I take a moment to put them in my wallet anyway.

"Ma'am, could you please go? Other people are waiting."

All eyes are on me as I vacate the salon. Normally, my brain would be pulsing from the embarrassment of making such a ridiculous spectacle of myself. But I don't worry about it too much because I'm ordinary now, which means no one will recognize me. Also, today I have more important things to think about.

Like food. If the credit cards no longer work, I'm officially out of business.

I return to Fig's apartment and have a brief skirmish with the doorman, who for a moment doesn't believe I'm the same person who left a few hours before. Once I pass the sniff test, I'm allowed to walk through the lobby and get on the elevator. I take off my mink and lay it across the banister on my way through the foyer.

I head straight for the kitchen and yank open the doors of Fig's twin Sub-Zs. All shelves are gleaming and empty except one, which holds small jars of olives, capers, sun-dried tomatoes and something called cornichons, which look suspiciously like pickles to me. I turn the jar over and look at the price tag. I guess if they called them pickles they couldn't charge $1.50 an ounce for them.

I return the jar to its place on the shelf, close the refrigerator door and start opening cupboards. There's nothing edible in any of them, just gleaming pots and pans, stacks of china and serving dishes. Fig does not have cupboard-type food. I'm thinking this is because Fig is a gourmet sort of person who does not eat anything processed, but then I go into the vast room Fig calls the pantry and find two boxes of designer crackers. I guess even gourmet people like Fig will keep some processed food on hand if it's obscenely expensive.

I ransack the bar and find a few small tins of smoked oysters and fish and also anchovies. Of course I realize anchovies are fish but in my mind they should be quarantined into their own separate category because they're completely disgusting.

I gather every edible item in the apartment and place it in a neat row on Fig's polished concrete countertop, which is the surface of choice among rich people who want their kitchens to appear spare and minimalist.

I stand back and assess the inventory. My stash of food has the same look as the kitchen—spare and minimalist. For a second, I start to panic. But then I realize the calorie content of this food is crazy high. I rummage through Fig's desk, find his calculator and some paper and spend some time adding up the total calories of all the food. Then I divide by 1750, which seems a reasonable number of calories for one overweight girl whom the universe has suddenly put on a diet.

According to the calculator, I have ten days of eating left. If you subtract the anchovies, it's only nine days and a few hours.

Suddenly, starving to death in America doesn't seem like such a farfetched possibility.

On Monday morning, I rise early and prepare for my interviews. My head aches from lack of caffeine because tea just doesn't do the trick.

Also, my mouth tastes funny from all the greasy, smoky sea critters I've been eating.

Needless to say, I do not linger over breakfast.

I'm out the door by eight a.m. and do not return until early evening. After a day of back-to-back interviews, I'm exhausted but I've learned many things about the world I didn't know before. Or maybe I knew them but I just hadn't thought of them before. They are, in no particular order:

1. Bad credit will keep you from getting a job.
2. Being fired from your last job will keep you from getting a job.
3. Even though hedge funds are supposed to make money in any kind of market, most of them don't. Hence, bad market conditions will keep you from getting a job if you're stupid enough to need a job in hedge funds.
4. Never eat a meal bigger than your head at a lunch interview. This doesn't impress anyone.
5. There is a special torture reserved for girls who spend all their money on Lanvin platform pumps and do not have enough left for cab fare or even a bus. The end result of this torture is that basically your little toe looks and feels like it's been smashed through a garlic press.
6. When blood drips out of your shoe onto your friend's white carpet while you're illegally squatting in his apartment, you will have a hell of a time getting it out.
7. It is impossible to find a water fountain anywhere in New York City, so broke and thirsty is a very bad combination.
8. If you're not planning to have lunch in a restaurant, don't even think about wandering in and using the bathroom.
9. Very thirsty people have to pee as much or more than anyone else.
10. Hunger and desperation on a job applicant smell worse than cat urine.

With these life lessons firmly in mind, and although it's not quite six p.m., I take a pill and go to bed.

On Tuesday morning, as I'm eating my ration of crackers with a lovely anchovy and Spanish olive tapenade, I remember a country song about a girl named Fancy, who was born dirt-poor and lived in a shack until her mother managed to scrape together enough cash to buy her a satin dancing dress.

The song isn't specific, but this dress somehow ended all of Fancy's problems.

I hum the melody to myself as I brush the taste of my anchovy-laced breakfast out of my mouth. Then I place my mink in a shopping bag and leave Fig's apartment. I'm wearing his sweatpants because they're warm and it's cold outside. Also, they're the only pants in the house that fit me in spite of my new diet. On top, I'm wearing a plaid coat-type garment Fig must use for hunting fox or quail or skeet or whatever they hunt on his family's farm in Virginia. Why such a garment would be here in New York is beyond me but I'm glad to have it because the mink's days in my possession are numbered.

At least I hope they're numbered. I'm armed with a list of consignment and specialty shops that deal in gently used fur, but it turns out that selling a gently used fur is not easy. As I make my way up Madison and down Fifth, I am chagrined to find the shops on my list are either closed or no longer exist.

As usual, the trend is over before I've gotten on board.

I wonder if I'd get arrested for hawking the mink on a street corner. Since I don't have bail money, I decide not to chance it.

I continue wandering down Fifth hoping to spot a random used fur shop. No such luck, but somewhere around Fifty-Second Street, not far from the St. John store where I bought a significant portion of my shoulder-pad infested former wardrobe, I see a small black woman lying on the sidewalk in front of a church. She's naked except for a green plastic garbage sack and is shaking uncontrollably, presumably from cold but maybe she's also having a seizure or something.

I look around at passersby, but no one catches my eye. More troubling, no one seems at all concerned about the shivering woman in the Hefty sack writhing at our feet.

I walk up the steps of the church but the front doors are locked. I hurry back down the stairs, trot around the writhing woman and poke my head around the corner of the church. There's another, smaller door at street level. This one is unlocked and I let myself into the basement of the church.

I stand in a warm, steamy hallway and look around. The space is not exactly dark, but it's shadowy because there's no fixture on the bare bulb hanging from the ceiling.

A man in khakis and a wrinkled white button-down cuts through the hallway and looks at me. His skin is so pasty against his dark hair I wonder if they ever let him out of this basement. "Five minutes," he says. He jerks his thumb back at the room he just came from. "Please wait in there."

As instructed, I step down the hallway and turn into the room, which is filled with cheap folding tables surrounded by an eclectic mix of dilapidated chairs.

I put my bag under one of the tables, sit down and wait for the man to come back and talk to me about what, if anything, should be done for the woman in the garbage sack.

The man never does come back, but other people, homeless-looking people, shuffle in over the next five minutes until the room is almost full. No one sits at the table with me, however. This rejection takes me back to third grade when I was the nerd with glasses who sat alone at lunch every day until I learned to hide my intelligence.

My trip down memory lane is enhanced by a small parade of women in hairnets who march through the room distributing brown trays to the people seated at the tables, including me.

I look down at my tray. There's a Styrofoam bowl of thin vegetable soup, a few hunks of cheap French bread and a small plastic cup filled with something too yellow and gross to be butter.

At this point, it occurs to me that the pasty-faced man thought I was homeless. I prepare to bolt with offended dignity until I realize he wasn't too far off the mark. If I hadn't had a key to Fig's apartment, I could have easily wound up like the woman in the garbage bag outside.

I look around the room but I don't see her anywhere. The diners are eating silently with their faces glued to their trays. The stingy soup drips off their plastic spoons like water.

I pick up my spoon and stir my soup. A few hunks of celery float up from the bottom but not much else. It's mostly just broth.

I take a second and study my tray. Other than the bread and the table-ware, this lunch is identical to the noontime fare served to the well-heeled diners at Fred's. I am struck by the odd notion that people at both extremes of the social spectrum are subsisting on this sock water. It pleases me to know that the food choices stay the same even as one slams into the bottom of the economic hierarchy.

As I eat my soup, or really, just let it slide down my throat because chewing is definitely not required, one thing becomes very clear. Watery soup like this may be the norm but it will not serve the needs of the homeless or the alarmingly thin women who shop among them.

When I leave the church, the woman in the garbage sack is gone.

I would like to wander aimlessly around the city because that would paint a dramatic scene to match my mood but my little toe hurts too damn bad. Also, I'm already forlorn, saturated with cold and very hungry.

I return to my posh new digs and think of the broken-down twin beds I saw in the church basement. As I'm eating my dinner, which con-sists of three crackers and four smoked oysters, I know I should feel fortunate but all I am is pissed. This would never happen to Fig. If Fig needs cash, he calls his banker and draws money from his trust. If he needs companionship, he calls any one of a dozen girls clamoring to date him. If he's hungry, he calls Gourmet Gallery and groceries magically appear.

Fig's life is so flipping easy. Even if I had someone to call, and I don't, because no one in my family has any money, I no longer have the techno-logical capability because my cell phone stopped working this morning. In a way, this pleases me because I no longer have to worry about the scary landlord's phone number showing up in my caller ID.

78

I'm chewing my last cracker when Fig's kitchen phone catches my eye. I walk over, pick it up and listen to the dial tone. There's a speed-dial list taped to the receiver. Gourmet Gallery is number five. I press the button and wait.

"Gourmet Gallery. Hello, Mr. Anton."

"Uh, yes," I say. "We'd like some groceries delivered."

"Certainly, ma'am. Your standard order?"

I nod until I realize he can't hear my head rattling. "Yes, and please add a dozen assorted donuts and a bag of Cool Ranch Doritos."

"What size bag, ma'am?"

"Family size will be fine."

"We'll be there in an hour," he says.

Just enough time for me to take a hot bubble bath.

In spite of the calming bath, I'm nervous when the delivery arrives. Fortunately, the kid from the store doesn't even attempt to collect money from me. "Can you add a tip for yourself to the account?"

"It's already built in," he says. "Have a good night."

That's the thing about really rich people. They never have to touch money. Or even think about it.

I dive into the donuts immediately. I don't even wait to unpack the rest of the groceries. I sink down on the kitchen floor with the box on my lap. Glazed, blueberry, chocolate-frosted, maple, Boston creme. At first, they're delicious. Then I start to feel a little sick and I have to take smaller and smaller bites. I nibble off each donut in turn so no particular taste will overwhelm, which enables me to keep going until all the donuts are gone.

When it's over, I push the empty box to the floor and stand up. I feel out of control, freaky and ashamed, like a heroin addict who just stole from her last friend to cover her latest fix. Which is exactly what I just did except my fix was food.

I stand at the kitchen sink fighting not to throw up and wonder why I continue hurting myself this way. I have no idea, except that sometimes it feels like my job.

I wonder what life would feel like if I just quit doing it.

When I wake up on Wednesday, I'm thirsty and groggy. I know my post-binge face will be as puffy as a prizefighter's. I don't even bother to look.

I've slept in Fig's sweatpants and T-shirt so there's no need to get dressed. I go straight to the kitchen and pull the grocery bags out of the refrigerators, where I shoved them just before I staggered off to bed.

I'm desperately hoping there's coffee hidden among my ill-gotten groceries and I giggle when I find it. I also find organic half-and-half. I dump coffee and boiling water into Fig's French press without regard to the ratio other than I make sure there's a lot of coffee.

While the coffee steeps, I take the groceries out of the sacks and arrange them by category on the refrigerator shelves. There's meat, chicken and fish; specialty cheeses; fruits and vegetables; organic milk and butter and some kind of eggs made with flaxseed.

Fig certainly knows how to live.

I sit down on a bar stool along the kitchen island and sip my coffee, which tastes so good I want to weep. The whole experience is so profound I feel like I'm in one of those cloying Taster's Choice commercials.

I'm no longer mad at Fig. I'm just thankful to have all these groceries. Like any good junkie in the calm of a post-fix haze, I resolve to cover the charge to his account before he's even aware of what happened.

He is my only friend, after all.

I also resolve to make this food last as long as I can. And to find a job that will generate immediate cash flow, however small, so I don't get into this verge-of-starving spot again.

I think about making myself an egg for breakfast but I'm not hungry yet. Probably won't be for several hours, maybe not until tomorrow. I think about diving into the Doritos just for fun but I'm actually more excited to go out and look for work.

All I want is a job that lets me walk a lot. Preferably one that's close to home so I can sleep in a little.

I get dressed in a pair of Fig's jeans, which are tight everywhere but at least I can get them on. His old blue sweatshirt completes my ensemble. I put on a little makeup and tuck my hair in a clip. I hate the new color but

SOUP IN THE CITY

at least it coats all the damage, so the strands aren't quite as crunchy as they used to be.

I leave Fig's building and walk slowly up Columbus Avenue. The first help-wanted sign I see is in the window of Gourmet Gallery, the source of my recent salvation. I take this as a good omen and enter the store. For a second, I wonder if I should take the sign from the window and hand it to the store manager in a confident gesture that would say, "You've found your girl." I don't, though, because it might make him mad and I think this would be a good place for me to work. Maybe I'd get a discount on groceries.

I go up to one of the cashiers and point to the window. "I saw your help-wanted sign."

She sizes me up. "It's not for cashier," she says, crossing her arms. "It's a delivery job."

This means tips. "Perfect." I smile but she doesn't say anything. "Do I need to fill out an application or something?"

She just stares at me. I stare back. Eventually, her head starts to shake in a teensy-tiny twitch that might mean no or might mean she has some kind of palsy.

I look around the store and then back at her. "Should I speak to the manager?"

She opens her eyes wide, like she can't believe I'm such a trouble-maker. Then she reaches under the counter that divides us and pulls out a notepad of applications. She rips off the top sheet and hands it to me. "Fill this out. I'll give it to him when he comes back."

I look at the questions and nod. "May I borrow a pen?"

She pulls one out of her hair, which is teased into a beehive so high she could easily have a whole package of Bics in there, and hands it to me.

"Thanks." I turn away, walk to the counter next to the coin-counting machine and scan the questions. The form wants to know if I speak English, if I'm authorized to work in the United States and if I've ever been to jail, arrested or wanted for any criminal violations.

This is going to be a piece of cake. I take my time writing each answer because neatness definitely counts. When I'm finished, I know I've passed the application with flying colors. I sign it and hand it back to the cashier, which irritates her because she's busy inspecting her fingernails. They're acrylic and need to be filled but maybe she's a little short on cash right now.

She doesn't bother looking at the application. She just tucks it under the counter.

"Thanks," I say. "When should I check back?" I remember from high school how to find a job like this. You always have to check back.

"What?" she asks.

"When should I check back? About the job? With the manager?"

She scowls. "Tomorrow, I guess." She turns away from me and resumes studying her fingernails.

"Okay," I say. "Thanks."

I leave the store, return to Fig's apartment and press number five on his speed dial.

A man answers. "Gourmet Gallery."

"Hello," I say. "Can you tell me the manager's name?"

"The owner's name is Joe. Is there a problem, ma'am?"

"No problem at all," I say. "Will he be in today?"

"He comes in every morning at six."

"Thank you very much." I hang up, go back to the store and ask a teenaged clerk if he knows where Joe is. The clerk leads me into the backroom where a balding, fifty-ish man with just a hint of plumber's crack is digging through the bottom drawer of a metal file cabinet.

"Joe, this girl is here to see you." The clerk leaves and Joe stands and squints at me.

"Hello." I extend my hand. "I applied for the delivery job. My name is Avery."

"Did you fill out an application?"

I nod. "This morning. I'm ready to start work today."

"You're a citizen?"

I keep nodding. "I live just around the corner."

He looks bleakly at me. "I take it you can read, too."

"Of course."

"English?"

"Absolutely."

"Let me get this straight," he says. "You read and speak English, live in this neighborhood and are eligible to work in this country, and you want to work *here*?"

"Yes, please."

He takes off his apron and hands it to me. "Well, you better get started before you change your mind. I'll go get the paperwork."

I spend the day organizing a huge refrigerator called a walk-in and stocking shelves with canned goods. I won't start deliveries until I'm familiar with all the products and where they're kept in the store.

When my shift is over, my arms and feet ache and I'm hungry. It's the good kind of hungry that comes from hard work and an empty stomach and not my usual freaky, over-caffeinated need to eat born of frustration, agitation and paranoia.

I haven't felt this feeling in a long time.

I hang my apron on a hook in the backroom and clock out. Joe is there. "By the way," I ask. "What does this job pay?"

"You make $7.15 an hour."

"Really," I say. "I would have thought it would at least be minimum wage."

"That is minimum wage." He points to a bulletin board on the wall. "I put you on the schedule from noon to nine Saturday through Wednesday. You get a half-hour dinner break at four-thirty."

This is more than forty hours a week. "Do I get health insurance?"

"You're on a probationary period right now," he says. "After that, we'll see."

"Okay," I say. "See you Saturday."

When I get home, I'm too tired to eat. I fall into bed and sleep for eleven hours straight. Without pills.

On Saturday, I'm sitting at Fig's counter sipping his coffee and wondering how I can make it through my first full day of work when the receipt from the grocery delivery catches my eye. It's $310. I do some quick mental math. This is roughly the amount of money I will earn in a week at my new job at Gourmet Gallery.

Before taxes, of course.

And the really sad thing is a substantial amount of that food is gone already, because I was home alone with it all day yesterday.

I pour more coffee and wonder how the employees in that store can afford to eat. The obvious answer is they're eating something other than the food they sell.

I take a shower and get dressed for work in Fig's blue sweatshirt and another pair of his jeans.

On my way out the door, I grab two apples and a hunk of cheese for my dinner break. I spend the day unpacking cases of canned soup and salivating over the smell of McDonald's French fries wafting from the back room.

Shortly before my shift ends, I'm replacing last month's magazines with the new editions when The Tool and some other guy, maybe from Chicago but maybe not, enter the store.

The Tool's apartment is near Lincoln Center. Too far away for him to shop here regularly. He's carrying a bouquet of flowers and a bottle of wine. I'm guessing he's going to a dinner party until he grabs a soon-to-be-retired issue of Cream My Puff. With this kind of reading in hand, I can't imagine where he's headed. I just hope he doesn't recognize me, partly because he was the go-between with my former landlord and also because he would laugh his ass off if he knew I was working in a grocery store. I release my hair from its clip so it hangs around my face and keep my eyes on the magazines in front of me.

He doesn't even look at me. He and his friend leave the store without incident.

I keep working and try to pretend nothing happened. But the truth is I would give anything for a few bucks so I could go to McDonald's like my more affluent co-workers.

CHAPTER 6:

Soup Salvation

- - - - - - -

DECEMBER 20, 2007 – JANUARY 31, 2008

After five long days at work, I'm standing at Fig's open refrigerators looking for something to eat when I come face to face with the reason New Yorkers eat every meal out. While they're at work, the groceries just sit in the dark of their refrigerators and rot.

I completely forgot about the fish that was delivered last week and it's really stinking up the fridge. I dump it in the trash can, carry the bag to the garbage chute and walk back to the refrigerator through an ammonia-like cloud of bad fish smell.

Unfortunately, the rotten fish was the last of the food. Today is December twentieth and I don't get paid until the fifth of January. As I rummage under the sink for a garbage bag, I wonder what I'm going to eat until payday.

Fig uses white garbage bags that aren't quite as big as the industrial-strength green ones currently making their way through the Fifth Avenue homeless scene. I pull a new garbage bag off the roll and hold it up for size, wondering if it would fit me if I suddenly found myself on the street without clothing.

It wouldn't. Everything, even naked homelessness, is easier if you're thin.

I shake out the bag and line the can with it.

Today is my day off. All this week, as I was working, I had the nagging sense that work was taking up too much time because I have pressing things to take care of. But now that my day off is here, I can't for the life of me imagine why everything seemed so urgent.

Probably because it is. I just can't see it right now, because, as usual, I want to hide my head in the sand. Of course, this is a bad look for me because my butt is just too damn big for exposure at that angle.

I decide today would be a good day to go to my old building and collect my mail. I don't know what they've done with the stuff in my apartment, but I'm pretty sure they had no interest in my bills.

I walk over to the East Side to my old building. When I get there, I smile at the doorman and head across the lobby. I don't think he has any idea who I am but he lets me enter the mail room unimpeded. If I were trying to deliver food to someone, however, I'm sure he would have leaped across the counter to stop me because that kind of thing is just way too dangerous.

I've been away for two weeks so of course the mailbox is jammed. I take a plastic grocery sack out of my purse, fill it with mail and swing the bag at my side as I nonchalantly vacate the building.

I feel a pang as I stand on the familiar sidewalk of my old neighborhood. I wonder what would happen if I went upstairs. Maybe my things are still there. Maybe I could just go up there and hang out a while.

Maybe there's some food left in the cupboards.

I turn around and go back into the building.

"Forget something?" the doorman asks.

I smile and nod. Maybe he does know who I am.

When I get upstairs, I knock on the door. No one answers. I knock again, harder this time. Still nothing.

I hang the plastic bag around my wrist and slide my key into the deadbolt. I allow myself a brief glimpse of hope but it won't turn.

I am literally locked out of life as I knew it, which frankly feels pretty shitty.

I return to street level and exit my building for the last time. As I walk back to Fig's, the weight of my outstanding bills cuts a little red streak through the puffy flesh on my forearm.

When I get back to the apartment, I make myself another pot of coffee and dump the bills out on the table. I desperately want something sweet, like a pecan sticky bun or some cinnamon-maple coffee cake, but of course there's no cash for that. All I can do is add extra sugar to my coffee, which turns out to be disgusting. I dump out the syrupy concoction, pour myself another cup and sit down with the bills.

I look at the nasty white envelopes for a moment and then shove them aside in favor of catalogs and other colored mail. I drink two cups of coffee while I peruse clothes I can't wear and furnishings I can't afford for a home I do not possess. Then I open the Christmas card from my grandma, which contains twenty dollars and an admonishment to buy myself something I need. My grandma is a waitress at a truck stop on the state line between Idaho and Washington but she always manages to send me a little something for Christmas.

This reminds me that Christmas is in five days. I'm working, of course, which means I need to celebrate my holiday now. I abandon the mail in Fig's kitchen and take my newly-acquired cash to Gourmet Gallery.

My step quickens as I walk to my favorite aisle. I'm dizzy with lust as I scan boxes of cookies, donuts and snack cakes on one side, chips and popcorn products on the other. Because funds are limited, I walk up and down the aisle carefully planning my purchases. I'll need something sweet and cakey, something salty and crunchy and something cold and creamy. All in large quantities, of course.

This is the first time I ever looked at prices in a grocery store. I add up various potential treat combinations and calculate my employee discount.

Each time, I come up short.

The longer I stand in the aisle, the more deflated I feel. And I can't help but hear the niggling little voice in my head, maybe mine but probably my grandma's, that says I don't need this garbage.

In fact, I need to spend my last twenty dollars on pseudo-food about as much as I need to smash each knuckle on my right hand with a ballpeen hammer. My grandma would tell me to buy a bag of dried beans and an onion and cook up a pot of food that would last a week.

I am propelled out of the junk food aisle by a force outside myself. The experience feels even more out-of-body as I stand and study the bags of dried beans. This is not something I imagined my New York self would ever do.

Although I'm not a native New Yorker, I am fully assimilated into the culture, which means I do not cook. I have not gone so deep into the lifestyle that I use my refrigerator for garbage storage like Courtney, who has a severe roach phobia, but I'm close. When my sister was visiting and wanted a scrambled egg, I picked up the phone and ordered it. Five or six restaurants in a two-block radius of my old apartment recognize my voice and know my address and credit card number from memory. They know my food preferences better than any man I've ever dated. Better than my mother.

For this reason, buying a bag of dried beans in Manhattan is a momentous occurrence. I am not afraid, however, because I come from cooking roots. My sister not only bakes her own bread, she does so with flour she grinds herself, from actual wheat kernels. In any of my relatives' homes, when one potato hits the frying pan, ten pounds of his brothers and sisters go down in flames with him. Although I come from a logging town, the women in my family cook like farmers' wives. They bake pies from scratch. Stouffers does not exist for them, even with coupons. I decide to draw on this legacy and make soup my familial contribution.

There is only one bag of beans in our store that comes with a flavor packet. Since I can't afford spices, this is the one I select. The soup recipe on the back of the bean package calls for ham. I go to the meat section, where it quickly becomes clear I can't afford ham. But I can afford a pound of turkey bacon because it's on sale. I grab a package, go to the produce aisle and select one large onion.

I take my humble purchases to the register. Rita, the girl with the beehive and acrylic nails, is working. "You making soup?"

"In theory," I say. I'm mesmerized by the way she tucks my purchases into a plastic sack because her hands move in an odd, overly affected way. Probably to avoid snagging her nails on anything.

She hands me my change. "There's some celery in the back that was pulled this morning. Might be good enough to cut up and use for soup."

I thank her, go in the back and fetch a few handfuls of the most youthful-looking celery and return to Fig's apartment.

As soon as I'm in the door, I yank the beans out of the grocery bag and study the recipe. There are two methods for pre-soaking the beans: the overnight method, where you put them in water in the refrigerator, and the quick-start method, where you simmer them on the stove for an hour.

Because I'm an instant gratification sort of girl, I choose the latter.

While the beans simmer, I chop the onions, bacon and celery. I'm not that great of a chopper so the pieces aren't that small and they're certainly not uniform but I decide they'll do. I brown them in a sauce pan and set them aside while the beans finish softening.

After a while, I start to feel like I'm on a cooking show. I wipe up the counters and scour the sink until an hour has passed. I pull the lid off the bean pot in great anticipation but my face falls at what I see inside.

The water is black, which troubles me greatly. Of course the recipe says nothing about this.

I call my grandma but she's not home. I leave her a message thanking her for the money, return to the stove and contemplate the steaming black water in the pot.

Recipe or no recipe, I'm sure this can't go into the soup. I dump the contents of the pot into Fig's gleaming colander, rinse the beans with the sprayer thingy and watch the black water wash down Fig's stainless-steel sink like it never even happened. I set the colander aside, again feeling like a TV-show chef, and wash and dry the pot.

I return the clean beans to the clean pot, add the browned bacon and vegetables and sprinkle in the contents of the flavor packet. Then I pour a quart of fresh water over everything, put the pot back on the stove and cover it. The lid fits tightly, like a good lid should.

I watch *Sex and the City* while the soup cooks, getting up to stir once in a while. After two episodes, it starts to smell like soup. I let it simmer for a third episode and then help myself to a bowl.

It tastes like soup. I'm amazed and thrilled and shocked I could be so happy over a simple pot of bean with bacon.

I report to work on Christmas day feeling surprisingly good. I expected to feel morose but the truth is I'm just happy to have somewhere to go.

My Christmas present from my boss is that today I get to deliver groceries. I start by packing the orders. The first calls for a package of celery, a jar of diet mayo, two cans of water-packed tuna, ten frozen diet dinners and a case of Diet Coke. A calorie counter if I ever saw one.

The second order is for an Atkins person. I pack eggs, cheese, bacon, steak, iceberg lettuce, blue cheese dressing and, not surprisingly, a rather large box of sugar-free, chocolate-flavored laxatives.

Not one order contains typical holiday fare, which is what I would have expected to pack on Christmas day. The other thing I would have expected is large parties but everyone, including the emaciated calorie counter and the beefy Atkins diet guy, is home alone. And no one has put up any decorations.

Later in the day a new trend emerges—Christmas parties attended exclusively by non-Christians. Between five and six p.m., I make deliveries to no fewer than four gatherings of attractive, well-dressed Jewish people gorging on Chinese takeout.

At one such function, a dark-haired guy with a Long Island accent and heartbreakingly beautiful blue eyes asks me my name as he reaches for his money clip.

"Avery," I say.

He peels off a twenty. "Merry Christmas, Avery." He pats my arm through Fig's hunting coat and hands me the money.

He's clearly Jewish, so I appreciate him appreciating my holiday. "Le Chayim." I smile and tuck the money into Fig's jeans as I walk away.

I return home that night with eighty-five dollars in tips and a bottle of Chardonnay to go with my soup. I am encouraged by my glimpses of the lonely and the not-so. For some reason, it no longer seems so difficult to cross to the other side. I have no idea how I got so stuck before.

A few days later, I'm applying makeup for work, a little more than I usually do, when Fig's phone rings.

It's the doorman. "You have a visitor," he says. "Nicole Ashley."

For a second, my throat won't work. What the hell is she doing here?

"Ma'am?" the doorman asks.

"Send her up." He seems to understand me even though my voice comes out like a croak.

I frantically race to the kitchen sink, turn on the faucet full blast and shove the watering can underneath the stream. When it's full, I lug it to the front door and stand there waiting for her knock. She rings the bell. I wait for the chimes to stop and then open the door.

Nicole Ashley smells like fresh air and the new kind of Chanel Number Five. She must weigh all of ninety pounds.

"Hi," I say. "It'll just take me a second to finish this stuff and then I'll be out of here." I lumber across the tile like a water buffalo and start dousing the plants on the far side of the foyer.

"That's okay," she says. "I'm actually here to see you."

I look up. "Me?" I ask. "Really?" Then I put my head down and keep watering.

"Anton has been trying to call you but your phone isn't working. He was worried."

"Oh, yeah. Sorry about that. I got a new cell phone and forgot to give him the number. I'll e-mail it to him."

"Why don't you give it to me, too?" she asks. "It would save me from having to come over here in the future."

Yes, why don't I? Because that part was a big, fat lie, that's why. I move to a new section of plants. "You know," I say. "It's new and I don't remember it right now. Why don't I e-mail it to you, too?"

"Okay." She pulls a small, leather-bound notepad out of her purse and writes her e-mail address on it. She rips off the page and hands it to me.

"Thanks," I say. "How are things going for you?"

She looks surprised. "Fine, I guess." She eyes me suspiciously, like maybe I'm going to hit her. I wonder if Fig has told her I'm violent.

"You miss him?" I ask.

Her face hardens. "I just wonder why he didn't want me to water his plants."

She studies me coolly but I have no answer for this. I shrug. "Maybe he didn't want to bother you."

"Maybe," she says. She hesitates for a split second, then turns on her heel and exits the scene. "See you later, I guess."

I walk back into the kitchen and look at the pot of onion and pancetta soup simmering on the stove. I wonder if she's also wondering why this apartment smells like soup. And whether she'll be catty enough to tell Fig.

I spend the next few days delivering food for New Year's parties. The holiday passes uneventfully and I'm glad when it's over. In January, the deliveries lighten up a bit because everyone's got their own little New Year's revolution going on. There's very little junk food in any of the orders. I notice this trend for about two weeks, and then the crap starts to creep back in.

By mid-January, I've received one paycheck, most of which went to pay off Fig's account, and have accumulated almost $700 in tips. Although I don't want to, I use some of my tips to buy a pay-as-you-go cell phone. It seems like the only thing I can do since I told the big lie about having a new cell phone.

I e-mail the number to Fig along with a breezy and fairly accurate description of what I've been doing. Staying busy, meeting lots of people and getting lots of exercise. Plants are fine, I tell him.

In just a few minutes, I get his two-word response. "No worries," he writes.

I have no idea what time it is in New Zealand but I'm guessing he's keeping some odd hours because I know everything is turned on its head down there. Also, in light of his brevity, it occurs to me he may have met someone, which might explain why Ashley Nicole was so testy the other day.

But I can't concern myself with these kinds of things. I have two refrigerators full of vegetables that need cooking right away.

Ever since that day when I took a few hunks of flaccid celery from the back room, Joe has counted on me to haul away the vegetables not suitable for display. He sent me home with bags of them almost every night this week. There's so much I commandeered my grocery delivery cart for personal use. To preserve this excess, I've been making soup like a crazy woman and storing it in Fig's massive freezers.

Just in case things get tight again.

Last night I came home with another cartful of surplus vegetables. To supplement the free produce, I used some of my tips to buy a couple roasting chickens, a few pounds of buffalo burger and several kinds of fresh herbs. It all cost less than half of one of my sushi dinners from the old days.

I need to get everything made into soup and put in the freezer before it goes bad, so today, my day off, I have a whole lot of cooking to do. I spend an hour perusing soup recipes online and then adapting them to what I have on hand. The rest of the day is devoted to washing, chopping, seasoning, simmering, stirring and skimming. After several hours, I'm greasy and the kitchen is greasier. I put three huge stockpots of soup in the refrigerators to cool and scrub the kitchen. Then I take a quick shower and go to Fig's closet for a clean pair of jeans.

I pull a pair off the hanger and slide into them. They go on easy. The monumental implication of this ease eludes me for a few seconds, until I'm reaching for a fresh shirt and I feel the jeans move with me instead of cutting into my flesh like they usually do. This delicious feeling, the give of previously unforgiving fabric, jolts me into a new dimension. A skinnier dimension.

There's actually enough room between me and the jeans that I could tuck in my T-shirt if I wanted to, but I don't bother because I'm not going anywhere. I pad into the kitchen, enjoying the feeling of clean floors under my bare feet, and fix myself a soup sampler for dinner. I've made chicken soup with organic brown basmati rice, roasted red pepper soup and vegetable beef soup, or actually vegetable buffalo but somehow that just doesn't sound right.

I pour myself a glass of wine and take my tray into the den, where I watch *Sex and the City* videos without getting mad at all.

CHAPTER 7:

Soup in the City

- - - - - - -

FEBRUARY 2008

I've been working at the store for about six weeks when I report for my Saturday shift and Rita comes out from behind her register and follows me into the back room. She stands in the doorway inspecting me while I put a few containers of soup in the employee refrigerator and clock in.

"You're losing weight," she says. "It's all that soup you're eating."

I nod at her as I tie my apron on. "You might be right. This morning I actually had to cinch my jeans with a belt. *That* hasn't happened in a while."

"For me, either," she says. She pats her hips and makes a face. Rita has three kids and lives in Queens. I'm not exactly sure where that is but evidently it involves a lengthy commute. Most days, she brings a plastic container of some kind of tortilla/cheese/hamburger combination that smells delicious but which is probably pretty fattening.

"I have plenty of soup," I say. "Do you want me to bring some extra for you?"

"Oh, I'm fine. I just bring my leftovers from supper." She turns to leave. "But thanks."

"No problem. Let me know if you change your mind."

On my break that day, I take one of my plastic containers out of the refrigerator, pour the contents into a chipped white bowl and set it in the microwave, which is none too clean. While the soup heats, I shove the cold, dirty soup container into a plastic grocery sack to take home and run through the dishwasher.

I'm washing the soup off my hands when it occurs to me that the whole aesthetic of bringing lunch to work is just nasty. No wonder Rita doesn't want any of my soup. Digging into someone else's cold plastic container from home definitely doesn't inspire any confidence about the quality of the meal inside, which is unfortunate because it would be nice if Rita or some of the other employees would help me eat the soup. Fig's freezers are overflowing with the stuff.

The next morning, I get up early, fix myself two eggs and toast and then head out in search of a cool kitchen store I saw once during a marathon barhop with Fig. It was somewhere on Columbus Avenue uptown from his place. I walk all the way up to Ninety-Fifth without seeing it so I cross the street and walk down the other side.

I find the store in the low Eighties. Not at all where I remembered, which is one indication I'm not a true New Yorker. Real New Yorkers can give you the cross streets of any business in Manhattan. Also, if you try to lie to them and pretend you live at Eighty-Second and Madison or wherever, they'll ask what corner and then tell you that's impossible because that's where the Duane Reade is.

Anyway, as I remembered, the store's window is filled with little ivory crocks. They look like they'd hold a generous single serving of soup and they have their own little lids. I go into the store and pick one up. It's heavy and kind of rough and feels good in my hand.

A saleswoman approaches me and smiles. "May I help?" She's wearing a long skirt and stands with her toes pointed out, like a ballerina.

"Are these microwaveable?"

She nods. "And dishwasher-safe. They're adorable, aren't they?"

"How much?" I ask.

"Eighty dollars."

"You're kidding. Eighty bucks?"

"We only sell to the trade," she says. "That's the price by the dozen."

I think quickly. I really want these crocks. "What's the minimum order?" I ask. "I'd like these for my soup business."

"You're in the soup business?" She walks behind the counter and consults a black binder. "You'll need to order a minimum of two dozen."

"Okay," I say. I have no idea what I'm going to do with twenty-four of these crocks. All I know is I have to have them.

She pulls out an order sheet and looks up at me. "What's the name of your soup business?"

"Soup."

I watch as she writes the word on the order sheet.

She looks up. "Is that it? Soup?"

I hesitate for only a second and smile when a name comes to me. "Soup in the City."

"Cute." She writes the name on the order sheet and takes my address. "What does the business do?"

"It's kind of a soup diet. Homemade soup delivered to your door every day. You lose weight, save money. That sort of thing."

"Really?" she asks. "And this is your business?"

I nod. "It's new and I'm still working out some of the kinks. But I've lost a ton of weight and have slashed my food budget to the bone."

"Are you accepting new customers?" she asks. "Because I'd like to sign up for something like that."

"Great." I pause and think for a minute. When I start talking again, a sales pitch flies out of my mouth like it's been incubating there for months. "Well, we provide lunch and dinner Monday through Friday. The soup is delivered to your door before you go to work. Or at work, if you prefer. You return the prior day's containers when you get your soup the next day."

"You're going to need more than two dozen crocks," she says. "I have tons of friends who would sign up for this. How much did you say it was?"

"It's seventeen dollars a day." Now that I'm in the food delivery business, I know this is the price at which nine out of ten people will hand you a twenty and tell you to keep the change.

"When can I get started?" she asks.

"Tomorrow?"

"Perfect. I'd like it delivered here. I'm Joanne, by the way." She reaches out and shakes my hand.

I'm so excited to have a customer I increase my order by a factor of six, which seems perfectly sane until I realize I just spent the better part of my life savings. I leave the store imagining twelve dozen crocks following merrily behind me.

When I return home from work that night, the doorman tells me he put some boxes in the foyer. I study his face for a second, wondering if he's suspicious of the contents or whether I'm just paranoid. I've heard these co-ops can get a little fussy about what goes on inside the units. I can just bet they won't be happy if they find out I'm running an up-and-coming soup delivery business from within their hallowed halls.

I try not to think about this as I go upstairs to deal with the crocks. Twelve dozen turns out to be a lot more than I expected. I haul them, box by box, into the kitchen and run them through Fig's dishwasher, which takes five separate cycles during which time I whip up soup for tomorrow. I make a batch of chicken soup with fresh rosemary and thyme and a roasted tomato soup from a recipe I found on the Internet.

I'm up very late. When the crocks are clean, I have nowhere to put them but on towels along the length of Fig's fourteen-foot dining room table. I'm not planning on doing much entertaining, but somehow the crocks' takeover of the dining room bothers me. Probably because I'm a nutcase to have ordered so many crocks.

I get up early Monday morning and deliver two crocks of soup to Joanne. As expected, I get twenty dollars for my trouble, which almost pays for the ingredients in all the soup I made last night.

Now I just need more clients. I think about this as I walk down Central Park West to Fig's building. The walk takes a while so I decide it would be nice to concentrate the clients in the vicinity of my temporary home.

Kind of like the way my grocery route is organized. I'm busy all day at my regular job, but I never venture further than six uptown and three cross-town blocks from the store.

As I make my grocery rounds that day, a marketing idea begins to take shape. I could simply distribute flyers for my soup business while I'm delivering the groceries. This feels slightly inappropriate at first, but I decide there's really no harm in it. After all, everyone in Manhattan is bombarded with take-out menus from every direction. They practically stick to you like lint as you walk down the street. Also, I'll still buy the food the customers are eating from Gourmet Gallery, so the store won't lose any business. It'll just sell the groceries to me instead of directly to the consumer.

I don't know how to reconcile this with my employee discount or all the free vegetables Joe gives me but I'm sure I'll work it out somehow. Maybe I'll bring soup to work for all the employees.

Anyway, I feel strongly this is the right thing to do because there are people on my route who could use some soup. The chronic dieter with her never-ending stream of frozen dinners comes to mind, as does the mother of three who subsists entirely on fish sticks, chicken fingers and instant mashed potatoes.

My mind races with ideas as I rush through my deliveries. I return home that night lugging groceries for two more batches of soup, this time minestrone and Spanish garlic soup, with the text for my flyer already written in my head. While the soup simmers, I sit down at my laptop and pound out a very simple flyer. "Soup in the City. Homemade soup to feed your soul, not your size. Save money and slide into your skinny jeans. Daily delivery Monday through Friday."

I e-mail the file to Kinko's and order five hundred copies printed on pink-and-white-striped cardstock that reminds me of an old-fashioned candy bag. I have no idea if this is a good marketing move but at this point I'm too bleary-eyed to care.

After a quick shower, I change the voice mail greeting on my new phone and collapse into bed.

On Tuesday, I rise early and deliver two more crocks of soup to my client. "How was the first day?" I ask.

"Delicious," she says, handing me another twenty. "I wasn't hungry at all, but I think I could use some instruction on how the diet works."

I hand her change but she waves it away. "Do you have particular questions?" I ask.

"Well, I guess so," she says. "Like, what am I supposed to have for breakfast?"

I think about my breakfasts over the last few weeks. "Whatever you want. Eggs and toast, oatmeal, even a waffle here and there. Eat whatever sounds good that morning."

"Whatever I want?" She exhales in frustration. "I want enchiladas and beef stroganoff."

"Then eat that. The point of having what you want for breakfast is not to deprive yourself or you'll freak out. Just relax and enjoy."

"What about wine?"

"I have a large glass almost every night. Or three. I'm still losing."

"Red or white?"

"Live dangerously," I say. "Feel free to go both ways as you prefer on any given night."

She laughs.

"Are we good now?"

"Okay," she says. "See you tomorrow."

I stop by Kinko's and pay cash for the flyers. This eats up $165 of my tips but I think it will be worth it.

I go to work with fifty flyers tucked in my back pocket. It takes me a little while to get up the courage, but about an hour into my deliveries, I'm at the calorie counter's apartment and I feel brave enough to hand her one. "I'm also delivering homemade soup in the mornings."

She takes the flyer and reads it. The skin on her hand is drawn too tightly across her bones. "Is this how you're losing so much weight?"

I ignore the "so much" and smile at her. "It is," I say. "It's the first thing that ever worked for me. And I'm saving money. I used to eat too much take-out."

"I'd love to eat take-out," she says. "But it's too fattening."

"Why don't you give this a try? It might be a nice break from frozen dinners."

She signs up. By the end of the day, I've distributed my fifty flyers and have seven new customers.

As I make clam chowder and navy bean soup that night, I'm happy. Very tired, but happy.

On Wednesday morning, I collect almost two hundred dollars from my soup clients. I take it to the store, buy more groceries to make soup that night and haul them back to the apartment. Then I have a huge bowl of oatmeal with raisins and head back to the store to report for work.

I'm standing in the dairy aisle packing my first order when this guy, this tall, well-built guy, comes up to me, obviously looking for something. He's wearing nondescript jeans and a brown suede jacket. If it's not Armani, it's a very good approximation. He has dark hair, short but not military, and nice brown eyes.

"Do you work here?" he asks.

I glance down at the apron I'm wearing and look back at him. "Did you need something?"

"Sorry," he says. "That was stupid. I've seen you here the last couple weeks." He holds out his hand. "I'm Kevin McCall. I live a few blocks from here and I was hoping you'd let me take you to dinner sometime."

Now this is just too much. Can't he see I'm a total loser? I have no idea what to say, but his hand is still extended so I shake it to avoid being impolite.

He grins at me, at which point I guess I'm supposed to say something. "My sister's name is McCall."

"Really," he says. "What's yours?"

"Avery."

"Your name is Avery McCall?"

"No," I say. "McCall is her first name."

"McCall Avery?" he asks.

Now we're in a Nicole Ashley/Ashley Nicole quandary that is making my head hurt. I take a deep breath and exhale loudly. "My name is Avery St. George. My sister is McCall St. George." I glance at him. He seems to expect more so I continue. "We were named after towns in Idaho. My other sister is Meridian." I realize how stupid this sounds and turn back to my dairy products. Surely he will now see the colossal mistake he made in approaching me and beat a hasty retreat.

But when I look up, he's still standing there. Still smiling at me. "Are you from Idaho?"

"I guess so. My family is still there."

"So maybe I can take you out for a potato. How does that sound?"

I guess that sounds about as good as anything. Still, I can't believe he's asking me out. "I don't know," I say. "Will this potato be fried?"

"It'll be triple-fried if that's what you want. Are you into gravy?"

"For me it's all about the ketchup," I say. "Maybe we're incompatible." I scan the dairy case searching for fat-free half-and-half. "And I don't even know you. Maybe you're a freak or something."

"I'm a regular customer here. I come in at least once a week and buy totally normal groceries. So just tell me when I should pick you up and I'll let you get back to work."

Now here's the thing about New York. Guys just tell you where to meet so they don't have to catch a cab to your place and then pay for another cab to the restaurant.

"You want to pick me up?" This encounter is growing more surreal by the second.

"I wouldn't have it any other way," he says. "Just tell me when and where."

"Saturday night. Ten o'clock." I'm off on Friday but for some reason I'm reluctant to give up my evening at home.

"Are you that girl who doesn't eat until midnight?"

"I get off work at nine," I say. "That's the best I can do."

"Good," he says. "For a second I thought you were too cool for me."

I don't bother to tell him there's not much danger of that. I take a notepad out of my apron, pull a pen out of my hair and write down Fig's address. "Just tell the doorman the apartment number. He'll call up for me."

He takes the paper from me and reads it. I'm expecting a reaction to the address but he doesn't flinch at all. Maybe he doesn't know New York very well.

"Okay, Avery." He shakes my hand again. "I'll see you Saturday."

When I get home from work that night I'm exhausted and it's no wonder. I've worked five days straight and made soup late into the night for the last four nights. I have tons of soup in the freezer and am tempted to give my clients frozen soup tomorrow but that feels a little like cheating because it might not be as good as fresh.

So I stay up late one more night and make an Asian-inspired soup with ginger and shrimp. It's a pretty skinny soup so the other one, potato-leek soup with kale, is a little more substantial.

The next day is Valentine's Day, so I give each of my clients a little dark chocolate heart in red foil to go with their soup. Some of them are surprised they can have chocolate on the soup diet and it occurs to me I should have explained things better, because the basic idea is that if you eat soup for lunch and dinner, you can have anything you want at the other times. The point is you don't really want a whole bunch of other stuff throughout the day, especially garbage food, because it's difficult to be freaky about food when you're full of good soup.

Also, it turns out that a few clients are a little hungry after the soup sometimes, which of course happens to the best of us. I suggest apples with a little cheese or natural peanut butter. This snack always keeps me going, yet the weight just keeps melting away. Lately I've been noticing how sharp my hip bones are when I roll over in bed.

When I'm finished with deliveries, I have a little over four hundred dollars in my pocket. I'm heading up Fifth Avenue in search of an appropriate date outfit when I get waylaid by another sighting of the woman in the garbage sack.

She's on the same corner in front of the same church in the same green sack. Even the convulsions look a little too familiar.

I march around the corner of the church and let myself in through the side door. I don't see the pasty-faced guy but there is a woman checking things off on a clipboard, which is always a good indication of authority.

"Excuse me," I say.

She looks up from her clipboard. "May I help you?"

"I guess I'm concerned about the woman in the garbage sack out front. Do you know anything about that?"

The woman rolls her eyes. "She has an apartment in Harlem. Her little garbage sack thing is a complete scam."

For a second, I can't believe anyone would go to such lengths to put one over on people. Then I remember a certain sable coat tucked safely away in the vault at my bank and I'm not quite so indignant.

The woman continues. "We just can't seem to get rid of her and frankly it really hurts the work we do when she's out there rolling around like that."

"People won't come to church because of her?"

"No," she says. "People still come, but the congregation is starting to feel a little unsympathetic. Our donations have fallen off 10 percent since she's been out there."

I take a flyer out of my pocket. "Speaking of donations, I have a little soup delivery business that generates a pretty significant surplus each day. I was wondering if you'd like to take the leftovers off my hands."

She reads the flyer and eyes me suspiciously.

"Seriously," I say. "It's all frozen and ready to go. All you have to do is thaw it out."

"You make the soup and it goes straight to the freezer? It's not parked in a warming dish for days on end?"

"Once it's made, it goes into the refrigerator to cool. The next morning, whatever isn't used goes straight from refrigerator to freezer."

"Can you deliver it here?"

This is not exactly convenient for me but it would avoid scrutiny from Fig's doormen, who seem to be monitoring my comings and goings with more interest every day.

"Sure," I say. "It would be easiest to bring it on Thursdays."

"That's perfect. Weekends are our busiest times."

"People are hungrier?"

"Fewer shelters are open." She hands me her card. "I'm the director here."

I read the card. Her name is Roberta Small.

"I'm Avery St. George." We shake hands. "I'll be back in an hour with the soup."

"You're bringing soup today?"

"Absolutely. I'm running out of freezer space."

I leave the church and head across the park to Fig's. When I get there, I pack as much soup as I can into my grocery delivery cart, which is basically a large metal basket on wheels with a long handle. The basket is lined with a clean, thick blanket to insulate the soup and protect it from the doorman's prying eyes. I throw another blanket over the top and wheel the frozen soup out of the building.

It should only take about twenty minutes to pull the cart across the park but my phone is ringing off the hook and I have to keep stopping to talk to new customers and answer questions about the soup diet. Can they have wine? What about dairy? What if they're craving jerk sauce like crazy? To which I respond yes, yes and go to Jamaica.

When I finally get to the church, my arms are aching from pulling the cart under the weight of all the soup. But I'm very glad I found someone to take it off my hands. Even with this donation, Fig's freezers are so chock full I'm afraid to open the doors because bricks of frozen soup keep falling out on the floor and I definitely can't afford a broken toe right now.

I park the cart just inside the door and walk down the hall looking for Roberta Small. She's sitting at a desk in a small office. "I have the soup," I say. "Where should I put it?"

"Let's take a look." She stands up and we walk down the hall to the cart. I remove the top blanket to reveal an abundance of square, flat bricks of frozen soup neatly contained in clear plastic freezer bags. On each bag I've written the type of soup and date made in black Magic Marker, a trick I learned from my grandma in her jam-making days.

"This is great," Roberta says. "Let's just bring it in here."

I follow her into the kitchen, wheeling the cart behind me, and she and I stack the soup in a large rectangular freezer.

I promise to bring more soup next week. When I leave the church, I think about shopping for a date outfit but decide against it. Dragging my cart around in the department stores would be too weird.

Kevin McCall will just have to take me as I am.

On Saturday night at ten o'clock sharp, I'm wrapped up in one of my wrap dresses when the doorman calls on Fig's phone.

"Kevin McCall is here to see you."

"Thank you," I say. "I'll be right down."

I put on my mink, pick up my purse and ride the elevator down to the lobby.

Kevin McCall is indeed waiting and looking pretty cute in his brown suede coat and just the right amount of nervous.

"Hi," he says. "Good to see you."

I smile and wave a teensy little wave at him. For some reason, I feel too shy to speak in front of the doorman. Kevin puts his hand on the small of my back as we leave the building.

"Wow," he says. "This is soft." He rubs my coat for a second. "Is it fur?"

"It's mink. It's sheared so it's just the softest part of the fur."

There's a cab waiting at the curb. He opens the door for me and I slide across the back seat. He climbs in beside me and shuts the door.

"I thought we'd have dinner in the Village," he says. "Is that okay?"

I smile and nod. He tells the driver the address and the cab zooms forward and darts into traffic.

"So how was your day?" he asks.

"Fine. I worked all day. Nothing too eventful."

He nods. I can't see his face very well in the dark of the cab. "I worked, too. Then I helped my mom with some stuff."

"Are you from here?"

"I've lived in the city all my life," he says. "Just around the corner from you, in fact."

"Hmm," I say. He doesn't seem at all interested in the incongruity of my address and my job. For a second I feel the need to explain and then decide against it. "What did you work on today?"

"I'm a graphic artist," he says. "Today I worked on the art for a book cover."

"Really? What kind of book?"

"It's a novel about a disgruntled pilot who goes nuts and starts crashing planes."

As I think about this, I can feel a wrinkle forming between my eyes where my Botox is wearing off. "How many planes could one person crash? Wouldn't the first one put him out of business?"

"That's right," he says. "It's not a very good novel."

I process this for a minute. Maybe I should become a novelist. I'm envisioning myself at book signings and wondering what I'd wear for my appearance on Larry King Live when the silence in the cab starts to seem awkward.

"And what did you help your mom with?" I ask.

He grins at me and laughs a little. "It's a little too random to explain," he says. "Maybe later."

Silence again, but I'm too exhausted to do anything about it. I put in a long week and just finished a nine-hour day. I sit back in the cab and decide to allow myself the luxury of saying nothing.

"So thanks for coming out," he says. "I know you must be tired, so I won't keep you out too late."

"You know, I'm actually surprised at how tired I am. It just hit me. I guess I've been staying up a little too late this week."

"Yeah?" he asks. "Doing what?"

I eye him warily. Suddenly, his abrupt entry into my life seems a little too convenient. Maybe he's a spy planted by Gourmet Gallery. Or the co-op board in Fig's building. "It's a little too random to explain."

"Fair enough," he says. We sit in silence for a few minutes and then the cab pulls up in front of the restaurant. He pays the fare, which makes me feel funny. I never know what I'm supposed to do about the money thing. I'm dreading the moment when the check comes.

I slide out of the cab and stand on the sidewalk while he gets out. "Thanks," I say.

"My pleasure." He holds the door open for me to enter the restaurant.

I was expecting him to take me to some special French fry place but fortunately he's not that dorky or obvious. He's selected a little bistro I've never heard of. It's cozy and nice. Not too fancy but not too casual either.

The prices are reasonable but I order with care anyway. The quiche is twelve dollars and comes with a side salad.

"Do you want wine?" he asks.

I smile. "I actually like that more than potatoes."

"Chardonnay?"

I smile again and nod a little. He orders a bottle.

We spend our time during dinner discussing random bits of nothing, which I find surprisingly pleasant. The wine is good and that makes things a little easier.

When dinner's over, the waiter brings the check and sets it smack dab between us. Kevin McCall reaches for it immediately and pulls it to his side of the table.

I'm about to thank him again but he interrupts me. "Thank you for having dinner with me, Avery St. George. This was very nice."

I'm thinking it was very nice too, until I'm back in the apartment and I realize he didn't ask for my number or say he would call me or anything.

I decide this is probably for the best. I have a lot going on and I just don't have the energy to try to impress anyone right now.

The next morning is Sunday, so I don't have deliveries. But I do have to put in my shift at the store. I know I should get up early and organize my new customers into a delivery route, or maybe get a jump on making the soup I'm going to need for the next few days. If not that, I could go get groceries, or look up recipes online, or figure out a system to keep track of my receipts so my life isn't a total train wreck at tax time.

But all I do is lie in bed not wanting to do any of it. It would take a humongous metal spatula and three or four very motivated men to scrape me off the mattress right now.

According to Fig's clock, which is some kind of nuclear clock that projects the time onto the ceiling, I have to be to work in less than two hours. And then I have to make soup after that. And go to bed late and get up early and deliver it to my thirty or so clients. And then go to work, make more soup, go to bed late and get up and do it all over again.

I have no idea how I'm going to keep up with all this. The lure of a massive dose of caffeine is the only thing that gets me on my feet. I don't bother to shower or put on makeup because I'm definitely not going to distribute any flyers or try to solicit for any new business today.

In fact, now that I think about it, I might not have enough crocks for all the customers I have right now. Which means I have to haul my sorry carcass back up to the crock store and buy some.

I grab wads of cash off the dresser, stuff it into Fig's jeans and schlep to Starbucks for many shots of espresso with a little steamed milk. There's no time for sweetener. I grab a few napkins on my way out and gulp my drink as I head over to Central Park West to try to catch a cab. I can't see a yellow car to save my soul, but I keep looking over my shoulder as I walk uptown just in case.

By the time I get to the store, my feet and legs are killing me and the words running through my head are definitely not the kind of thing I would ever say out loud.

Unless, of course, the store is out of crocks and can't get them for me until Thursday, in which case the objectionable words come streaming out of my mouth in a veritable fountain of impotent, frustrated, sleep-deprived rage.

I don't really realize what I'm doing until I look up and see Joanne's mouth wide open. Her eyes are even wider. I stop talking and clap my hand over my filthy mouth. She's not only my crock supplier but my first client and here I am swearing like a sailor in front of her.

I keep my hand pressed across my face until I've counted to five. "I'm sorry," I say. "I have no idea what got into me. Please have the crocks delivered as quickly as you can and I'll just pay for everything now and shut up."

She consults a file and adds some numbers on her calculator. The new crocks are over a thousand dollars.

I stand at the register sorting and counting money for several minutes. She stands and watches but is unusually quiet. She's probably afraid of me now that I've shown myself to be a volatile, angry freak.

I am indulging in the idea that I might be able to afford to quit my grocery job when I realize I don't actually have enough money to pay for the crocks. I count it out twice but come up short both times.

"I'm sorry," I say. "This is all I have. Can I pay the rest on Friday?"

"That's fine," she says.

I apologize again and turn to leave.

"Avery," she says.

I stop and look back at her. She's smiling.

"I've lost another four pounds. I thought you might want to know. So get some rest and keep up the good work."

I smile, raise my fist and shake it in a victorious sort of way that says defeat is not an option. Then I turn and leave the store. The smile falls off my face as I gingerly walk down Columbus Avenue. My feet are so sore it feels like I'm walking on bloody stumps. And of course there's not a cab in sight.

Kevin McCall is loitering outside Gourmet Gallery when I limp up to the entrance. Actually, he's just leaning against the wall looking about as cute as anyone can look, but my impression of him is of course colored by the fact that I've already declared the day to be a total disaster and nothing is going to change that.

He stands up straight and walks toward me. "Are you limping?"

I nod. "I've been walking too much. Occupational hazard."

"Do you have time to get some coffee?"

I pull my cell phone out of Fig's jeans and check the time. "I have half an hour."

As we walk across the street to Starbucks, I'm hobbling like one of those Chinese women with bound feet.

"This isn't going to work at all," he says. "You're a mess." He sits me down at a table. "What do you want?"

"Plain coffee is fine. With a little half-and-half."

I watch him order the coffee and doctor it up. He has long legs and moves like one of those relaxed guys who never get uptight about anything.

These guys, of course, do not exist in the neurotic, adrenalin-driven world of hedge funds. I don't know anyone like him, except maybe Fig. But anyone with all Fig's money would of course be relaxed all the time so with Fig maybe it's not a naturally occurring condition. Kevin McCall, on the other hand, seems like he was born that way.

He returns with the coffee. "I have an idea."

"You want to play hooky and ride unicycles all day?"

"No," he says. "But that's a great idea." He takes a sip of his coffee. "What I was going to say is I can help you with your deliveries today."

I tap the bottom of my cup on the table. Hot coffee sloshes out of the lid and he hands me a napkin.

"Seriously," he says. "My mom has one of those motorized scooters, like a wheelchair but more agile, and you can ride it. I'll walk alongside and pull the grocery cart."

I smile. Kevin McCall is completely unconcerned about his impression on other people, which is exactly what I need right now. "You'd do that?"

"Sure," he says. "It'll be fun."

He leaves me at Starbucks. Ten minutes later, he comes back riding on a bright yellow scooter. I get up and walk out to the curb. He looks ridiculous, which I find absolutely thrilling. I can't stop smiling. "Are we allowed to run this on sidewalk?"

He stands up and points to the blue placard affixed to the handlebar. "Yes, because you're handicapped."

I sit down on the scooter. "You got that right."

He shows me how to operate it and we make our way to the corner and cross the street at the light. I navigate my way down the sidewalk and stop just short of the entrance to Gourmet Gallery.

"Okay," he says. "So how do we do this?"

"I have to go inside and pack the orders. Then I'll bring the cart outside and we can go."

"You sure I can't help with that?"

This guy is getting cuter by the second. "I'm pretty sure but let me go check." I get off the scooter and go inside to find Joe. I am really limping by the time I get to the backroom.

"Whoa," Joe says. "What happened?"

"You hired a tenderfoot. But don't worry. I brought fresh horses. Can my friend help me today?"

Joe raises his eyebrows. "That's a good friend. I don't care. Just get my groceries delivered and don't kill yourselves."

I limp out to Kevin and get back on the scooter. "We're good," I say. "Joe says you can help." I giggle as I drive the scooter across the automatic door pad into the store.

I watch from the scooter while Kevin becomes my surrogate body. He clocks me in, grabs a delivery cart and walks to the phone where the first stack of orders is waiting.

As we move through the aisles packing the deliveries, he takes it all so seriously I have to smile. He's very careful to keep the frozen foods together and make sure nothing gets smashed by canned goods. He doesn't even seem embarrassed when we have to pack feminine hygiene products. Also, he looks very professional in his apron with a pencil behind his ear.

We leave the store in good time. He's definitely quicker at packing than me. I laugh again when I go through the automatic door. I don't know why, but it seems a little crazy to drive through a doorway.

The deliveries are eye-opening. No one wants to look at me or hand me the money now that I'm handicapped. They just want to deal with Kevin.

When our cart is empty, we head back to the store. I'm scooting slowly along the sidewalk and he's walking beside me.

"How'd you get this scooter, anyway?"

"It's my mom's."

"She's handicapped?"

He doesn't respond. Maybe this is not the correct term anymore. "Physically challenged?" I ask. "Walking impaired?"

He looks at the sidewalk for a few seconds and then straight ahead. "She's morbidly obese. She could walk if she lost weight but she's just too heavy right now."

I bite my upper lip and concentrate on driving. Suddenly, the scooter doesn't seem fun anymore. I have no idea what to say. "I'm sorry," is all I can think of.

"It's okay," he says. "We don't have to talk about it."

We're silent for about half a block. "Does she live with you?"

He shakes his head. "That would be enabling. She's on her own but she still manages to get her hands on way too much food."

"Can she work?"

"She works for a call center from her apartment. It's all on the phone so she never has to leave. Her apartment is paid for and she makes enough to cover the maintenance. And take-out, of course."

"But she could use this scooter to get around if she wanted to?"

"She could but she doesn't," he says. "I don't think she's left her place in a year. But I keep it charged up just in case."

"Has it always been this way?"

He shakes his head. "That's the crazy thing. It's just since my dad died. They had tons of friends before that. Went out all the time. I just don't get it."

I do, but I don't say anything.

"So you don't have to worry about me being a wacko. I had a totally normal childhood. Totally normal family. My mom just isn't handling her widowhood very well."

I nod. "I understand. It must be tough."

At some point around eight, Joe takes pity on Kevin and lets us off early. He shakes Kevin's hand and thanks him profusely. Me, however, Joe doesn't feel too sorry for. All I get is a scolding to buy some new shoes.

I drive the scooter out on the sidewalk, put it in park and stand up. "Thanks so much. I couldn't have done it without you."

"Glad to do it," Kevin says. "It was fun."

I smile, look down the block toward Fig's apartment and then look back at Kevin. "I'd like to take you to dinner or something but I actually have to get home and make a bunch of soup tonight."

"Oh, sure." He nods like this is an excuse he gets from girls all the time. "I understand."

"So I was wondering if you'd want to come over and keep me company. We could order in sushi and I have some wine . . ."

"Do you make good soup?" he asks.

I shrug. "I guess so."

"Why don't we just have that, then?"

Yes, why not. We go back into the store, get some groceries and go to my place. The scooter leaves the doorman in quite a dither but there's really nothing he can do. It is for the handicapped, after all.

When we enter the apartment, I watch Kevin for a reaction. Still nothing. I take off my shoes and slide into the kitchen in my socks. He follows and sits down on a barstool at the island while I open a bottle of wine.

We toast and he takes a couple long drinks. Then he pauses and looks at me over his wine glass.

"Okay," he says. "I can't stand it anymore." He sets his glass down, stands up and waves his arms around the apartment. "What the hell is going on here? Do you deliver groceries as some kind of community outreach effort?"

I start laughing. "Thank God. I was starting to think you were an earthworm."

He shakes his head. "No one could be that oblivious." He sits back down and gulps more wine. "This is a crazy apartment. Surely you know this."

I nod. "I know. It's my friend's. He's away for the winter and I'm watering his plants."

Kevin looks at me and smirks a little. "Watering his plants?"

"No, no," I say. "It's nothing like that. He has a girlfriend and it's not me. I'm actually squatting here without his knowledge. I lost my job and my apartment in the sub-prime mortgage crisis so I moved in here until I can figure something out."

"What's with the soup?"

"I started making soup because I didn't have any money and it was all I could afford to eat. Then some people started buying it from me and now I have a little business called Soup in the City. I deliver soup to my clients every morning."

"And groceries all afternoon," he says. "No wonder your feet are trashed."

"Exactly. But I have some bills to clean up so I have to keep going until I get back on my feet."

"That's only going to work if you have any feet left," he says. "In fact, I think you should sit down."

I plop a big sack of vegetables into the sink. "I have to wash these first. I'll sit down while I chop."

He stands up, walks around the island and picks up a small paring knife. "You sit down now," he says, pointing the knife at me like he means to do something with it. "I'll wash."

I scamper around the other side of the island, sit down in his chair and watch him wash the vegetables. He slides my wine glass and a cutting board over to me. "Start chopping," he says. "I'm hungry." He tosses a pile of wet carrots at me. "What are we making, anyway?"

"Tomato bisque and turkey vegetable."

"Is that one soup or two?"

"It's two." We drink and chop and cook. Both soups turn out delicious, but not as delicious as the good night kiss he gives me when he leaves.

After my day on the scooter, my feet are a little better and I make it through the next morning's soup deliveries without much trouble. I even have enough time to stop for new shoes before reporting to my other job. I ask the salesman to throw the old pair away and I wear the new ones out of the store. They feel pretty good, so I think I'll be able to make it through the day.

Kevin is waiting outside the store with the scooter when I arrive. I laugh when I see him and hold up my hands. "No handicap today," I say. "I'm fine."

"How'd it go with the soup?"

"I have too many customers. So many people are calling I'm running out of minutes on my cell phone if you can believe it."

"Sounds like a good problem to have," he says. "But I believe it. It's good soup."

Now I don't know what to say. I'm suddenly aware that this is the second day in a row he's been loitering outside my place of business, which probably is a good sign that he's a desperate loser with nowhere to go and nothing to do. "So," I say. "What are you doing?"

"I just came by to make sure you're okay. Now I guess I'll meet some friends for basketball and then I have some work to do."

"The bad book cover?"

He laughs. "Let's hope it's a good cover for a bad book. I should finish it up tonight."

"Then what?"

"Then I'm between projects. I usually only work about one week a month."

"Oh." I try to sound neutral but instead come across like I'm worried that he's a desperate loser with nowhere to go, nothing to do and nothing to spend. I sigh. "Well, I guess I better get to it."

"Okay," he says. He rubs his hands on his jeans. "What would you think about giving me your number so I can quit stalking you at your place of employment?"

I hand him one of my flyers. "It's at the bottom."

He glances at the flyer, folds it and tucks it into his pocket. "Okay," he says. "I gotta go. I'll call you later."

"Okay," I say. "Bye." I go into the store feeling like a huge idiot but I'm not sure why.

Kevin doesn't call me for two days, which is enough time for me to stop worrying that he's a freak and start worrying that he's not going to call. When the phone finally rings, I decide to stop analyzing and just be happy to hear from him.

"Hi, Avery," he says. "How's your day going?"

"Fine, thanks." I'm deliberately short because I don't want him to turn into one of those chat-on-the-phone guys. The Tool used to do that all the time. He'd call me almost every day to keep tabs on what I was up to, but wouldn't say anything about what he was doing and would almost never ask me out.

This is how New York guys keep you on a string while they hunt for the bigger, better deal. It's really bad out there, and heaven help you if you're dealing with a guy who sends text messages.

"Well, anyway," Kevin says. "I was wondering if you'd like to get together again. Maybe tomorrow?"

This diving-right-in thing Kevin McCall does is so shocking I can't even remember what day it is. "What's tomorrow?"

"Well, I was thinking we could go out for a burger and then see a movie or something."

"No," I say. "I mean, what day is tomorrow?"

"Oh," he says. "It's Thursday."

Thursday is my day off, at least from the store, which means I can make soup in the afternoon and go out that night. "That would work," I say. "What time?"

"I'll pick you up at seven?"

"Okay," I say. "See you tomorrow."

So now I have another date with Kevin McCall, who evidently is the kind of guy who eats burgers. This tells me he's not fucked up about food, which is a very refreshing change from all those hedge fund guys with their macrobiotic eating disorders.

CHAPTER 8:

Fear and Rejection in Manhattan

- - - - - - -

MARCH 1 – 15, 2008

I don't see Kevin for a while following our burger date. He calls and asks a few times, but every time I have to say no because I'm busy with work or soup or both and when I'm not busy I'm exhausted.

Finally, I call him on a Thursday morning, exactly two weeks after our last date, and ask if he wants to walk across the park with me to take soup to the church. He seems surprised but happy at the invitation and in thirty minutes is standing in my kitchen helping me load up a cartful of frozen soup.

As we walk across the park, I feel sort of light, like I'm floating. I stop walking to get my bearings, but as soon as I start walking I feel it again. It's the strangest feeling I've had in my life.

Kevin turns around and looks at me. "You coming?"

"Yeah," I say. "I just feel a little funny." I decide it's because Kevin is pulling the cart and I'm unaccustomed to moving around without its weight dragging behind me. But when he stops to answer his phone and I take a turn with the cart, I still feel funny.

Kevin ends the call and takes the cart again. I start walking and skipping and hopping, trying to figure out where this ethereal feeling is coming from, and I stop cold when I do.

My thighs no longer rub together when I walk.

I'm standing in shock with my mouth open as Kevin gets further and further away. Eventually, he turns around and sees that I'm lagging. He sets the cart upright and runs back at me. He's running really fast, like he's the kind of football player who does the tackling.

I cower in one place because I've never been athletic and I have no reaction skills. Just before he gets to me, he slows to a brisk trot. Then he scoops me up in both arms, runs in a wide circle and literally carries me back to the cart.

I had no idea this was possible, but it is extremely fun to be jostled in a running man's arms, especially when he doesn't groan or collapse or anything.

When we get to the church, I introduce Kevin to Roberta Small. They shake hands and I'm glad he's the type of guy who smiles and doesn't say a lot of stupid things if he's nervous.

"How's it going with the soup?" I ask.

"It's a Godsend," she says. "We had very few donations this week and one day our cook called in sick. It was so nice to have on hand when we got pinched. And our diners really love it."

"Great," I say. "I'll see you next week."

We leave the church and walk up Fifth Avenue. Kevin is pulling the cart with one hand and holding my hand with the other. Our arms are swinging between us.

"I have an idea," he says.

"Unicycles?"

He stops swinging and looks at me. "What's with you and the unicycles? Do you really know how to ride one?"

I smile a closed-lipped smile and look at the ground modestly as we walk. "I do. I guess I'm hoping for a chance to show off my only athletic ability."

"Well, that's going to have to wait, because today we're going to get you some new jeans."

I ignore him and keep walking. He's crazy if he thinks I'm trying on jeans in front of him.

"Seriously," he says. He ducks behind me and clasps his hands around my hips. "There's way too much fabric here."

SOUP IN THE CITY

People are streaming around us on the sidewalk but not paying any attention to us at all. I look down. Sure enough, Kevin's hands are overflowing with denim.

I wriggle out of his grasp and trudge forward.

He gets up off the sidewalk and follows me. "If you want to be the soup diet guru of Manhattan, you can't keep hiding inside these jeans. They're too big for you."

I shift my eyes from side to side. This is not going to happen. "I'd rather pull out my toenails with needle-nose pliers."

"Oh, come on," he says. "What's the big deal? It'll be fun." He opens the door to the Gap and yanks me inside. The store is thumping with music and there are tourists everywhere. "Let's find a salesgirl." He leaves me and the grocery cart near women's jeans. I stare at the floor, wishing it would swallow me.

He returns with a teeny little blonde girl named Britney and points at me.

"She needs new jeans," he says. "Can you help?"

"Sure," she giggles. She's wearing a little blue top that's puffy around her midriff. It makes her hips look even tinier than they really are.

Kevin looks at me and I give him the best stink-eye I can muster. Wisely, he looks back at Britney before he turns into a pillar of stone. "Can she just wait in the dressing room and we'll pick out some jeans and bring them to her?"

"Sure," Britney says. "This way." I half-heartedly follow for a few steps. When I try to veer off course, Kevin is right behind me, grabbing my shoulders and nudging me back on track.

Britney is wearing a bracelet made of faded pink telephone cord that has a key attached. She rolls the bracelet off her wrist and unlocks a dressing room door. "What size are you?" Her voice carries like a car alarm.

"I have no idea." I enter the dressing room without looking at her and slump down on the bench. Mercifully, Britney and the evil person known as Kevin McCall shut the door and leave me alone.

I hate them both.

Fifteen minutes later, they return with jeans. Britney is carrying a tall stack of folded jeans neatly balanced across both hands. Kevin's offering is messier. He has many pairs hanging on his left arm and one pair tossed casually over his right shoulder like a dishtowel.

He gathers the jeans he's carrying into a wad and hands them to me. "These were on clearance so try them first." He turns and takes the folded jeans out of Britney's arms. "This is the full-price stuff, just in case." He sets the stack on the bench next to me. I give him another stink-eye and he backs out of the dressing room. "We'll check on you in a while." Then he lowers his voice. "Don't kill anyone. It's just jeans."

He shuts the door and leaves me to my misery, which threatens to flood my small cubicle when I realize Kevin the sadist has brought clearance jeans with tags marked "Pencil Cut" in sizes two and four.

Of course, the reason these jeans are on the clearance rack is no one could hope to wear them, even in skinny Manhattan. In fact, the demand is so low they're marked down to $8.99.

I pout for a minute and then look around the dressing room and decide what the hell. No one but me and the pervert manning the surveillance camera will witness this little debacle. If Kevin asks I can always tell him the jeans were unfortunately way too big through the thighs. I kick off my shoes, stand up and release the buckle on my belt. Fig's jeans fall to the floor in a heap. Because these jeans have been quite loyal to me, I bend over, shake them out and place them neatly on the bench.

I unfold the first pair of pencil cuts and step into them. I scrunch my eyes closed and pull them up. The experience is amazing. They slide right on. I mean easily, without any tugging or swearing at all.

I zip up the jeans and examine from all angles. They look terrific. These size-four, chain-store, pencil-cut jeans look terrific, which means my soup diet has accomplished the impossible. I feel the overwhelming urge to run through the streets of Manhattan shrieking at the top of my lungs.

Instead, I calmly put on my shoes and go out to the cashier to pay for my amazing new jeans. Then I find Kevin so we can hustle our butts to Kinko's and order more flyers.

Afterward, we stop at a sushi place for lunch. While we wait for the food, Kevin leans back in his chair.

"I'm glad I got to see you today," he says. "This is nice."

I nod. "I'm sorry. I've just been so busy lately."

He looks up as the waitress sets two steaming mugs of tea in front of us. When she leaves, he looks back at me. "Do you want to be?"

"Not really. But I don't know what else to do at this point. I'll need enough money to get my own apartment pretty soon, so I just have to keep going for now."

"That's tough," he says.

"Thanks." I wrap my fingers around my mug. "But you don't have to feel sorry for me. I got myself into this and I can certainly shovel my way out."

"I'm actually feeling sorry for me. I'd like to spend more time with you, Avery."

I don't know what to say to this so I take a sip of tea. And then another and another.

"I'm sorry," he says. "I know I sound like a big sap but I don't meet girls like you very often. Or ever, if you want the truth."

I scratch my neck, which is suddenly very itchy. "Girls like me?"

"You know," he says. "Who aren't looking for a meal ticket and have more going on than their latest pair of shoes."

All I can do with this is nod and look around for the waitress. I wish she'd hurry so I can get home and make the goddamn soup so I can go to bed and get up and do it all over again tomorrow. As the weeks grind on, I move slower and get less sleep, which makes me even more tired and hence even slower. The vicious cycle has escalated into a mind-numbing, never-ending haze that makes me feel like a prisoner of war in some kind of third-world work camp.

Then I realize I'm ignoring Kevin, who has been talking the whole time. "I'm sorry," I say. "What did you say?"

Kevin roughs up his chopsticks as the waitress sets down the food. "It's nothing," he says. "I was just saying I haven't worked since that last cover we talked about."

I cross my arms and give him a couple once-overs. "You know, you look like an able-bodied young man with a little too much time on his hands. Would you like a job delivering soup five days a week?"

He crosses his arms and stares back. "Well, yes, ma'am. I think I might."

"I'll pay two dollars per delivery and you'll get tips, too. Should come to around five dollars per customer."

He squints and rubs his forehead with his index finger. "Now aren't you forgetting something?"

"Like what?"

"Well, like certain fringe benefits." He raises his eyebrows and stares at me like I should know what he's talking about, but unfortunately I'm clueless.

"I'm sorry," I say. "I don't have a benefits package."

He laughs. "I'm talking about soup. I'd like to take soup to my mom."

"Oh," I say. "Of course. And anyone else in your family. There's plenty to go around."

As we leave the restaurant, I feel a little bit lighter. Now I'll be able to use my mornings to make soup and actually get to sleep at a decent hour.

The next morning, Kevin reports for work promptly at seven. When I open the door, he's standing there with a tray of Starbucks. I silently bless him as he follows me through the foyer and into the kitchen.

"Does your doorman hate you?" he asks.

I look at Kevin in alarm. I forgot to warn him that the doormen can't know about the soup. "What happened?"

"Nothing," he says. "He just looked like he wanted to carve my liver."

I take the lid off my coffee and savor the first sip. "I think he's suspicious of all the comings and goings with the grocery cart."

"How many times do you bring it in and out?"

"Too many. I leave a couple times in the morning with soup and return with empty crocks. Then I take the cart back out to work and come back in with groceries that night."

"Can he see what's in the cart?"

"No. I always cover it with a blanket. And I wrap the crocks in little hand towels to keep them from rattling."

"Well, maybe that's part of the problem. He probably thinks you're running a meth lab up here or something."

I shake my head. "The problem is I'm not supposed to be running a business from here. I'll have to find another place to live." I look around Fig's spacious, well-appointed kitchen and sigh as I envision the hovel I'll be able to afford. Making soup on a hot plate won't be easy, but I guess I can do it if I have to. I push my hair out of my eyes with my forearm and start ladling soup into crocks. "I'll find a new apartment without a doorman."

"An elevator building without a doorman is going to be tough," he says. "And you have to have an elevator."

Suddenly I feel tired. I stop ladling, slump against the counter behind me and stare at all the soup. "You know," I say. "This is probably just as illegal as a meth lab. I'm sure the city requires licenses and inspections for this sort of thing. I should find a commercial kitchen that will let me make soup."

"What about the kitchen at Gourmet Gallery? I'm sure you could work something out with Joe."

"Yeah," I say. "At $7.15 an hour. He'd want all the profits because he owns the store. I'm just a minimum-wage grunt there."

"You sure?" Kevin asks. "He seems like a good guy. Maybe he'd partner up with you on the soup thing."

I shake my head. "I'd need to file for a trademark on the name first. Otherwise it would be too easy for someone to steal it from me."

"Someone meaning Joe?"

"Well, anyone. I really should get it done but I think it's complicated. And probably expensive."

Kevin doesn't say anything and I get the feeling he thinks I'm a paranoid jerk.

"Anyway," I say. "I haven't had time to worry about that kind of thing."

"Okay," he says. He pulls the cart out of the kitchen and waves over his shoulder. "I'll see you later."

On Saturday morning, after two days off from Gourmet Gallery, I can barely stand the idea of going back to deliver groceries. It's all I can do to tear myself away from Fig's soup cookbooks and report to the store for my shift.

Joe is in the backroom going over some paperwork when I get there. "Hey, Joe." I find my time card and clock in.

He snorts a little but doesn't look up from his papers.

As I go through my day, I wonder why I'm so reluctant to quit. I'm clearing more than five hundred dollars a day on the soup business, even after paying Kevin, and I'm running myself ragged and ignoring my more profitable venture. Delivering groceries is starting to feel very much like stepping over dollars to pick up pennies.

When I go to the store to pack my next round of orders, I stop by the backroom to talk to Joe. I stand at his desk feeling a little nervous and a lot like an asshole, but I'm not sure why.

He's still doing paperwork and is still grumpy. "What is it, Avery?"

"Well, I need to talk to you about something."

He looks up. "You're giving notice?"

Now how did he know that? I look at my hands. My nails are ragged and my cuticles are dry and cracked. "I guess so. But I'll keep working until you can find a replacement."

"Like that's gonna happen." He sounds complimentary and irritated at the same time. "I knew you wouldn't stay forever. Just finish your shift today and we'll call it good."

I'm sad as I finish out the rest of my deliveries. When I get back to the store, Joe is gone. I clock out for the final time and leave a goodbye note on his desk.

I'm still a little melancholy the next morning, but I hustle out of bed and get myself to a nail salon for an early-morning manicure before the Sunday throngs get too thick. It feels so good I treat myself to a pedicure, too.

I feel a little twinge of guilt at my extravagance when I pay the tab, but I'm planning to spend the day promoting Soup in the City and I have to look good for that, so I consider the forty-five bucks an investment in my future.

I stop at Starbucks and sip espresso while I wait for my polish to dry completely. Then I return to Fig's, take a shower and put on some makeup. I'm starting to feel like my old self again. Actually, like a new-and-improved version of my old self.

I fix myself a power breakfast of two eggs and a side of oatmeal with raisins so I have energy for my big marketing blitz. Then I grab a stack of flyers and head out to drum up some new customers.

Today my target area is the four-block radius around Fig's apartment. I plan to methodically distribute flyers at every strategic location. I'm not exactly sure what the strategic locations are, but I think they include every little store and bar with an ATM in the back. I figure I can set a stack of flyers somewhere near each machine and maybe get some attention that way. I also plan to offer a flyer to every person I pass and scatter them on tables in coffee shops and hotel lobbies. If I get really brave, I might walk into bakeries and ice cream stores and offer flyers to the counter staff. If anyone needs a healthier lunch, I'm sure it's these people. I won't bother with delis. They have their own soup, however inferior it might be.

In my mind, this all seems perfectly easy and natural. I can visualize people stopping to take my flyers and maybe even smiling and talking to me for a little while.

When I hit the sidewalk, however, I remember I'm in the middle of Manhattan, which is not exactly a stop-and-chat kind of place. I take a deep breath and try to hand out some flyers but everyone steers clear. They won't even look at me, much less stop and chat about soup. At this point it becomes apparent that I am an idiot. Just another loser with no job and something to sell.

What the hell was I thinking? These people don't want soup. And if they did, they could get it anywhere, at any time of the day or night, delivered in fifteen minutes or less.

After five solid minutes of rejection, it's clear that accosting people on the street isn't going to work. What I really need to do is get into the office buildings. Law firms, hedge funds, real estate brokers. The girls who work in those places have money and are always looking to lose weight.

Unfortunately, Sunday isn't the right day for that kind of marketing effort, but at least I can get outfitted for the task so I'm ready to go when the business world opens tomorrow morning. I decide a pink Chanel suit would be a lovely ensemble to wear while I'm marketing to the corporate world.

I walk to Chanel's flagship store on Fifty-Seventh Street and stand in the middle of the wide sidewalk staring at the entrance. The building's black façade is austere and cold, as are the mannequins in the windows. I feel like I'm poised at the edge of a flimsy bridge in high winds.

Frankly, I've been blown off this precarious perch many times before. And now, I definitely can't afford to drop three grand to outfit myself for some fucked-up fantasy that's never going to happen. I don't even have the balls to hand someone a flyer on the street. How do I think I'm going to get up the courage to walk into the office of some superior, already-thin hedge fund people and give them one of my stupid flyers? You can't even get past the lobbies of those buildings without an appointment anymore. What am I going to do? Call up ABC Investment Bank and tell them I need to stop by and sell soup to them?

I'm insane. That's all there is to it. And the only thing I can think to do about this is stop in a diner for some pancakes and try to get my wits about me. After all, it's Sunday and no one is working today. They're all sitting in diners having brunch, after which they'll go home and read the Sunday Times and take a nap.

So although I'm still full of eggs and oatmeal, I abandon my selling efforts in favor of finding a suitable place for a civilized little respite from my stressful day. I walk back to the West Side and find a good place on Columbus not far from Fig's building. I sit down in the only empty booth and scan the menu.

If I order eggs, they come with hash browns and toast but I can substitute pancakes for a dollar more. A side of pancakes, however, is only $1.50 and then I get the hash browns and toast, too, so that's what I order.

As the waitress is leaving, I decide I'm too hungry to wait and need an appetizer. "Do you have rice pudding?"

She turns and looks at me. "Yeah," she says. "It's pretty good."

"Can I have a side of that to start? I'm really hungry."

"Coming up." She leaves and returns with a good-sized bowl of rice pudding topped with whipped cream and sprinkled with cinnamon. I pick up my spoon, dip the tip into the pudding and take a small bite.

It's a little bland but it will keep me going until the real food arrives. The next time the waitress passes by, I ask for more cinnamon and also some nutmeg and that makes it a little better.

The pudding is almost gone when she comes back and plunks several plates down in front of me. Judging from the size of the pudding, I should have guessed the portions would be big here, but I'm still a little surprised at the volume of food in this breakfast.

She reaches for my pudding bowl to take it away but there are a few bites left. "No, no," I say. "I might need that."

She drops her trouble-making hand to her side. "Anything else?"

"Ketchup. And can I get a side of gravy?"

I don't think I like gravy, but Kevin mentioned gravy that first day he asked me out so maybe there's something to it.

"Brown?" she asks.

I have no idea what this means. "Whatever you usually serve."

She returns with ketchup and a bowl of gravy, which is as thick as the pudding and has a nasty-looking skin on it. "You sure eat a lot for a little girl."

I laugh a little. "Yeah," I say. "I guess I do."

She leaves me alone with my stash, at which point I stare at my plate like it's a dope-filled syringe I'm about to shoot up less than two hours out of rehab. I take a deep breath and pour some ketchup on the hash browns, just in case I want a little bite or two. After all, something salty might be a nice change after so much sweet pudding.

I pick up my fork and consider what to do. On the one hand, I don't really need this food. On the other hand, I'm quite thin these days. Even the waitress noticed. So even if I eat all the food on all these plates, I'll still be thin. So this one time, it seems okay. As long as it's just this one time, of course.

I dig in and start eating. I'm not used to this much food anymore, so it takes me a while but eventually I get it all down.

Then it occurs to me that I also can eat two pieces of cherry pie with ice cream. Even then, I'll still be thin.

When it's over, I can barely breathe. I give the astounded waitress some money, stagger out of the diner and go home and lie down. I'm way too sick to do anything else.

Later that afternoon, after I've made tomorrow's soup and I'm lying on Fig's couch contemplating the resurrection of my eating disorder, it occurs to me I didn't hear from Kevin the whole weekend. I realize this is probably because I've declined his last four invitations. Also, he knows I was working last night. But the fact is he could have asked me out for Friday when he finished the deliveries and he didn't. Maybe he feels uncomfortable now that he works for me, in which case I wish I hadn't hired him.

I always manage to screw this stuff up somehow. I roll over on my bloated stomach feeling quite confident I will be alone for the rest of my life. I'm in this rather fragile and pathetic state of mind when I get an e-mail from The Tool at around six Sunday night.

"What are you doing?" he wants to know. This question is The Tool's standard booty call.

When we were dating, the rare instances when I actually saw The Tool usually occurred on Sunday when he tired from all his weekend antics and wanted to be with someone who didn't require him to exert himself in any way. I was his doormat. The only effort he had to make was to occasionally wipe his feet across my ego.

I'm staring at the message and wondering what to do when my phone rings. It's Kevin. He's playing pool with some of his friends at a bar off Ninth Avenue and wants to know if I'd like to join them.

I briefly consider dashing off a vicious rejection to The Tool before I leave. Instead, I just press delete and go meet Kevin and his friends.

When I get to the bar, I decline to play pool. My stomach is still uncomfortably full and bending over a pool table might cause waistband-induced asphyxiation. I pass on the beer for the same reason.

Kevin orders a glass of ice water for me and leaves to finish a game while I chat with his friend Duncan.

Duncan is a very skinny guy who looks like Elvis Costello, dark glasses and all. He tells me he lives in old tenement housing in Hell's Kitchen, which is not too far from my, I mean, Fig's place, and went to school with Kevin. For the last eight years, he's been trying to make it as an actor on Broadway.

I can't decide if he's gay or not, but it doesn't matter. Mostly I'm interested in how he handles the rejection. "How do you get out of bed every morning?"

I'm expecting some kind of sales-training garbage about how every "no" puts you one step closer to a "yes" but Duncan is a little more morose than that.

"I have no idea," he says. "Now that you mention it, I probably should quit and get a real job."

"What would you do?"

"I don't know. I didn't exactly finish college."

"I know what you mean."

We sit glumly on our barstools, side by side with our backs to the bar, and watch Kevin take a shot. When he's finished, he walks over to us, leans between our shoulders and grabs his beer off the bar.

"What's wrong with you two?" he wants to know.

"Fear and rejection in Manhattan," I say.

Kevin glances at me and then glares at Duncan. "You're like an infectious disease. Would you cut it out?"

"She was depressed when she got here," Duncan says. "It's not my fault."

Kevin takes another drink of beer. "Somehow I don't quite believe you. Avery, I'll just finish this game and we can get out of here."

"No," I say. "It's okay. He's right. I came in this way."

"Why?" Kevin asks.

"It's too stupid to talk about," I say. "I just got sidelined by rejection today."

"What rejection?"

I shake my head. "I'm a loser at sales. I went out with big plans of promoting my soup business and now I just feel like an idiot."

"Well, that's completely understandable," Kevin says.

Duncan leaps off his chair like he was ejected from it and walks away. I want to do the same, but Kevin's now standing right in front of me with his hands on my knees. There's no escape, which means I have to sit there and blink at Kevin, wondering what to say next.

He laughs a little. "All I mean is you can't promote anything without a good logo. It's no wonder you're struggling." He reaches in his back pocket, pulls out a pink business card and hands it to me.

I take the card and look at it. It has my name and a caricature of me sipping soup off a large wooden stirring spoon. He's exaggerated my cheekbones and my figure but it's definitely me, right down to my cinched jeans and messy up-do, which he's somehow made elegant and sexy with artful little tendrils framing my perky face. All in all, Logo Avery is effortlessly cute and mischievous and stylish and exactly who I've always wanted to be.

I tap the card against my palm. Maybe Kevin McCall sees the world in a caricature sort of way, which might explain his rather inexplicable attraction to me.

"You don't like it," he says.

I look back at the card and shake my head. "No, no," I say. "Are you kidding? It's amazing. It's great. I love it."

It's just that I don't feel nearly as together as this girl looks. I hand the card back to him. "I think I'd be self-conscious to use this."

He's staring at me with his mouth open, like my head just spun around three times in one direction and then three times the other way.

"I like it," I say. "A lot. But it's not like I really look like that."

SOUP IN THE CITY

He makes a disgusted coughing sound. "Are you nuts? This is so you it looks more like you than you do. It's so you I can't stand it." He waves the card around in frustration. "This is the very *essence* of you."

"The essence of me is onions and chicken broth," I say. "Let's not get carried away."

He makes a face. "I'm keeping you away from Duncan from now on." He pounds the rest of his beer, sets the empty mug on the bar and waves at his friends. "We're outta here." He looks at me and jerks his thumb over his shoulder. "Let's go, grumpy."

I stand up and follow him. "Where are we going?"

"We're going to spiff up your flyer." He opens the door for me and I step past him onto the sidewalk. "You'll see. When we're finished you'll want to hand it to everyone you meet."

We walk briskly to the corner and stop and wait for the light.

"Okay," I say. "My flyer sucks. I get it. That still doesn't tell me where we're going."

"My place."

Kevin's place is a fifth-floor walkup a few blocks from Fig's apartment. There's no doorman. In the old days, this might have bothered me but now I can see the benefits of not being monitored by some overbearing uniformed thug every time you leave or enter your building.

Anyway, the stairs are long and steep. By the time we get to his front door, I'm breathing so hard I'm worried I might hack up a lung. To make matters worse, I'm trying to hide the panting from Kevin so he won't know I'm aerobically challenged, which means the oxygen deficiency is not going away anytime soon.

He unlocks two deadbolts, opens the door and lets it swing open. "Madam," he says.

I walk past him into a decent-sized studio apartment with wood floors and exposed brick walls. It's decorated like something you'd see in a book about optimal designs for small spaces. The room is saved from being pathologically tidy by the closet door, which is wide open. I count six shirts, one suit and five pairs of jeans hanging neatly on identical wooden hangers.

"Do you want something to drink?" He walks over to his desk in the corner and fiddles with his computer, which also must be a stereo because music comes out. I don't know what the music is but it's not Barry White so it doesn't bother me.

"Okay," I say. I can't take my eyes off his computer screen. If it were curved, it could almost be the screen in an IMAX theater.

"Pretty big, huh?" he asks.

"Well, they say size matters."

"Yeah," he says. "I heard that, too." He hands me a glass of white wine. "So what do you think?"

I sip my wine and look around the apartment. "It's nice."

"Yeah?"

I nod. "Actually, it's perfect. Everything you need and nothing you don't. I should try to find a place like this. Is it expensive?"

"Not bad," he says. "But I bought it a long time ago."

I'm always surprised when people buy studio apartments. "Really?"

"Well, I figured I could rent it out if I ever needed something bigger. It'd be easy to find a tenant this close to the park."

"What would it go for?"

"I could probably get a couple thousand a month. Maybe a little less with what's going on in real estate lately."

Suddenly, Fig's cavernous apartment seems empty and cold. I can't wait to get home to my computer and find myself a cute little studio close to the park. "So what are we going to do to fix my horrible flyer?"

He looks a little sheepish. "I actually did it already."

I smirk at him and look around the apartment. "Then what are we doing here, Kevin McCall?"

His eyebrows go up and he grins like he's been caught at something, which of course he has.

"Oh, I don't know," he says. "I guess I wanted to show it to you when there weren't so many distractions."

He walks to his desk, opens a drawer and pulls out the new flyer. He looks at it for a second and then hands it to me. The wording is the same, but the presentation is much more stylish. There's a silver soup spoon on a pink background, and the bowl of the spoon is overflowing with gold glitter in a perfect nod to the magic of soup.

The caricature of me, however, is nowhere in sight.

"Where's Logo Avery?"

"Oh," he says. "So now she wants to be on the flyer. Aren't you the girl who was too embarrassed?"

Now I'm caught. I don't know what to say so I drink wine and try to find a point of discussion in his apartment. Unfortunately, he's a minimalist so there are none. "Well," I say. "It sure is clean in here."

"Do you want to sit down? We could watch a movie or something."

I eye the brown leather couch, which is positioned on the wall opposite the giant computer screen.

"Seriously," he says. "Just a movie." He walks to a credenza under the window, opens it up and scans through his DVDs.

"I would have figured you for a Netflix guy."

"I am," he says. "These are just the things I watch again and again."

No one watches the same thing again and again. Except me, of course. "Why?"

"Well, as you can see, there's not much space here."

"No," I say. "Why do you watch them more than once?"

"I write screenplays. It helps me understand the structure of the movie."

"So the book cover thing?"

"Same as the soup deliveries," he says. "Pays the bills until I sell a script."

"How's that going?"

"Nothing yet, but I did land an agent a while back, so maybe something will pop soon." He pulls a DVD from the shelf. "How about *The Godfather*?"

I shrug. "Okay."

"Do you want popcorn?"

This is kind of scary because microwave kettle corn is one of my binge foods. "If you do."

He thinks for a second. "I'm okay. We can order in Chinese later if you want."

We sit down and watch *The Godfather*. At first, Kevin is pretty intent on the screen. He pauses the movie once in a while to point out things I wouldn't have noticed, which is kind of fun. He seems to know a lot about movies so maybe he'll actually sell a script someday.

Eventually, though, his arm is resting on the back of the couch and he's dropped the remote in favor of playing with my hair.

I'm surprised at my reaction. Normally, on the day of a big binge, I'd be completely disinterested because my stomach is totally splooged out. But this hair thing he's doing feels nice and before I know it, my eyes are closed and he's moved on to my neck and I'm not at all concerned about all the pancakes and crap I ate this morning.

This is obviously a problem because if this goes too far, Kevin McCall is going to discover how disgusting I am and I'm just not ready for that to happen right now.

But then he's kissing me and I'm even more surprised because I'm not doing any of my usual freaky things, such as constantly jockeying for the best aesthetic angle or doing serious battle in the clothing tug-of-war so I can delay or even avoid actually getting naked in the presence of another person.

So I decide to take the plunge and stay the night with Kevin McCall.

In the morning, it occurs to me that the experience was completely atypical for this city. In New York, there's always something weird, like maybe you haven't had a wax in a while and the guy slips and calls you a Chia Pet. Or maybe he wants you to wear his old NFL jersey because that way you can have sex but he doesn't have to actually look at you.

But that's not at all the way it was with Kevin and me. In fact, we were just like a couple you'd see in a movie, where it's totally normal and natural and neither party is at all disgusted by the other and everything is really nice.

This is the clincher for how I know I really like Kevin McCall. And the funny thing is I'm confident he feels the same. This, too, is a very rare occurrence in New York.

When the alarm rings, Kevin reaches over and slaps it silent. Then he lies back and gasps a few times, like the process of waking up hurts a little more than it should, which makes sense because it's six o'clock in the morning. In a few seconds, he rolls toward me and gives me a kiss. "Let's go," he says. "Soup waits for no man."

We get dressed, make the bed and head out. After a quick stop at Starbucks, we're at Fig's loading up the soup for the morning's deliveries.

Kevin gives me another kiss before he leaves with the soup. This has never happened before. It's definitely the kind of kiss that replaces the obligatory morning-after phone call, which obviously isn't an option because he's standing right in front of me.

When the kiss is over, I tell him goodbye, close the door and pause in the foyer. From long habit, I find myself poised on the edge of a big dramatic thing where I flip out and worry that the guy I just slept with is thinking about dumping me. This means I am now dangerously close to drowning myself in a vat of Ben & Jerry's.

Old habits die hard.

But as I'm walking back into the kitchen, my phone chimes with Kevin's ring.

I answer. "Hello?"

"It's me."

"Yes," I say. I wait to see if he's going to say anything, but he doesn't. "Did you forget something?"

He pauses for a moment. "I guess I just didn't want you to think I was the kind of guy who wouldn't call the next morning."

"Oh," I say. "I wouldn't think that."

"Of course not. But I just wanted to make sure."

We're silent again. I have the phone pressed to my ear and I'm trying to think of the perfect thing to say. Something clever but not jaded and appreciative but not too mushy or pathetic.

But he speaks first. "Anyway, I have a surprise for you. I'll bring it when I finish deliveries."

When he returns in a few hours, he has a decent-sized cardboard box under his arm. He brings it into the kitchen and sets it on the counter.

I giggle as I slice through the packing tape. The box contains stacks and stacks of the new flyers. I'm speechless for a second because I had no idea this kind of thing went on in the world. "You had them printed?"

He shrugs and looks a little sheepish. "I referred the last book I did to this guy, so he owed me a favor. He said he'd print your stuff and have it first thing this morning."

He reaches into the box, takes out a flyer and studies it. "I think they look pretty good."

"Oh," I say. "I do, too." I grab my own flyer and wave it around. "They look great. *Everyone* will want soup now."

"Well, these should keep you busy for a while. And he'll give us a deal when you need more."

"Great." I nod emphatically. "I'll let you know when I'm running low."

"Okay," he says. "I gotta go. I'll call you for dinner?"

I nod again. He kisses me and leaves.

When he's gone, I stand looking at the box wondering if he'll still like me when he figures out I'm too chicken to hand out flyers.

The next morning, I decide flyer distribution will have to wait because I must concentrate on finding my cute little studio apartment. I'm initially excited about this, but after a few hours online it all seems futile. I can't pass the credit check portion of the application process, much less the nasty part about income verification.

These are the reasons I wound up renting from the real estate equivalent of Tony Soprano in the first place.

I am feeling morose and somewhat desperate when Kevin returns from deliveries with the dirty crocks. To make matters worse, he plops down at the counter and announces I need to buy a van.

"A van?" I say. "I can't afford that."

"I know," he says. "But transportation costs are eating you alive. Plus it's getting warmer. You're going to need refrigeration."

He takes a stack of cash and cab receipts out of his pocket and plunks it on the counter while I fill the sink with sudsy water to soak yesterday's crocks.

"How much would a van cost?" I ask.

"Twenty thousand, give or take. You'll also need plates, registration and insurance. Can you swing that?"

"I don't see how. I'm using every extra dime to pay down debt."

"You're still generating a huge surplus of soup. Why don't you go out with some of your flyers and drum up more business?"

Yes, why not. I rest my forehead on the counter and consider the question. The truth is I really messed up when I quit my job at the grocery store. Before, I had an in with the customers. It was easy to sell to them when I was standing at their front doors, handing them groceries and they were happy to see me.

I don't say this to Kevin, though, because I'm afraid he thinks I did Joe dirty by not including him in the soup business. I might agree if I were actually going to make any money at this soup thing, but it's a moot point because the cost of a van is going to put me under.

I look up. "I have some administrative stuff to take care of today. Then I'll go out and sell."

"Okay," he says. "I guess I'll get going, then. See you later?"

I'm tempted to ask him if he wants to spend the day at the movies. But then he'd know what a slacker I am, so I just nod and promise to call him when I'm finished.

After Kevin leaves, I decide I'm morally obligated to spend some time getting a handle on the administrative end of Soup in the City. After all, that's what I said I was going to do.

I grab a cup of coffee, take a deep breath and sit down with the business records. I've been running the company's accounting through a manila envelope. When money comes in, I deposit it in the envelope. When I need money for crocks or ingredients or cab fare or whatever, it comes out of the envelope. All receipts are stored in a plastic grocery sack from Gourmet Gallery.

Whenever there's an accumulation of extra cash, I take it to the bank and put it in my checking account, where it's funneled out to my various creditors. As a result, the business never has more than a thousand dollars on hand.

But in spite of its current cash challenges, Soup in the City has a few things going for it. A good product, great flyers and two employees, one of whom actually seems fairly stable and dependable. What it doesn't have is a van or the money to buy a van. Also conspicuously absent are a bank account, a business license, a tax identification number or any kind of insurance, all of which I'm pretty sure are necessary in the current legal and regulatory environment.

I think about the girl in the logo and wonder if she'd look so damn perky if she had any sense that an administrative train wreck might be headed her way. I also wonder what the City of New York does to the proprietors of illegal soup kitchens.

I get online and look at official government web sites trying to figure out how to get all this stuff. I devote almost thirty minutes to the cause, but then I have to take a break because I'm hungry.

As I grab my coat and head out for some pancakes and eggs, I'm very upset at how the City of New York impedes legitimate business. The idea behind regulating the preparation and sale of food is to keep people from getting sick. Interestingly, though, no one is concerned about me making soup for myself in my own kitchen, or even eating out of a dumpster, for that matter. If I get sick, I guess the city figures I should be smart enough to quit eating the particular food that made me that way.

So really, the thrust of the food service regulatory regime is that the city needs to protect people whose food is prepared by someone else. On the surface, this makes sense, until I think about everyone whose food happens to be prepared by someone else without the benefit of these regulations. Parents with children come to mind. What about them? I'm sure their kitchens and methods of preparation and storage aren't even close to commercial standards. Yet somehow the offspring of the city's residents seem to do just fine on the food they get at home.

It's only when money changes hands that the city gets involved, which seems like a racket to me.

We learned about stuff like this in law school. The distinction between inherently bad things, like murder, and things that are bad merely because we say they're bad, like engaging in the ultra-dangerous activity of selling homemade soup without the requisite license.

I decide I'm hanging too close to the edge to worry about someone else's made-up problems. When I've clawed my way back a little, I'll sort myself out and get set up properly.

In the meantime, it's all about keeping my head above water.

When I return home from the diner, I find I've eaten a little too much and don't feel very well. I decide tomorrow will be the first day of my new life as an energetic marketing machine.

But when Wednesday rolls around, I don't think I can go out and distribute flyers, because I'm pretty sure I'm coming down with a terrible cold. And the morning after that, I have to stay in just to make sure.

By Friday, I'm disgusted with myself and I think Kevin is beginning to feel the same way. So when he comes to pick up the soup I make sure both the flyers and I are ready to go, meaning I'm dressed with makeup on and the flyers are stacked on the table in the foyer. This of course creates the impression I'm going out to take the city by storm and I don't bother to correct any disillusions he may have in that regard.

When he leaves, I clean up the kitchen, go out into the foyer and look at the flyers. I take a deep breath and even put on my shoes, but then I remember I haven't had breakfast, which I will definitely need if I'm going to tromp around the Upper West Side all day.

So even though I'm not remotely hungry, I fix myself a big bowl of pasta with pesto and sit down with Season Five of *Sex and the City*. I smile to myself because I also have cheesecake with lemon curd for dessert.

I realize this is quite a breakfast, but it's all I'm planning on eating today so I don't feel too bad about it.

But by the time I'm halfway through the pasta, I'm queasy from too much garlic, which I should have seen coming because it's not quite eight a.m. Also, this whole sick scene has a familiarity to it that makes my downward spiral all the more frightening.

I set the bowl on the table, lay back on the couch and watch *Sex and the City* in a dazed stupor. But I snap to rapt attention when I see Samantha standing on the street in front of her philandering boyfriend's apartment distributing pink sheets of paper pronouncing him to be a cheater and a liar.

She smiles and hands a pink flyer to each passerby with all the authority that comes from knowing she's disseminating valuable information. You can tell from her demeanor that she's performing a serious public service by getting the word out about this guy. The people on the street readily accept the flyers and don't throw them away or anything. Then a breeze comes up and she scatters the flyers in the wind, the implication being that everyone in the universe will be well served by Samantha's wisdom, so of course the weather gods must help in her distribution efforts.

Thus inspired, I get up and head for the shower to rid myself of the garlic stench. While I stand under the steamy spray, I brush my teeth with copious quantities of toothpaste and gargle with Fig's super-strong mouthwash. Then I towel off, fix my hair and apply the kind of meticulous makeup you might see on someone who works at the Chanel counter. When it's time to get dressed, I reach for my exercise pants straight away because confirmation that my pencil-cut jeans are too tight might just send me back to the couch for another week.

I grab a jacket and the flyers and head out to spread the word. People need to know about soup, whether they know it or not. And it's my job to tell them.

My efforts are of course made much easier by the fact that my flyers look absolutely amazing now.

CHAPTER 9:

Digging Deep

- - - - - - -

MARCH 15 – APRIL 17, 2007

I spend the next month conducting a concerted selling effort. Every morning, as soon as Kevin leaves with the soup, I hit the streets. Not every day is fantastic. In fact, on most days, there aren't even any fantastic moments. But I generally manage to keep going in spite of the rejection.

When I can't keep going, I give myself a break to regroup. I'm proud to say that only a few of these breaks involve eating five thousand calories' worth of pancakes.

So by the end of March, I can still wear my pencil-cut jeans and the business is so busy we need Duncan and Mark, another of Kevin's underemployed friends, to help with deliveries on a regular basis. By tax day, I have enough money to buy the van.

But I've been so busy I haven't been to the bank in a few weeks.

I gather all the money I've hidden around Fig's apartment, put it in a garbage sack and tie the sack around my waist. Although the functional nature of the accessory has a certain appeal, it's still a fanny pack so of course I cover it with a jacket so no one will think I'm a tourist from Wisconsin. Also, this way no one will be able to rip the bag off my waist before I get to the bank.

As usual, I'm in no mood to face my enemies at my bank's main branch so I walk ten blocks out of my way to a small satellite branch.

If the teller has any trouble with me pulling twenty-four thousand dollars out of a garbage sack and handing it to her, she doesn't show it. She just starts counting the money.

"These are my tips," I say.

She nods and writes the total on a deposit slip.

"Just in case you were wondering."

She ignores me and punches some numbers into a little machine that looks kind of like a cash register. Then she slides a deposit slip into a slot in the machine, which stamps it with something. She hands me the deposit slip. "Thank you," she says.

I put the deposit slip in my purse and leave the bank.

I'm tempted to celebrate by stopping at Louis Vuitton and buying one of those slim, oblong checkbooks but instead I do the responsible thing and go home and search the Internet for a cheap, short-term sublet with a big kitchen. I figure if I pay cash for the term of the lease the landlord won't bother with a credit check. This turns out to be sheer folly because everyone wants a credit check before they'll rent to me, which means no one is going to rent to me.

At this point it's clear that I am doomed to live at Fig's forever. Or at least until he gets home and kicks me out. The bright side is I can live in the van if I have to.

I don't have this kind of latitude with the business, however. Clearly, it needs a proper home, which I must find soon because the doorman situation is getting ridiculous. It's gotten so bad Kevin wants to move the soup in and out of the building in furniture crates and have me follow him through the lobby yelling about all the delivery mistakes.

I don't think this is going to work, because there's only so much furniture that can be delivered before people, meaning doormen, start to catch on. So I decide I must commit every spare moment to finding an appropriate kitchen for the business. Ideally, I'll find a restaurant that's only open for dinner that will let me rent early-morning use of their kitchen. I strap on my walking shoes and head out on reconnaissance.

SOUP IN THE CITY

The next day, having found nothing on the West Side, I'm traipsing around the Upper East Side scouting potential kitchen sites when my cell phone rings.

"Soup in the City," I say.

"Is this Avery?"

"Yes, it is. May I help you?"

"Avery, this is Sheridan Chance. I've been your customer for about three weeks now ... "

"Hi, Sheridan." I feel silly saying her name because it doesn't seem like a real name at all.

"Is now an okay time to talk?"

"Sure." Just then, I find a little restaurant with posted hours beginning at six p.m. daily. I peer in the window. "What's up?"

"Well, I'm a reporter at City Style magazine and I wanted to write a story about your amazing soup diet. I was hoping we could sit down so I could interview you."

"You want to interview me?" I sound squeaky. I stand up straight and turn away from the restaurant so I can concentrate. I swallow hard and take a deep breath to avoid more squeaking.

"Yes," she says. "Would next week work for you?"

"Okay," I say. "Where?"

"Your kitchen would be best for the photos. And can you ask some clients to come, too? Two or three should be enough."

"Sure," I say.

"Great. I'll set everything up and call you back with a time." She says goodbye and hangs up.

I put my phone on silent and pull on the door of the restaurant. I'm surprised when it opens.

I walk through the dining room and look around. Everything seems familiar. There's a bar on the left and tables on the right. I walk past the barstools toward the back. There are two unisex bathrooms right before the entrance to the swinging door to the kitchen, which also look familiar. I think I ate here with Courtney once when we were still friends, which would make sense because it's not far from her apartment.

I push open the kitchen door and stick my head inside. "Hello?"

A man's voice comes from around the corner. "We're closed. Come back at six."

I take a few steps into the kitchen. The man behind the voice is dark and wiry and on the smallish side. He's attacking dishes with a hose that hangs from the ceiling. Water sprays so violently from the nozzle it makes a ringing sound when it hits the metal bowl he's washing.

"I need to see the manager."

"We're not hiring."

"Are you the manager?"

"Yes," he says. "And the owner and the pastry chef and, right now, the dishwasher. What do you want?"

"I want to rent your kitchen in the mornings, Monday through Friday."

He glances at me as he dries the bowl with a very white towel. "What for?"

"Soup," I say. "I have a homemade soup business. I need a refrigerator and probably two of those shelves. I can be out by ten every morning."

"Nine-thirty," he says. "I start at ten."

"Fine."

"You can pay?" He eyes me suspiciously as he cracks eggs into the bowl he just washed.

"Within reason. What did you have in mind?"

"Two hundred a day. And you clean up. I have to clean, it's fifty bucks extra." He grabs a wire whisk and beats the eggs violently.

"How about one hundred and a pot of soup?"

He mulls this over while he whips the eggs. "You clean?"

"Very," I say.

"Because I run a really clean shop here."

Funny. He's not at all concerned if the soup is good. Just clean. "You won't have any concerns at all," I say, looking around. "The kitchen will be cleaner when we leave than when we got here."

"It can't get any cleaner," he says. "And that's the way I like it."

"It will be that clean then."

"What time do you want to come in?"

"Five?"

He wipes his brow with his sleeve and keeps whipping. "I don't know," he says. "I'll have to think about it."

"How about if I come in and clean?"

He looks up at me as if I just appeared from nowhere. "What?"

"How about if I come in one night and clean your kitchen? That way you can make sure it's clean enough."

He makes that face New Yorkers make when someone is being really stupid, like he has a very bad taste in his mouth. "Nah," he says. "I don't think so."

"Why?" I ask. "What do you have to lose?"

"Well, for one thing, you seem like a pain in the ass."

"What's your busiest night?" I ask. "Saturday? How about if I come in on Saturday and clean?"

He mulls this over while he pours the beaten egg whites into a pan. "Sunday morning. I'll be here at eleven to let you in and I'll come back at two."

"That's not much time."

"You're not going to have much time after you make soup, either," he says. "I need you out of my kitchen so I can start cooking."

"Deal. I'll see you at eleven on Sunday." I turn and scurry out of the kitchen before he can change his mind.

When I hit the sidewalk, I run smack dab into my old friend Courtney, who is hanging on the arm of a slightly paunchy guy in a cashmere sport coat. He grabs her around the waist and steadies her as she teeters on her heels.

"Sorry." I keep my head down hoping she doesn't recognize me.

"Avery?" She grabs me by the shoulders and pulls my face toward hers. "Avery, is that you?" She hugs me to her. It's a very profound hug the intensity of which seems mostly fueled by alcohol, which is strange because it's not quite three in the afternoon. When she lets go of me, she's practically bawling. "I've been worried sick about you. I've been calling and calling but I can never get through."

I take a closer look at the guy she's with. He's in his mid-fifties and has the smooth, clear skin of someone who can afford bi-weekly facials. He seems to believe this performance we're witnessing.

"I have a new cell phone," I say quietly.

If Courtney notices my lack of enthusiasm, she doesn't let on. She hugs me again and sways from side to side, like it's a slow dance and we're in junior high. "I missed you so much. When did you change your hair?"

All the swaying back and forth releases my bottled-up annoyance. I put up both hands and extricate myself from her drunken grasp. "You're kidding, right?"

"Of course not," she slurs. "We really need to reconnect. Give me your number right now." She thrusts her phone at me.

I just want this to be over, so I take the phone and dial my number into it. She promises to call and I walk away thinking about whether I'll answer if she does.

I'm almost to Fig's place when Kevin calls.

"How's your day going?" he asks.

"Let's see," I say. "I think I found a kitchen."

"That's great," he says. "How much?"

"A hundred a day. Plus a pot of soup."

"Ouch," he says. "Can you afford that?"

"I guess so. My main concern is the owner is a complete jerk."

"Can you hold out for something better?"

"I don't think so. I just got a call from City Style magazine and they want to interview me about the soup diet."

"Woo hoo!" Kevin is shouting so loudly I have to pull the phone away from my ear. "That's fantastic!" Even from arm's length, I can still hear him through the phone.

I smile and put the phone back to my head. "Yeah." I chuckle a little. "I guess it is, isn't it?"

"When's the article come out?"

"I don't know. But they want to interview me in the soup kitchen next week so I'm going to try to make it work with this guy."

"Well, that's great," Kevin says. "You'll be official, won't you?"

"I guess so. Do you think your mom would want to be interviewed for the article?"

"My mom?"

"The reporter wants to talk to some clients."

"I'll ask her," he says.

"No, no," I say. "That's okay. It might be too upsetting for her."

"I think it'd be great," he says. "She's lost some weight and is even getting out once in a while."

"Okay," I say. "Let me know. The other thing is I was wondering if you'd help me buy that van today."

He's silent.

"I mean, help me drive it."

"Sure," he says. "When?"

"Now?"

"I'll meet you at the lot."

Courtney calls first thing the next morning. I recognize the number on the caller ID so I know it's her before I answer. I don't know how to play this. On the one hand, I was kind of glad to see her yesterday. On the other hand, the feeling was very similar to how I imagine a dog would feel when his owner finally lets him out of the trunk of a car.

Also, I'm not so dumb I can't figure out that Courtney is full of crap. Worried my ass. I've had the same e-mail account since college. If she wanted to get in touch with me, she could have done so without any trouble at all.

I answer the phone on the last ring before it goes to voice mail. I decide to be breezy and light. She does the same. "Good morning, Avery." Her voice is sing-songy for a second, then matter-of-fact. "It's Courtney. Are you busy?"

"No," I say. "What's up?"

"Let's get together for lunch."

I am silent.

"Come on, Avery. Don't be like this."

"Why not?"

"Because we've been friends too long to let one stupid guy come between us. Stop being silly and have lunch with me."

I don't know what to say to her. Eventually, it just seems easier to agree. "Okay," I say. "But it will have to be later. I have some things to do this morning."

Namely, shop for my City Style interview.

"Fine," Courtney says. "Two o'clock at Fred's."

I hang up and walk to Henri Bendel for a little shopping before I meet Courtney.

Henri Bendel is a department store tucked in the middle of one of my favorite blocks on Fifth Avenue. As department stores go, it's on the smallish side and is decorated and laid out like the sprawling mansion of an eccentric aunt. Shopping there feels like wandering up a very broad, meandering staircase. At every turn you find a new room in which to hunt for treasure, both new and new-disguised-as-vintage.

I didn't used to like Henri Bendel that much, except for accessories, because the clothes are very stylish, which means they also are very slim. Today, though, I have a distinct feeling I'm about to have a new, more welcoming experience at Henri Bendel, which is good because spring is here and I need clothes.

I've decided to take the Kevin McCall approach to my new wardrobe. My closet will contain just a few of my very favorite things. No more overstuffed for me. In any area.

I spend most of the day at Henri Bendel. When I leave, I've purchased just two garments. One pair of dark-washed jeans that are quite flattering. In fact, too skinny is a phrase that wouldn't be out of the question when I'm wearing these jeans. I also bought one cashmere cardigan in periwinkle that will be perfect with the jeans and which also serves as the inspiration for the additional pieces I plan to buy, namely, one slim suit and one ball skirt, both of which I'll wear with the sweater and pearls.

The saleswoman tried to sell me T-shirts at eighty dollars per but I would have none of it. I can get the same thing at the Gap for less than ten.

When I get to Fred's, Courtney already has a table and is talking on her phone. She waves at me. I slide into the chair across from her, order iced tea and wait for her to wrap up her call.

The waiter brings the tea and whispers at me. "Would you like to order?" I look at Courtney. She's turned to the side with the phone clutched to her head and her finger pressed over her other ear so she doesn't have to listen to the waiter and me.

"No, thanks," I say. "We'll take a second."

Five minutes later, I'm still waiting. I'm about to get up and leave when Courtney finally says, "Listen, can I call you back? I'm being rude to my friend."

Now this is a first. Courtney is not exactly known for her empathy. She hangs up and puts her phone in her purse. "I'm so sorry about that. I'm looking for a job so I'm answering every call that comes in."

"What happened to yours?"

"I still have it, but there's no way I can sell that fund now. It completely tanked in the last few weeks."

"How bad?"

"Down 35 percent," she says. "The redemption requests are burning up the fax machine. It's just a matter of time."

"You think they'll let you go?"

She waves her dainty, well-manicured hand and makes a noise. "Let's not talk about me," she says. "You look amazing. What's going on with you?"

I'm relieved to see the waiter coming back so I don't have to answer this question. For some reason, I don't want her to know anything about my soup business. The waiter stands with order pad poised and looks at me. "Are you ready?"

"What's good?" I ask.

"The chicken soup is our specialty."

"Thanks." I scratch the back of my neck. "But I think I'd like a salad. Just make me a big bowl of vegetables with blue cheese dressing."

"Would you like chicken?" he asks.

I nod and hand him my menu. "That will be good. Thanks."

Courtney hands him her menu. "I'll have the soup."

The waiter writes down her order and leaves without saying anything to her. For a second I wonder if for once we have a waiter who likes me better than Courtney.

"You never eat soup," I say.

She wrinkles up her nose. "Everyone eats it. I thought I'd give it a try."

"So how's the job search going?"

"Fine," she says carefully. "Just looking for the right opportunity. I figure I have a couple of months before they let me go." The waiter comes with more iced tea. I watch as she stirs sugar into her glass. Suddenly, she looks like she's about to cry.

"Courtney, this isn't about the drawdown, is it?"

She presses her lips together and shakes her head. "No," she says. "They were going to fire me anyway. The truth is I haven't met my quota in over a year. They're only keeping me on so I can take the heat from all the investors. Once the screaming is over, I'm done."

"Ugh," I say. "Sounds nasty."

"It is. I'm just so glad I ran into you. It's been really tough not being able to talk to you."

I was feeling sorry for her, and actually a little connected, but now my bullshit monitor goes into overdrive. "Courtney, you never talk to me. In the entire history of our friendship, you've never had so much as a pimple you wanted to discuss."

As soon as the words come out of my mouth, I feel mean. She slumps a little.

"Well, what did you expect, Avery?" Her eyes glisten with tears. "Everything comes so easy for you. Did you really want to hear that the biggest account I can raise is a hundred thousand dollars from a dentist in Des Moines? That I'm a total loser at my job? Do you think it's easy being friends with someone like you?"

I sit back and look at her. She's suddenly so forlorn she looks a little soggy. "I had no idea you felt this way."

"Oh come on," she says, stabbing at her eyes with her napkin. "All Richard could talk about was Avery, Avery, Avery. How Avery is the best cap intro person he'd ever met. He's never seen anything like it. Eighty million dollars on one stinking sale. I was so jealous I hated you about half the time."

The waiter comes and sets our food in front of us. "Anything else?"

"No, thank you," we say in unison. He departs.

I pick up my fork and stab a tomato. "Well, I was jealous, too. I pretended everything was hunky-dory so you wouldn't see how fucked up things were for me."

"What was fucked up?" she asks. "You had more money than you knew what to do with, a great boyfriend, that beautiful coat. Everything seemed perfect."

My insides start twisting around at the memory of all the lies I told. "Well, it wasn't," I say. "It wasn't perfect at all. But I'm glad about one thing. I'm glad we're finally being honest with each other."

"Me, too," she says. She takes a bite of her soup, which looks more watery than I remembered.

"How is that?"

She laughs. "There isn't very much here, is there?"

"I guess we'll be having dessert, then."

By the time we've finished our crème brulée, things are good between us. Like old times, but better, because we actually have weekend plans to attend a party in the East Hampton home of the latest hedge fund manager she's seeing. So of course we have to spend the rest of the afternoon at Bergdorf's finding the perfect outfits for the party. This throws a huge, unexpected wrench in my minimalist wardrobe plans and puts me back in front of the eighty-dollar T-shirt firing squad.

This time, I do not emerge unscathed.

I'm loaded down with shopping bags on my way back to the West Side when my phone rings with Kevin's chime. I transfer all the bags to my left hand and answer the phone with my right.

As I walk and talk, it occurs to me that this is just the sort of afternoon I've been hoping for. Here I am, carrying my beautiful new wardrobe to my apartment on the park, after meeting my best girlfriend for lunch, when my adorable boyfriend calls to see how I'm doing.

Everything is finally coming together for me.

The whole experience would be perfect except for two things. First, the apartment isn't mine. I decide this is a minor point that shouldn't mar my enjoyment of this delicious moment. The other, major problem is that the bags are too damn heavy, which of course must be dealt with immediately. "Hang on a second," I say. "I have to change arms." I set my bags down on the sidewalk, switch my phone to the other hand and pick up the bags with my fresh arm.

"Change arms?"

"I needed a new outfit for the interview. Anyway, what's up?"

"Well, I was just calling to see if we're on for that thing on Saturday. I have to tell Duncan if we want the tickets."

"Oh, gosh," I say. "I'm so sorry. I just told my friend Courtney I'd go out to the Hamptons with her."

"The friend Courtney who's not really your friend?" He doesn't sound accusatory. Just curious. But still, I find the question irritating in spite of the fact that I may have whined about how Courtney dumped me on more than one occasion. I can't believe he was actually listening to all that drivel.

Anyway, the thought of expending energy getting Kevin up to speed is a little too much for me. I feel slightly bad about this. And slightly irritated.

"Avery?"

"We had lunch and worked some things out," I say. "Don't worry. She's been my friend for a long time."

"Yeah? Where's she been the last two months?"

"I don't know," I say evenly. "We got into a fight and lost touch for a while. Things are more complicated with girls."

He hesitates. I hope he won't say anything but I'm not that lucky. "Nothing's complicated, Avery. Even with girls. She wasn't around when things were hard for you. That tells you something. Or at least it should."

I roll my eyes and don't say anything.

"Avery?"

"Yes?"

"I'm just worried about you."

"Thank you." I want to say how I've noticed that people who profess to be worried about me tend in fact to be worried about something else, usually themselves, but instead I just change the subject. "Anyway, what about tonight?"

"Okay," he says. "But it's just pool and burgers. We do that all the time."

"Well, can't we go to that show next week?"

He sighs. "I guess so."

"Okay," I say. "Then I'll meet you for pool in an hour."

I stop by Fig's to drop off my bags and change into the outfit I bought for the party. I want to give it a test-run because there's nothing worse than being overly conscious of wearing brand-new clothes in a room full of people who wear them every day.

I've never bought an outfit like this before. It's very skinny white pants and a thin black sweater that looks totally ordinary until I turn around and you see that it's completely backless. The outfit is unusual because the white is on the bottom, which is not something you do if you have one extra ounce on you. Needless to say, I will not be eating burgers tonight.

I tease my hair into a little beehive, apply serious eyeliner and transfer the contents of the Birkin into my new spring bag, which cost two thousand dollars but which I had to have because it makes me think of buttery yellow cupcakes.

I leave the apartment feeling very much like Mary Tyler Moore back in her ultra-cute days when she was throwing hats in the air, which is the perfect way to feel when a reporter from City Style magazine calls you to let you know you will be the subject of a four-page feature article in their June issue and the photo shoot is set for Monday at three.

I'm grinning from ear to ear when I get to the bar. Kevin and five of his buddies are playing pool and drinking pitchers of beer.

He doesn't see me at first. I wave at his friends, sit down at the bar and watch him take a shot. When he stands up, I smile at him and he comes over.

"Holy shit," he says. He puts his hands under my hair, wraps his fingers around my neck and gives me a kiss on the mouth. "Where did you come from?"

"Bergdorf's." I spin halfway around on the barstool and show him my back. "You like?"

"Huh," is all he can manage. He leans over and whispers in my ear. "Don't show that to any of these idiots. They don't have any self-control at all."

"And you do?"

"Not enough." He takes some money out of his pocket and puts it on the bar. "Let's get out of here."

I punch him in the stomach and laugh and he grabs me with both hands and tickles me.

"Your shot, Kevin."

He releases me and takes a drink of his beer. "Don't go anywhere." He sets his glass down and picks up his cue. "I'll be right back."

As I watch him take the shot, I sort of wish I hadn't promised to go away with Courtney for the weekend.

CHAPTER 10:

Bright, Shiny People

APRIL 18 - 19, 2008

After soup delivery and clean-up Friday morning, Kevin and I are standing outside Fig's building waiting for the car to come by and pick me up.

It's not a rented car. It's a private car owned by the guy who's throwing the party. He's coming out in his helicopter after markets close. Courtney and I get to ride out with the car so everything he needs is there when he lands. This obviously means the car and probably Courtney and perhaps me, now that I think about it. But I push this thought aside and concentrate on saying goodbye to Kevin.

"I'm going to miss you," he says.

"I'll be back early Sunday," I say. "We can hang out after I clean the kitchen."

"No, we can't." He gives me a hug. "By then you'll be engaged to some rich guy with a plane and his own private island. I know what you girls do out there in the Hamptons."

I wriggle out of the hug. "This isn't about that. It's about Courtney."

"Yeah?" he asks. "What about Courtney?"

I shrug. "She's my friend."

"And she needs a chaperone? Or maybe a designated driver?"

Just then the car pulls up. Kevin watches the driver get out and load my bag in the trunk. Then he turns and looks at me. "Your friend Courtney already has a driver, Avery."

I have no idea where this hostility is coming from, and frankly, I don't want to know. Without a word, I get in the car and nod for the driver to shut the door behind me.

I stare straight ahead as the car pulls away from the curb.

"Who's that?" Courtney asks, craning her neck to look through the rear window. "Are you seeing him?"

"Yeah." I sigh. "I guess I am."

"He's cute." She settles back in her seat. "What does he do?"

"I guess he's an artist."

"Well, now. That's quite a bit of guessing, isn't it? Was he giving you shit?"

I sigh again. "I don't think he understands why I'm going to the Hamptons this weekend."

Courtney laughs. "Of course he doesn't. Men who can't afford the Hamptons never understand it, do they?"

I look out the window. "I guess not."

"Just give him a little while to cool off. And call him every three hours. He'll be fine."

"Every three hours?"

"So he knows you miss him even though you're having a fabulous time in the Hamptons."

I look out the window and don't say anything.

"Oh, come on," she says. "We're going to have a blast."

I turn and look at her. "Why would I call someone every three hours to show I want to be with him when I'm choosing to be somewhere else?"

"Oh, Avery. You always did see the world too much in black and white. The point is to have some fun. Do you know how to do that?"

I look at my hands and don't answer.

"No," she says. "You don't. And it's high time you learned. I can't have my best friend moping around all weekend. The trick to getting invited places is to have more fun, to be more fun, than anyone else."

So this is why she never invited me anywhere. And now that we're being honest with each other, she's telling me, without telling me, so I don't screw up again.

"Okay," I say. "I can do that."

"Of course you can," she says. "Or we're sending you back to the minor leagues." She laughs like this is a very funny joke but I know it isn't.

We're silent as the car moves through Manhattan. The driver guns it at each intersection, so we're thrown around in the back and it's uncomfortable to talk. Finally, we're going through a tunnel to get off the island. I don't know which one, because although I've lived in New York quite a while, I still have no idea which bridges and tunnels go to which places.

When we come out of the tunnel, I'm hungry. "Are we stopping for lunch?"

Courtney rummages in her bag and comes up with a rather large bottle of pills. She shakes some into her palm and hands them to me. "Here," she says. "Keep these in your purse."

"What is it?" I dump the loose pills into my change purse and snap it closed.

"You can't really eat at these things," she says. "The pills will help."

So that's her secret. Courtney uses diet pills. I am initially alarmed and upset, but at least she's finally letting me in on her strategies for success.

In a couple of hours, we're pulling up to the house. I'm expecting one of those massive gray monstrosities that look like a museum, but the house is actually a reasonably-sized Cape Cod, meaning it's only about six thousand square feet. Of course it's right on the water. It's too large to be a cottage but it's just as charming, right down to the tulip-lined front walk.

I stand looking at the house while the driver unloads our bags and hauls them up to the porch.

"He's married, isn't he?" I ask Courtney.

"Why would you think that?" Her voice is a little too smooth.

"This is a married house if I ever saw one."

"He's getting divorced." She leaves me standing on the driveway and walks up to the house.

I follow several feet behind. "Of course he is."

If she hears me, she pretends not to. She takes a key out of her purse, opens the door and stands aside for the driver to enter with the bags.

I walk slowly into the house. It's all fresh flowers and yellow carpet and gleaming crystal. A restful weekend retreat for the elegant woman who's unfortunate enough to be married to Courtney's boyfriend.

"What's his name, anyway?"

"Ira."

I make a face at her. "Is he thinking of changing it?"

She laughs. "I don't know. Maybe you could suggest it." She picks up her bag and walks down the hall. "Let's get changed and go for a swim."

I follow her down the hallway. "I can't believe you're sleeping with a guy named Ira."

She looks at me over her shoulder. "Who says I'm sleeping with him?"

I'm about to say something really snide and sarcastic when I realize she's serious. "You're not?"

"Of course not. He's married." She stops in the hall. "This is your room. I'm right next door."

I peek into the room, which is very cheery thanks to a wall of windows overlooking the water. It's like a little girl's room for grown-ups, with a full-sized canopy, Yves Delormes bedding and white furniture. "How many times have you been here?"

"A lot," she says. "More since he separated from his wife. But you don't have to be ashamed of me. I always have my own room."

I roll my eyes, wheel my bag into my room and change into my new swimsuit. I'm still red from my recent bikini wax so I slip on the matching skirt. And a sweater. It's really too cold to swim, anyway.

I leave my room and wander back into the living room, where I find Courtney looking through a stack of magazines. "We can take these out to the pool," she says. "Do you have sunscreen?"

"I don't really burn." I look out the window. "And it's not that bright out there."

"Must be nice." She tucks her red hair under a huge hat and slathers lotion on her face.

"Shall we take a drink?" I ask.

"There's a bar outside." She picks up the magazines and we walk out to the pool. It has a disappearing edge, like a pool in a fancy hotel.

Courtney and I spend the rest of the afternoon drinking wine and reading magazines. I look up from the latest issue of City Style when I hear the helicopter. It's a small black dot on the horizon. For a second, I feel like we're under attack. "I guess that's Ira, huh?"

"Yup," she says. "The weekend has begun." She stands up, adjusts her bikini bottom and picks up her towel.

"Where are you going?"

"To brush my teeth," she says. "I'll be right back."

She disappears into the house, leaving me alone at the pool to deal with Ira. I watch as the chopper lands on the helicopter pad, which is not far from the pool deck, and unloads three men. Two are young and slim so I know the paunchy guy in the pink shirt is Ira.

The men duck down and run out from under the blades. When they're clear, the chopper lifts off the pad and heads back to the city. Or at least in a direction I assume is back to the city. The men disappear for a second while they're down on the beach. I see their heads again as they walk up the steps to the pool deck and let themselves in through a small gate.

Ira takes off his glasses and squints at me. "Avery?"

I stand up and smile. "Hi," I say. "How are you?" The last part comes out too loud because the helicopter is pretty far away now.

"I'm Ira," he says. "We kind of met on the street the other day."

"Thanks for having me," I say, shaking his hand. "This is a beautiful house."

He smiles and points to each of his friends in turn. "This is Blake Snyder and Jeff Singer."

By the time we're done with the handshakes, I've already forgotten which friend is Blake Snyder and which friend is Jeff Singer. One is blonde and one is dark so it shouldn't be too tough to keep them straight. Maybe Courtney will know. I look around but she's nowhere in sight. I silently curse her and wonder what the hell I'm supposed to do now.

"What are we drinking?" The dark-haired guy looks at the blonde guy and waits for an answer.

"Scotch," the other one says.

"Scotch it is. Avery, do you need anything?"

I shake my head. Blake and Jeff walk to the bar, leaving Ira and me alone by the chaise lounges.

"Courtney's inside," I say, sitting down in my chaise lounge.

Ira nods, sits down on Courtney's chair and picks up the magazine I was just reading. He thumbs through it. "Did you girls have a nice afternoon?"

"We did. It was a little too cold to swim but . . ."

He looks up from the magazine. "The pool is heated. You can swim in it year-round." He seems annoyed, maybe because Courtney did not brag up the features of the pool.

"Oh," I say. "Well, I'll be sure to do that then."

He doesn't respond. He sets the magazine on my chair, so close it actually bumps my hip, and gets up and walks to the bar. "Stand aside," he says. Blake and Jeff take their faces out of their buckets of scotch long enough to move around to the other side of the bar.

Ira ducks behind the bar and comes up with a blender. He fills it with ice and yells at me. "Avery, do you like margaritas?"

"Sure," I say. "Who doesn't?"

The truth is I do not like margaritas at all. The sugar makes me freaky and crazy and ice-cold booze always goes straight to my head. But I'm guessing the truth would be decidedly un-fun, so I keep this to myself.

Ira, on the other hand, must be nuts about margaritas. He sloshes a bunch of stuff into the blender and fires it up with an enthusiastic fling of his arm, like he's a finalist in an air-guitar contest.

He blends for a few minutes and then uses a spoon to coax the margaritas out of the blender and into two glasses. He picks them up and brings them over to me. "This is great. Courtney won't drink margaritas. Too fattening."

I accept the glass from him. "No salt?"

"Oh, sorry," he says. "I don't use it. It's bad for my blood pressure. Do you want me to get some for you?"

I look at the glass. "No, thank you. This'll be fine."

We clink glasses and Ira takes a few generous gulps. I pretend to take a sip. Then we sit back in our chaise lounges and stare at the ocean or the sound or whatever it is.

"So Courtney says you do some cap intro."

I glance at Ira and look back at the water. "I have," I say. "Not so much anymore."

"Modesty is not a virtue I appreciate, Avery. Courtney says your smallest sale was eighty million."

I take a gulp of my margarita. "Well, that's true."

He laughs. "I like you, Avery. All the guys I've been talking to can't shut up about themselves. They want five hundred grand a year and cars and drivers and eight weeks' vacation. You seem a lot more reasonable."

I clutch the stem of my glass. "Really." I close my mouth and nod a few times, as if this idea of reasonableness is so profound there's nothing left to discuss.

He sits up and turns toward me, putting both feet on the ground between our chaise lounges. "Listen," he says. "My fund is just over a billion dollars. I should be at three billion and I'm not because the genius I hired to head up marketing couldn't sell beer at a ballgame."

Ira is resting his elbows on his knees, which puts his hands a little too close to my bare legs. I shift in my chair to put a little distance between us.

"So what do you think?" he asks.

I stare at him thoughtfully and nod a few more times. I'm starting to feel like one of those Weebles-Wobble toys. He takes a gulp of margarita and looks at me, obviously waiting for me to say something.

"So you got rid of your last guy?" I ask.

Ira shakes his head. "No can do. I gave that son-of-a-bitch a three-year contract and I'm not going to buy him out for sitting on his ass. You'd have to come in under him, but we'd both know where you'd really be. And Courtney, of course. You two have sold together before, right?"

The only thing Courtney and I ever sold together was a block of raffle tickets for a fundraiser at Yale. I rub my chin and look away.

And lo and behold, there's Courtney looking spiffy in clean clothes and fresh makeup.

Ira stands up, walks over to her and gives her a kiss on the cheek, which is innocent enough, but it's accompanied by a hey-baby kind of bear hug that seems not quite as platonic as Courtney might like.

At least in front of me, anyway.

"So how are things going out here?" she asks. "Are you two getting along?" She sits down at the end of my chair and looks at me with rapt attention while Ira goes to fetch a drink for her.

"I think he's offering me a job," I say in a low voice. "Do you know anything about that?"

She glances over her shoulder and sees Ira approaching with a glass of wine. She looks back at me and flares her eyes so I know I'm supposed to stop talking. Ira hands her the wine and sits down on the chair next to us.

"You know," I say. "I'm getting a little cold. I think I'll go get dressed." I get up and pick up my towel. I walk a few steps toward the house but then turn back to pick up my margarita. If I can't eat, I have to get calories from somewhere.

Once inside, I grab my cell phone and flip through the missed calls. None are from Kevin. I spend five minutes listening to messages, mostly about soup, and another twenty minutes returning calls and talking about soup.

My phone starts making the low-battery sound so I cut my last call short and rummage through my bag for my charger. I can't find it but I'm sure it's in there somewhere. I take a quick shower, wrap myself up in a thirsty yellow towel and return to my bag. By the time I'm dressed, it's clear my cell phone charger is not along for the ride. I pick up my phone and flip through the names in my phone book so I can write down Kevin's number and call him from another line.

But just as I'm selecting his name, the phone powers off. I'm cussing at the maddening little song it's playing when Courtney sticks her head in the door. "What's the matter?" she wants to know.

"My phone just died. I forgot the charger and I don't know Kevin's number."

"Is he the artist?"

I nod and try to power my phone on. It's completely dead.

"It's no big deal, Avery. We'll just check your messages later and you can get his number from that."

"If he leaves me a message."

"He will," she says. "Anyway, are you ready? Everyone wants to go out for some drinks before dinner."

"I thought no one ate at these things." I walk into the bathroom to apply cosmetics. Courtney follows me and sits on the toilet seat.

"It's such bullshit," she says. "The guys can do whatever they want. But once there was this girl who ate a fairly substantial amount and they called her a heifer behind her back for the entire weekend."

I lean into the mirror to get a better look as I apply mascara. "Was she fat?"

"Well, no, but she wasn't exactly thin."

"So what's this thing about the job?" I ask. "Did you know about that?"

"I'm surprised he brought it up already. We talked about it but it's still very much in the idea stages."

"Okay," I say. "So what's the idea?"

Courtney gets up and shuts the bedroom door. And the bathroom door. She sits back on the toilet and speaks in low tones. "Ira doesn't like his marketing guy. He wants us to come in and raise some money so he can fire him."

I pretend not to know about the three-year contract. "Why can't he fire him now?"

"It's complicated. He's the son of a big investor and he doesn't want to let him go until we bring in some other big investors."

"Who's the big investor?"

"His wife."

I set down my hairspray, cross my arms and look at Courtney. "You must be joking."

She shakes her head. "She has family money. She seeded the fund with the first hundred million. If we can replace that, Ira will fire the son and then we can divvy up his salary."

"It's not his son?"

She shakes her head. "Ira doesn't have kids. If he did I wouldn't be interested."

I resume teasing my hair. "If you're so interested in Ira, why would you want to work for him? Wouldn't girlfriend status be a little more fun?"

She puts her finger to her lips and shushes me. "He'll hear you."

I put my comb down and look at her. "What am I doing here, Courtney?"

"You're having a great time and getting a great job."

"I think I'm helping you get a great job."

"So what?" she asks. "I told him I could get you and that we'd work together. What do you care?"

"How does he even know about me?"

"Richard," she says. "I told you he couldn't shut up about you."

"I don't know, Courtney. This all seems a little strange."

"Oh, God, Avery. Don't be such a prude. How do you think this stuff works? You think you put on a prim little suit and go to an uptight little interview and you walk into a half-a-million-dollar job? Grow up. Business and pleasure go hand in hand and they always have."

"Somehow I don't think he's going to pay half a million." I pause to apply lipstick. "He was bitching about that to me before."

"No," she says. "But he'll split it between us and we'll get another half-million when we get rid of Jeff. That's five hundred grand a year for each of us. Do you really want to screw this up?"

"Jeff?" I ask. I duck down like there's a chance he's looking through the window at us. "The son is one of those guys out there?"

She looks at me like a horn just started growing out of my forehead. "Of course. So don't get any wild ideas about family loyalty. He hates his mother as much as anyone."

"Which one is he?" I ask.

"The dark-haired one. Why?"

"Just trying to keep everything straight, I guess." Ira's son-of-a-bitch comment now has a whole new meaning. "So let's recap. We're here on a job interview. Father and stepson are going to spend the weekend checking us out. If we pass muster, we start working for them. If all goes as planned, we raise a bunch of money and Ira throws his stepson out on his ear, just like his wife."

"Exactly," she says. "And you can keep the job because I won't need it anymore."

"Because by then you'll be upgraded to wife status."

She sips her wine and smiles at me. "That's the idea anyway."

"Well, that's a perfect plan," I say. "How long did it take you to think of this?"

She stands up. She's not smiling anymore. "Not long at all, Avery. It's amazing how quickly things come together when everyone gets what they want."

She leaves me alone with my makeup, at which point all I want is to sit down with a huge pie and a gallon of ice cream. Since this is definitely not on the agenda, it's clear to me that not everyone is getting what they want, which is how I know Courtney's plan has a few holes in it.

The other thing I want is to shove my clothes back in my bag, get out of this house and go back to the city.

Trouble is I have no idea how to escape. If my phone worked, I would call a car service and sneak out before anyone knew I was gone. But the fact is I probably didn't bring enough cash for a car back to the city. I could take a train, except that would involve checking a schedule and getting to the station on time. This kind of intricate planning would probably necessitate assistance from the other house-guests, which might embarrass Courtney. And I definitely don't think I could figure that stuff out on my own, because I don't even know which stations are near here and how long it takes to get to them. For that matter, I don't even know for sure if there are trains that go back to the city. Carrie Bradshaw was sent home from the Hamptons on a train once, but maybe that was a different part of the Hamptons or maybe it was pure fiction inserted by the *Sex and the City* writers to make for a better script.

Now that I think about it, the whole train thing must be a big lie because everyone takes a Jitney or a helicopter to the Hamptons. You never hear about someone taking a train. Ever.

So unless I can find a Jitney, whatever that is, it seems I'm stuck here for the weekend.

All through that evening, as our little Machiavellian entourage hops from bar to bar to bar with no food in sight, I use Courtney's phone to check my voice mail. There are lots of messages from clients and prospective clients, but none from Kevin.

By eleven o'clock, I'm drowning in a deadly cocktail of vodka mixed with that bad feeling you get when you realize you've blown it with a very nice person who has determined you're not so nice.

I take a sip of my drink and slam into my limit. In trading, I think they call this a hard stop. I can't have one more drop of alcohol and I can't hear "no messages" one more time. I shove my drink and the phone at Courtney.

She barely glances at me. "Just keep it," she says. "You'll need it later."

I'm not sure if she's talking about the drink or the phone, but I'm done with both and I tell her as much.

She doesn't hear me, though, because she's turned back to listen to Ira, who is going on and on about planes and how you need at least three so you're prepared for long distances and short distances and also when you need to get somewhere really, really fast.

Jeff, the dark-haired guy from the helicopter, is sitting on the other side of me with nothing better to do than talk to me and anaesthetize himself from the boredom of it all with copious quantities of Jack Daniels.

His buddy Blake has abandoned us in favor of a skinny blonde at the bar. Her face is too long and her chest bones stick out in a funny way but she's blonde and has big fake boobs so I guess that's all that matters.

The waitress arrives at our table with another tray of drinks and Jeff hands her a hundred-dollar bill. One thing I've noticed about these hedge fund guys is no one ever runs a tab. Vying to pay for each round is just too much sport for them to give up.

Jeff puts his wallet in his pocket and turns to me. "Don't worry," he says. "He'll call."

I'm drooping from not enough food and way too much booze and suddenly find I no longer have the energy for subterfuge. "Yeah," I say dully. "How do you know?"

"He'd be an idiot not to," Jeff says. "And you don't really look like you'd date an idiot."

My only response is a small snort.

"What?" he asks. "Is he an idiot?"

"I don't think so," I slur. "But clearly you've never been a single girl in Manhattan. It's the most vicious dating pool on the planet. Nice women date idiots all the time."

He takes a short drink and glances at Ira. "Yeah, I guess you're right about that."

"What time is it?"

Jeff looks at his phone. "Almost midnight."

"I can't do this anymore."

"Do you want to go home?"

"No." I shake my head vigorously. "I can no longer pretend I don't need food."

The waitress returns and hands Jeff a stack of bills. He fishes out a twenty and gives it back to her. "Can we have menus?" he asks.

"The kitchen is closed except for burgers and clam strips."

I rest my elbows on the table and clutch my head with both hands. Jeff looks at me and then back at the waitress. "We'll take two of each."

"And fries," I mutter into the table.

He leans over. "What?"

I look up at him. "Fries," I say. "We need fries. And cheese and bacon on the burgers."

He looks at the waitress. "Did you get that?"

"Hard not to." She tucks her pen behind her ear, picks up her tray and leaves.

When she brings the food, Courtney and Ira descend on our plates like hungry vultures.

So much for Courtney and her magic pills.

The next morning, I get up and get dressed. I don't bother with a shower or makeup because Courtney is a late riser and I want to get the lay of the land before she comes out of her room. I go out into the kitchen, where I find Jeff and Blake devouring a huge American breakfast involving many items that can only be served drowning in buckets of syrup.

They look up as I enter. Jeff is holding a fork that's dripping syrup from a massive bite of French toast. "Good morning," he says. "You're just in time for French toast."

I'm still full from our little fried food extravaganza last night. "No thanks," I say. "Just coffee." I walk across the kitchen, pour myself a cup and put a little swig of half-and-half in it.

"How'd you sleep?" Jeff asks.

"Fine." I sip my coffee. "You?"

"Could have been better," he says.

I take my coffee and walk to the window. It's gray and cold outside.

"So we're on our own today," Jeff says. "What do you want to do?"

I turn and look at him. "What do you mean?"

"Courtney and Ira went back to the city."

"When?"

"Last night. They had a little change in plans."

"Oh." Next time I'll think twice about hanging around somewhere to be polite to Courtney. "I don't get it. Isn't there some kind of party tonight?"

Jeff takes a few bites of food before he answers. "That's the change in plans. Turns out my mom is hosting this little shindig and not Ira."

"Well, I guess I should get back to the city, then. Is there a train or something?"

"You don't want to do that," Jeff says. "It's going to be a great party."

"I'm sure it is," I say. "But it's really not my thing anymore. I only came here for Courtney."

"Bullshit," Jeff says. "She's not that interesting. You're here about the job, and now that she's out of the way we can actually talk about it."

"To tell you the truth, Jeff, this whole thing feels like one big goat rope. I really don't want to get involved."

"I'm not sure what a goat rope is," he says. "But it sounds like Courtney could use one. The fact is Ira's out of the picture and so is Courtney."

"I thought Ira was in charge of hiring."

"Ira's in charge of being Ira and that's it," Jeff says. "Not only is my mom the major investor in the fund, she owns 100 percent of the management company. She canned his philandering ass last night."

"Oh, I get it." I'm so excited to have figured it out I don't bother to censor myself. "You're a spy. That's why you haven't raised any money."

Jeff shakes his head. "I haven't raised any money because I don't have the foggiest clue how to do it. But Richard says you do. When I first heard you were friends with Courtney, I was not enthusiastic. But you're nothing like her. So hang out, meet my mom and see if this is a job you'd like to have."

I think about this. With that kind of job, my debts would be ancient history in short order. I'd have verifiable income so I could get an apartment. I could stockpile a bunch of money so I don't wind up homeless again. I'd diversify my income stream so if the soup thing tanked, I'd still have some money coming in. And I actually like Jeff. He kind of reminds me of Fig.

I look at Blake. "What's your role in all this? Are you a marketing guy, too?"

Blake shoves his last bite of food in his mouth, gets up and takes his plate to the sink. "I run the trading desk." He scrapes his plate and puts it in the dishwasher. "I'll see you guys later."

I watch him walk out of the kitchen.

"Just ignore him," Jeff says. "He's pissed that girl wouldn't go home with him last night. Anyway, we can take the boat out while they get the house ready for the party."

I look out the window at the gray sky. "It's freezing out there."

"I'll loan you some rain gear," he says. "It'll be fun."

I sip coffee and look around the kitchen. "Can I use your phone?"

He shakes his head, stands up and starts clearing the table. "You can use it when we get back. Leave it alone for a while. Enjoy your day. He'll call."

For some reason, I find myself nodding. Probably because I don't want Jeff to see my desperation. And I don't want to feel it myself. I decide I'll just go back to the city tomorrow and act like nothing happened. After all, guys hate to talk about the little bumps in the road. I'm sure if I just keep my mouth shut, everything will be fine.

"Okay," I say. "I guess I'll go sailing."

Jeff slides some French toast and hash browns onto a plate and shoves it in my direction. "You have to eat breakfast first. We're going to be out there a while."

I pick up a fork and eat as instructed.

When we return from sailing late that afternoon, all I can think about is getting to the phone and checking my messages. I hastily strip out of my rain gear and stand impatiently on the deck waiting for glacially slow Jeff to do the same.

Jeff nods at the kitchen window as he steps out of his rain pants. "That's my mom and her sister." I look and see two very thin, dark-haired women perched on barstools drinking wine.

They turn and look at us when we enter the kitchen. They are mirror images of each other. It's so freaky I have to look away.

Fortunately, there's a lot to look at because the kitchen is infested with an army of frantic catering people. A man named Hector is darting about in a chef's outfit shouting orders, having seemingly assumed all headaches, stress and responsibility for the party.

This is probably why the hostess and her sister are so calm.

I wipe my hands on my jeans as we approach. In spite of the best rain gear money can buy, I feel a little damp and a lot disheveled. Also, I haven't brushed my teeth all day and the syrup and coffee from this morning are making my breath smell like a wet sheep, so of course I feel great about meeting two impeccably groomed, very wealthy women.

"Aunt Claire and Mom, this is my friend Avery St. George," Jeff says. "Avery, this is my mom's sister, my Aunt Claire, and my mother, Candace."

The aunt and the mom extend their hands in turn. They're so graceful I feel like I should be kissing someone's ring or something, but I manage to do the right thing and execute a couple simple handshakes.

"Welcome, Avery. It's nice to have you," the mom says. "Jeff, pour Avery a glass of wine. I'm sure she could use one after a day on the water."

I smile and try not to say too much to avoid breathing my nasty breath on them.

"How was sailing?" the aunt wants to know. She has one of those smooth, elegant foreheads that don't move when she smiles.

I accept the glass of wine from Jeff and look down at myself. "A little wet. Maybe I should go change?"

"Of course, dear," the mother says. "We'll have a drink before the guests arrive."

I borrow Jeff's phone, excuse myself and go into my bedroom with my very generous glass of wine. I'm surprised when I enter because the room is so clean and tidy. I left the bed in a rumpled mess but now it's made up with fresh sheets. Also, last night's clothes, which I abandoned on the floor, have been cleaned, pressed and hung up, like I'm in a spa or something. I hope the staff won't mention to the hostess what a slob I am.

I quickly check for a message from Kevin. When there isn't one, I slam down some wine and try to stay calm as I take stock of my soggy appearance in the mirror.

I decide I don't have time to shower because blowing out my hair would take too long. I read somewhere that the ability to get gorgeously dressed in no time at all is critical to a brilliant social life. Still, my efforts at hair and makeup are delayed because some well-intentioned housekeeper has hidden all my stuff and I have to keep rifling through drawers looking for this and that.

When I emerge from the bedroom, it's been almost an hour since I went in.

Jeff and his mom and aunt are in the living room drinking martinis. I feel a little light-headed from the wine so I take a deep breath before I walk into the room. "Good evening," I say.

Jeff stands as I enter. His reflexive, old-fashioned manners seem to have an on-off switch that is activated by his mother's presence, which is kind of cute. "Good evening, Avery." He is smiling broadly, like we're in a play and he's terribly amused by it. "Would you like a martini?"

"Sure." I hand him his phone and then sit in a small love seat not far from Jeff's chair and directly across the room from the couch where his mother and aunt are seated. In spite of my growing misery, I'm happy about the outfit I chose. When I'm sitting, it's so plain you hardly notice it, so it seems very tasteful and appropriate for conversation with someone's mother. Once the party gets going and everyone is moving around, though, the backless part of the sweater will be just surprising enough that I won't disappear into the crowd.

"So how do you two know each other?" his mom asks.

I look at Jeff, who is standing behind the bar stabbing an olive for my martini.

"She's interviewing for the marketing position, Mom." He walks across the room and hands me my drink. The glass is so large I feel like I'm down the rabbit hole and everything is off-kilter, size-wise. I hold the drink carefully in both hands and take a small sip while Jeff walks over to his own chair, picks up a similarly large martini and returns to the love seat to sit beside me.

"Well that's marvelous," his mom says. "I love to see a woman doing well in business. Isn't that marvelous, Claire?"

Aunt Claire sips her martini. "It is indeed marvelous." These women are so identical it's freaking me out.

"Avery, tell us about that," the mom says. "How did you get started?"

"Well," I say. "There's not much to tell. I interned at McKinlay & Company in my last summer of law school. I got to know some of the players and saw an opportunity to introduce a bank to a hedge fund I liked. The bank wound up investing. It was more a fluke than anything else."

"How much did the bank invest?"

"Eighty million." I say it quietly, so it doesn't sound like bragging, but I'm afraid it comes off that way anyway.

"And that's a large amount?"

"It's respectable. I don't know if I'd call it large. As you know, the numbers can get really big in this business."

The mom looks at the aunt and raises her eyebrows in an I-told-you-so sort of way. Then she looks back at me. "Yes, I'm learning that. It's a very exciting business, isn't it?"

"Sometimes," I say. "It can be a hard business, too. But I guess that's true with anything."

"Well, that's delightful. Now if you'll excuse me, I think I'll go freshen up before my guests arrive." She stands and smoothes her hair.

Jeff stands and kisses his mom's cheek as she leaves the room. Then he sits back down and looks at Aunt Claire, who is glaring at him.

"Jeff, this is getting out of hand," she says. "You have to talk some sense into her."

"As much as I wish I could, Aunt Claire, I can't stop a freight train."

"Well, something has to be done. This just can't go on." She stares at him expectantly, but Jeff doesn't say anything. He polishes off his martini and gets up and walks to the bar.

"May I fix you another drink, Aunt Claire?"

"No, thank you. I've had quite enough. Excuse me."

She puts her drink down, stands and leaves the room.

Jeff shakes new martinis and pours them into icy cold glasses. "Don't worry about that, Avery. It's just old family politics. It has nothing to do with you."

I decide to take him at his word. I have no interest in becoming a guest star in their long-running family drama, especially since no one bothered to give me the script. I down the rest of my drink and relax back into the cushions. "Are they twins?"

He nods. "It's creepy as hell, isn't it?"

"Identical?"

"Yeah, but it's strange because they're nothing alike other than the way they look." He steps out from behind the bar, hands me a fresh martini and holds up his glass for a toast. "Here's to a more enlightened approach."

I hold my glass in front of me and eye him over the rim. "I don't really understand what we're toasting to."

"My mother's kind of shaking things up in our family. I think it's cool."

"Well, I can certainly agree with that." I clink my glass against his. "What's she up to? And why does your Aunt hate it so much?"

He flops down on the loveseat beside me. "Well, of course it's all about the money."

"Isn't everything?" I'm trying to be funny, but I hate how the words sound when they come out of my mouth.

He nods and drinks two big swallows of martini. "In Aunt Claire's mind, it's morally reprehensible to earn money when you're stinking rich."

"Which you obviously are."

"Right," he says. "But for her, it's mostly about where the money came from. Not really how much there is."

Even through my gin-soaked haze, this sounds way too familiar. "Really," I say. "Where did it come from?"

He puts his fingers to his lips and pretends to take a drag. "Tobacco," he says. "Aunt Claire feels guilty about our sordid beginnings, and she thinks everyone else in the family should, too. But it's total bullshit. Not all of us are happy as cogs in the charity machine."

He gets up and paces around the living room, sloshing martini on his mom's perfect yellow carpet. "And the other thing is she doesn't think my mom's smart enough to run a hedge fund, which is damn insulting if you ask me." He looks back at me. "What do you think?"

All I can think about is Fig. "I think I know your cousin."

"Anton?" he asks. "I should have known." He tips his glass in my direction and then takes another drink. "I guess that's the call you've been waiting for?"

"No, no," I say. "Nothing like that. We've been friends since NYU. He's in New Zealand right now anyway."

"Not anymore," Jeff says. "He'll be in New York tomorrow for a little Coming-to-Jesus with Aunt Claire."

"Why?" I ask. "He hasn't been *working*, has he?"

"She's been getting complaints from the co-op board that some girl is running an illegal restaurant in his apartment."

"They called his mom?"

Jeff looks sharply at me, at which point I realize I'm shouting. I take a drink and try to calm myself but when I stop drinking I laugh like a crazy person. "I mean, why would they do that?"

"She owns the apartment," Jeff says quietly. "And she's the trustee of his trust so I'm sure he's shitting bricks about now. It's kind of a big deal." He looks at his watch. "Anyway, we have better things to do than worry about that, don't you think?"

"Oh, of course," I say, sliding off the loveseat. I'm a little unsteady on my feet. "I'll just go freshen up before everyone gets here. Do you think I could borrow your phone again?"

He winks at me and hands me his phone. "Good luck."

Good luck, indeed. I walk down the hall to my room like I'm on the way to my own execution. My heart is pounding and I'm dizzy. I lock the door, lie on the bed and wait for the room to stop spinning. After a few minutes, I dial Jeff's phone to check my messages.

Sure enough, there's one from Fig.

"Avery, it's me. I just landed in L.A. I'm coming in on the red-eye. I don't know what's going on but my mom thinks someone is running a food take-out business from my apartment. I hope that's not the case, but if it is, I trust that you'll get it the hell out of there before she shows up tomorrow." He pauses for a long time. Then he says, "I guess that's it. I'll be in the city tomorrow to deal with my mother."

This is the end of the message and, I fear, the end of Fig and Figlet.

I look at the clock on the bedside table. It's almost eight. If I leave now, I should make it back to the city before midnight. I'll probably need five hours to get the apartment in white-glove condition, which should help grease the wheels for Fig tomorrow. From what I know about mothers, particularly mothers like Claire, clean always helps.

As I throw my stuff in my bag, I try to come up with a reasonable explanation for my sudden departure from the Hamptons. None seem plausible, particularly since I'm going to be named as the soup culprit in this little debacle at some point very soon. Claire is going to put two and two together, if she hasn't already, because there just aren't that many Averys in the world.

On this logic, I decide there's no reason to try to float some cockamamie spiel for my abrupt return to New York. Better to just get the hell out of there, clean up my mess and hope Fig doesn't suffer too much as a result of my never-ending fuck-ups.

I zip my bag closed and check myself in the mirror.

I feel like death but I actually look okay. My hair has that tousled look I covet and never seem to be able to create on purpose. I sneak out of the party dragging my bag behind me.

Fortunately, the few guests who have arrived are clustered in small groups and engrossed in lively conversation. No one even looks at me, in spite of my amazing sweater. I let myself out the front door and bounce my bag down the steps. As I expected, there are about five Lincolns parked in front of the house. Their drivers are standing in a cluster, smoking and talking.

They look up as I approach.

"Yes, ma'am," one of them says.

"Excuse me," I say. "I need a ride back to the city. Can any of you guys help me out?"

"Now?" one asks.

"Yes," I say. "Right away."

They look at each other and back at me. "We're working," another says. "We can't leave right now."

"Oh, I know. But maybe you know someone, or maybe one of you could take me to the train." I look around. "Is there a train station near here?"

One guy tosses his cigarette to the pavement and crushes it under his heel. "I could take you to the train. I don't know if they're still running, though."

"It's worth a shot," I say. "Let's do it."

He grabs the handle of my bag and wheels it to the car. As I follow, the other drivers make little hooting sounds that I guess are the Hamptons version of cat-calls.

There's no traffic and my driver goes very fast. At the train station, he gets out of the car and takes my bag out of the trunk. I give him fifty dollars and he agrees to wait in case there are no trains. I grab my bag and sprint up the stairs into the station. I had no idea I could go so fast under that kind of weight.

The next train to the city departs in thirty-five minutes. I buy a ticket, walk out onto the platform and wave it at the driver. He salutes me, gets in the car and drives away.

I sit on a bench and dig through my bag for my periwinkle cashmere sweater. Then I remember it's hanging in the guest room closet along with my new skinny jeans. Two more innocent casualties of the weekend. I wonder what the death toll will be when it's all over.

CHAPTER 11:

The Demographic of My Discontent

- - - - - - -

SUNDAY, APRIL 20, 2008

It's after midnight by the time I get to Fig's apartment. I don't even acknowledge the doorman as I enter.

It takes about an hour for me to locate and pack my things. When I'm finished, I haul my bag and the crocks to the front door and then proceed to scrub away every shred of evidence that I was ever there.

I work fast, but it takes a long time because I'm scrubbing almost ten thousand square feet. When the apartment has been sanitized, I return Fig's things to his bathroom in a manner I hope is reasonably similar to the way they were arranged before.

I have no idea what time it is when I leave the apartment, but it's still dark out and it's raining so hard the drops are bouncing off the ground like in a movie. In spite of the downpour, however, I don't want any help from my enemy the doorman, so I drag my bag and the cart full of crocks down the street and try to hail my own cab. This takes quite a while thanks to the deluge, so I'm soaked to the skin when a cab finally pulls over.

The driver gets out and hefts my stuff into the trunk while I slosh into the back seat.

He gets in the driver's seat and slams the door. "Where to?"

I take a moment to consider the question. "A hotel, I guess."

"What?"

He's looking straight ahead so it's no wonder he can't hear me. I lean forward and yell at the back of his fat head. "A hotel. I don't care which one. Just anywhere."

He just sits there like a useless lump. "A hotel, you want. What hotel?"

Some people have absolutely no imagination at all. "Can't you just drive until we see one?" I roll my eyes in disgust. Too late, I realize he's watching me in the rear-view mirror.

"Lady, I don't have time for this shit." He's staring at me with his beady eyes, which are set too close in his meaty, stupid face.

"You don't have time to drive? Isn't that what you do? Drive the car and get paid for it?"

"I can't drive the car without a direction."

"Sure you can. Just put the car in drive, put your stupid foot on the stupid gas and keep going until you see a hotel."

For the first time, he turns his head and looks at me. He's glaring like a vicious bull and all I can hear is his heavy breathing and the windshield wipers, which suddenly seem quite loud in the close quarters of the cab. Then he turns, opens the door, and gets out of the cab with the same hasty, angry movements my dad used one time before I knew rearview mirrors existed and he saw me spit out my tongue at him.

For a second, I'm very afraid the driver is going to yank me out of the car and paddle me but all he does is open the trunk and toss my stuff through the rain in the direction of the curb.

Then he yanks my door open. "Get out."

"What?"

"Get out of my cab."

I just stare at him.

"Lady, get the hell out of my cab before I drag you out."

I slide away from him, open the other door and get out on the street side. Asshole doesn't seem so scary with a car between us. I stand motionless until I see which way he's going to go. When he starts walking around the front of the cab, I go the other direction and walk behind it to the sidewalk. My bag is toppled over in the gutter with dirty water streaming around it like a corpse gunned down in a drive-by. The cart is next to it with pieces of broken crocks scattered around like shrapnel.

I stand on the curb and wait for the cab to pull away. Then I reach down, pull my stuff out of the muck and trudge uptown through blinding rain. I stop for cash at an ATM, walk a few more blocks and duck into a by-the-week motel that is more likely one of those by-the-hour places.

The clerk looks up from his magazine as I enter. I'm so wet my hair is dripping in my face like I just got out of a swimming pool.

"I need a room, please."

He looks me up and down a few times. "It's nine hundred a week."

His voice is not unpleasant but he resembles Charles Manson a little more than I would like. I don't say anything. I just blink at him and wonder if this is a good idea.

"Okay," he says. "For you, eight hundred."

His willingness to negotiate and the absence of the tell-tale swastika tattoo make me a little more comfortable. "I'll give you six, but only if the sheets are clean."

For a second, he looks like he's going to argue with me. I just cross my arms and wait. Eventually he gets up, goes into a room behind the counter and returns with a set of sheets and one folded towel.

Water is pouring off me onto the floor in a little puddle around my feet. "Do you think I could have two towels? I'm kind of wet here."

He scowls a little but leaves and returns with another towel. I pick it up and sniff. It smells clean so I wipe my face and then count out the bills. He hands me a key. It's an actual key, not one of those credit cards real hotels use as keys these days. I try not to think about how many duplicates he has behind the counter as I wheel my bag to the elevator and take it up to my room on the fourth floor.

I bolt the door, take two steps inside the room and peel off my wet clothes. The thought of a hot shower is so delicious I decide I'm willing to tolerate the filthy bathroom, which I can smell from where I'm standing in the foyer. But when I step onto the tile, my bare feet stick to the floor. I leap off the gummy tile and back onto the carpet. No shower is worth standing on whatever is on that floor.

I pick up my wet clothes and sling them across the radiator to dry. I'm so tired I don't even have the energy to change the sheets. All I can do is spread my clean sheets out on the bed and try to sleep underneath my two towels. I'm shivering, so at some point I get up and crank up the heat as high as it will go.

When the room is warmer, I still can't sleep because the heat intensifies the urine odor wafting from the bathroom. And maybe from the mattress.

I close my eyes and try not to think about this.

About ten minutes after I finally fall asleep, I'm awakened by the sound of traffic, which I haven't heard in a while. Generally, a thirty-million-dollar apartment is a pretty reliable prophylactic insulating one from the more objectionable aspects of city life.

This new place, on the other hand, feels like a Petri dish perched on a dirty sidewalk in the seediest part of Times Square.

The sun is up now. In the cold light of day, I'm very disturbed because I'm pretty sure the carpet's current color of charcoal gray is not its original hue. I tiptoe naked across the filthy rug, slide my bare feet into my damp sling-backs and open my bag in search of something to wear.

The search is rather frantic because I really have to pee. Unfortunately, everything in the bag is soaked with muddy gutter water except my jazz-singer dress, which was spared because it's still wrapped in its original protective bag from Saks.

I stand up and strut to the radiator in a tight-legged way that must look very strange but which keeps me from adding to the room's urine problem. Thanks to the heat, my clothes from last night are no longer soaking. Just damp. I put them on, grab my purse and bolt out the door in search of a tolerable bathroom.

In New York City, Starbucks locks its bathrooms so only paying customers can use them, which means you generally can count on them to be clean and well-stocked. I speed-walk to the nearest store, order a triple tall cappuccino and ask for the key to the ladies' room.

I watch as the clerk reaches for the key, lifts it from its hook and hands it to me. Either I'm on drugs or she's moving in slow motion. I snatch it from her fingers and scurry away, almost certain I'm not going to make it. It takes me three tries to unlock the door, at which point I have to pee so badly I'm paralyzed from the waist down. Any movement at all will open the floodgates. I gaze longingly at the toilet, which is only a few feet away, and decide I'm just going to have to brace myself and make a run for it.

I unfasten my skinny white pants as I fling myself across the room toward the toilet. When I get there, I'm so relieved I could cry.

In the calm that follows, I stand at the sink washing my hands and inspecting my face. Most of last night's eyeliner is still there, but it's a few inches lower than it should be. I wet a tissue and clean up the mess as best I can. Then I search in my bag for a clip because my hair looks like a crow slept in it. I pull it back, twist it up and fasten it into place. Last, I brush my teeth and apply powder and lip gloss. When I'm finished, I hope I look more like someone coming in from a hard night and less like the victim of a heinous crime.

I exit the bathroom and find my cappuccino waiting for me on the counter. I pick it up and hand the girl the bathroom key. "Thanks."

"You're welcome." She tips her head toward me and whispers. "You look a lot better."

My face hurts as I smile at her. I don't know where I got the idea no one can see me when I look like hell.

I take my drink to a table. My backless sweater feels extremely conspicuous and inappropriate so I turn my chair to the wall before I sit down. A dark-haired guy in a black jacket is staring at me. He looks away when I catch him at it.

After a few sips of coffee, I pull my cell phone charger out of my purse, plug it into the outlet underneath my table and connect the other end to my cell phone. I let the phone charge a few minutes and then turn it on and check my messages. There's one from Courtney. "Hi, Avery. Sorry for jumping ship in the Hamptons. Hope you made it back okay. Call me when you can."

There's one from Sheridan Chance. "Avery, it's Sheridan. Hope you're having a nice weekend. Just wanted to confirm that we're on for tomorrow. Give me a call."

The final message is from a man. At first, I feel a little jolt of excitement because I think it's Kevin. But the jolt turns into full-blown electric shock treatment when I realize it's my old landlord's gravelly voice. "Avery St. George," he says. "You owe us back rent plus late penalties and interest. If we don't have the money—and I mean cash—by noon Monday you can expect a visit from our collector."

I don't know what their interest rate is, but I'm sure it's far more abusive than the measly 18 percent I pay everywhere else. All-in, they probably want more than twenty-five grand. Trouble is I don't have the money. I paid cash for the van and used everything else to pay down my outstanding debts.

Except, of course, this particular debt.

I quickly delete the message, slap the phone shut and drop it with a clatter. I'm trying to suppress my impending convulsions and avoid a full-blown seizure when the phone starts vibrating from an incoming call. I sit back and watch it slither across the table like a tarantula.

I can't bring myself to touch the phone while it's jerking around like that. When it stops moving, I pick up a Starbucks napkin, wrap it around the phone and turn it over to see who called. It's Sheridan again. She doesn't leave a message, probably because she's getting irritated at my lack of response. Without thinking, I hit the talk button and call her back, which is a mistake because I'm in no shape to talk to anyone now that I'm being hunted by The Collector.

"Oh, hi Avery," she says. "Sorry to bug you on Sunday but I'm worried about the interviews tomorrow."

"No trouble." My voice is hoarse and I swallow some coffee, which goes straight to my heart like a shot of adrenalin. I clutch the table so I won't spin off into the universe.

"Avery, are you there?"

I lean forward and hide my face in the crook of my arm. If I can't see the room, it doesn't spin so much. "I'm here."

"Are you okay? You sound kind of muffled."

Snuffed might be a better descriptor. "I'm fine. I have two clients who agreed to be interviewed."

"Who is it?" she asks. "Can you describe them to me?"

"Well, one is my boyfriend's mother." I pause when it occurs to me that boyfriend might not be a word I get to use anymore. "Anyway, she's the client who lost the most weight so far so I thought she'd be good."

"How much has she lost?"

"Almost thirty pounds. I'd say she has another hundred and fifty to go."

"Oh," Sheridan says. She sounds disappointed. "Who's the other person?"

"My first client. She owns the store that supplies the crocks."

"How old is she?"

"Oh, I'd guess around fifty."

Sheridan clicks her tongue against her teeth. "I'm sorry, Avery, but I don't think those clients will work for the interview."

"Really."

"Well, it's just that City Style writes for a certain demographic. We'd like to photograph very young, very attractive women for the piece. I guess I should have been more specific."

I look around the Starbucks. The guy in the black jacket is still staring at me. This time, he doesn't look away. I try to listen to Sheridan but I can't really pay attention. All I can think about is whether this guy's The Collector. I jerk the charger out of the wall, pick up my purse and head for the door with the phone clutched to my head. The charger cord is dangling from my ear like a tube hooked to the head of a marauding mental patient.

I pause at the door and turn around. Black Jacket Man is on the move and heading my way. I push out of the store and hit the sidewalk running. Sheridan is still talking but I have no idea what she's saying.

I sprint to the end of the block, fling myself around the corner and run until lack of oxygen forces me to stop. I look over my shoulder to see if that guy is following me. Fortunately, he isn't.

"Avery?" Sheridan asks. "Are you there?"

"I'm here," I gasp.

"Are you running?"

"No," I say, which is true because now the best I can do is a not-so-brisk walk. However, I am panting into the phone. I turn the mouthpiece upward so she won't know I'm a mouth-breather.

"Well," she says. "Getting back to the interviews. Do you have any clients who are under, say, thirty, and size two or below?"

I look over my shoulder again. "I'm not sure," I say, craning my neck to peer through the pedestrians. I can't see the guy anywhere. "Do you want me to find someone and call you back?"

"As quickly as you can. I have the photographer lined up for tomorrow so we'll need to get someone right away."

"Okay," I say. "Will do."

I duck into a diner and sit at a booth. All I want to do is call Kevin. I yank the dangling charger cord out of my phone and dial his number.

He lets the phone ring a few more times than usual before he answers. "Yeah," he says. It's a staccato word, like he doesn't have much time.

"It's me," I say. "Avery."

"I know." Neither of us speaks for a while. I consider telling him I'm being chased by a henchman of Guido the Angry Landlord but the truth is everyone walking past the diner window seems totally ordinary and not at all interested in me. Also, it sounds like a bullshit story made up to generate sympathy and if Kevin is mad at me that's the last thing I want from him.

"Anyway," I say. "I'm back in the city."

"Right."

"Okay." I take a deep breath. "Well, I guess I just called to let you know your mom is off the hook for the interview tomorrow."

"They're not doing it?"

"No," I say. "They are. It's just that they're bringing a photographer and they want someone more..." I stop talking when I realize there's no way I can finish this sentence without sounding like a complete jerk.

"More what?" he asks.

I look around the diner and don't say anything. I feel like I'm sliding into a swamp and there's nothing to grab onto.

194

SOUP IN THE CITY

"Avery, my mom got a new outfit and actually went out and got her hair done. What do you want me to say to her?"

"I'm sorry. I guess I wasn't thinking about the demographic. City Style wants a model type for the interview."

His silence feels angry.

"So if you could just give me some names of the thinnest, most attractive clients, I'll call them and try to set something up for tomorrow."

He rattles off three names so quickly I don't have time to write them down.

"Thanks," I say. "I guess I can try to remember that."

I stare at the table and wait for a response. He's silent for at least six blinks. Finally he speaks. "When did you get back?"

"Last night."

"I know," he says. "I called your apartment this morning and some guy answered."

"Kevin, that was . . ."

"I gotta go, Avery." He hangs up.

I sit in stunned silence for a few minutes. Then I call him back.

"What?" he says.

Although I have no idea what to say, I feel pressure to say something quickly. "So you're not going to do the deliveries tomorrow?" is the best I can do. Instantly, I regret the words.

He sighs. "I feel like too much of a dumb ass, Avery. Why don't you find someone who fits into your demographic a little better?"

My mouth is open but I am unable to make a sound.

"Okay, then," he says. "Goodbye." He hangs up again.

I close my phone and sit in the diner in a daze. For one fleeting second, I think about calling Fig so he can talk me down from the tower. But then I remember his Coming-to-Jesus meeting with his mom and the co-op board, so I'm pretty sure he doesn't want to hear about me and my problems right now.

I know I should get up and do something, but I'm brittle and numb and paralyzed. Last time I felt like this I was sitting on my ass in the snow with a compound fracture, desperate and yet powerless to actually get down the mountain.

However, this time feels worse because the cute guy from ski patrol is definitely not coming to rescue me.

Which is unfortunate because I really need to get moving. I should call around and see if I can find a delivery person. I should look through the client list to see if I can pick out the names of the thin, pretty girls Kevin mentioned so I can try to convince them to become part of my demographic. I should figure out a way to reconcile with Fig and Kevin and everyone else who hates me.

I should take a shower because my last one occurred more than forty-eight hours ago.

But then I remember I have to meet the jerk at the restaurant at eleven to scrub his kitchen. I buy myself another cappuccino and schlep over to Duane Reade for cleaning products.

The jerk is waiting outside the restaurant when I get there.

"You're late," he says.

I look at my cell phone. "One minute isn't late."

"Well, you should have been early. Come on." He pulls the door open and walks into the restaurant. I pause on the sidewalk and consider how good it would feel to unload on this guy. But I check myself when I realize that if I don't ingratiate myself with him in the next three hours, Soup in the City is probably dead in the water.

I follow him into the kitchen.

"So here you go," he says. "All the cleaning stuff is in that closet. I'll be back at two."

He stands against the wall with his arms folded and watches as I walk over to the closet. "Are you cleaning in that getup?"

"It's a special occasion, isn't it?" I yank open the closet door and study the cleaning implements crammed inside. When I look up, the jerk is still looking at me.

"What's your name, anyway?" he wants to know.

"Avery," I say, yanking a broom out of the wreckage. "You?"

"Mac."

"Well, Mac, it's nice to meet you. Now if you'll just get out of here, I'll clean this kitchen."

"Don't swear at me," he says. "I don't have to put up with that crap."

I pause and replay my last words in my head. "I didn't swear."

"No," he says. "But you were thinking about it." He ducks out of the kitchen and leaves me alone to clean.

The thing no one knows about me is I clean better than anyone. I learned in high school when I helped my Grandma with her cleaning business.

When you're cleaning a really messy place, the first thing you have to do is put everything away. I look around the kitchen and realize that Mac may be an asshole but at least he plays fair. All the dishes are clean and shelved, so although the kitchen is encrusted in a layer of baked-on grease, I won't have to struggle with the challenge of putting things away when I have no idea where they go.

The next step is to sweep every surface, starting high and going low. There's no sense sweeping a floor only to spatter it with crumbs from the counters above. By the time I'm finished sweeping, I've dumped the industrial-sized dust pan at least three times.

After that, you scrub. There are a few tricks to scrubbing. First you fill a bucket with the hottest water you can stand. It definitely helps to wear rubber gloves. Then you dump ten or twenty clean washrags in the bucket and fill a spray bottle with three parts hot water and one part Simple Green. You spray the cleaning solution on the dirty surface, scrub with one of those yellow sponges with the scratchy green side, and then wipe off the cleaner and the muck with a hot, damp rag. When the rag is dirty, you toss it aside, grab another one and keep going.

At all times, you carry an old toothbrush in your back pocket to get into the nasty little nooks and crannies.

When you get to the floors, you start all over again. Spray, scrub and wipe. It sounds easy but it's a punishing, hands-and-knees sort of task. When I'm finished, my white pants are completely ruined but there was no way around it. No one ever cleaned a floor sloshing dirty water around with a sloppy old mop.

Shortly before two, I'm standing in the sparkling kitchen sipping what's left of my cold cappuccino. I'm confident Mac will be amazed. He may think he had a clean kitchen, but I found filth in places I'm sure he never even considered.

Sure enough, when he comes in he's speechless. He just stands there, looking around the kitchen in awe.

"I'll be back in two hours with my equipment," I say. "And I cleared off that shelf for my pans. You'll have to arrange the walk-in so I have at least four feet of space on two shelves."

I toss my empty Starbucks cup into the shiny-clean garbage can on my way out.

I'm standing on the curb outside the restaurant trying to catch a cab when it occurs to me no cab is going to pick me up because I look like a greasy filth monger. But there's no time to go back to my hovel, I mean, hotel, to take a shower. The crock store closes at four on Sundays and I need pans and knives and chopping boards and all the other stuff I took for granted when I was at Fig's.

Finally, I'm forced to take two buses over to the Upper West Side. I look bad, even for the bus. When it stops a block from the crock store, I'm so tired I can barely stagger down the steps.

Joanne stares at me when I come through the door. "What happened to you?"

I try to laugh it off. "It's a war zone out there, let me tell you."

She just shakes her head and keeps staring.

"Anyway," I say. "I need all new crocks." I pull a list from my purse and read the rest of the order. "And pots, knives, strainers, spoons and chopping boards."

"Should I throw in a food processor?"

I can't believe I didn't think of this before. It will save me hours of chopping time. "Definitely," I say. "The biggest one you have."

198

SOUP IN THE CITY

She hustles around the store putting the order together. When she's finished, there are many large boxes stacked next to the counter. "Shall we deliver it?"

"Unfortunately I need it now. Can you call a Town Car for me?"

She glances at my pants and then looks away. "Okay," she says. "Just a second." She picks up the phone behind the counter and dials. "Where do you want to go?"

I give her the address of the restaurant. When the car's on the way, she helps me carry everything out to the curb to wait for it.

She gives me a hug, goes back into the store and comes out with one of her calico skirts. "Here," she says. "Use this until you can get home to change."

The skirt is a long, tiered number with lace sewn around each seam. It has an elastic waistband and looks like something Laura Ingalls Wilder might have worn. It's way too big for me, but I have no other options at the moment. I slip it on over my filthy white pants. With the backless sweater and heels, I'm pretty sure I look like an Amish hooker.

As I stand and wait for the car, I make many resolutions so I'll never have to run around like a total wacko again. First, Courtney and the Hamptons no longer exist in my world. Second, I will give the soup business all the care and attention it deserves. Third, I will shower daily, no matter how disgusting the bathtub may be.

I blow my schmucky hair out of my face and decide I will find the strength to keep going. All I have to do is get this stuff to the restaurant, get to bed and endure one very early and crazy morning of shopping for groceries, washing the crocks and making soup in time for deliveries.

Then I remember I no longer have a delivery guy. I don't even have keys to the goddamn van. Kevin has them.

I've never hated anyone so much in all my life.

An hour later, I'm riding on the edge of rage when the Town Car finally comes and picks up me and the stuff to take us to the East Side. Of course the restaurant is already open when we get there.

The driver helps me stack the boxes by the door. I don't really want to leave them on the street but I can't see any other option. I rush into the restaurant and look around. Mac isn't anywhere in sight so I go up to the bartender, who is pouring a sidecar.

I lean over the bar. "I'm Avery. I'm here to see about unloading some stuff in the kitchen."

He looks up and squints at me but doesn't say anything.

"I'm renting the kitchen in the mornings."

"Oh, yeah." He looks down and garnishes the sidecar with a cherry and an orange slice. "You're the soup girl."

It sounds so dorky when he says it but I have no choice but to own up to my status as the soup girl. "Yes," I say. "I guess I am."

He points towards the back of the dining room. I thank him and head back there. Mac is sitting in the last booth going over the reservation book.

"You're here," he says. He doesn't look up from his book. "Just a second." When he's finished, he closes the book and looks at me. "You ready to unload your stuff?"

I barely have the energy to respond. "Yes." The word is so quiet I'm not sure he hears it.

But he must have, because eventually he jerks his head toward the kitchen. "Go in there and get Chuck. He'll help you with your stuff. When you're done, come see me and I'll get you a key."

I go into the kitchen and ask for Chuck. The dishwasher rips off his gloves and curses, so I'm guessing he's Chuck. I watch him stomp away. He stops at the top of the stairs on the far side of the kitchen and turns and looks at me. "Are you coming?"

I nod and follow him down the stairs. He flicks a light switch at the bottom and we walk through the cellar to the stairway thingy that comes up through the sidewalk. He pulls out the bar that holds the doors shut and pushes them open without apparent regard for any pedestrians unfortunate enough to be standing on them.

The boxes are still stacked on the sidewalk where I left them. I turn back to point them out to Chuck, but he's disappeared back into the hole. Evidently I am supposed to carry all this stuff through the creepy little cellar myself.

At this point, I hate Chuck even more than I hate Kevin.

It takes me twenty minutes and many trips to haul the boxes into the kitchen. When I'm finished, my four-inch heels are pressing into my feet like thumbscrews. I want to take the shoes off and throw them at somebody. Just then, Mac sticks his ugly face around the corner. "You ready to learn how the alarm system works?"

"I'm really tired," I say. "Let's go over it tomorrow."

"I'm not meeting you here at five a.m.," he says. "Let's do it now."

He hands me a key and shows me how to use the alarm system. This straightforward process takes twenty minutes longer than it should because for some reason he feels he must run through the same simple procedure at least ten times.

"Okay," I say. "I've got it."

"One more time," he says. "I don't want to be pulled out of bed at the butt-crack of dawn because you weren't paying attention."

I can't afford to alienate Mac now, so I put a cork in my irritation and watch one more time.

When kindergarten is finally over for the day, I manage a tight-lipped goodbye, grab a cab to the hovel and collapse into bed. I'm way too tired to sleep but it doesn't matter. Just laying there feels so good I don't ever want to get up.

As I lay there, I wonder why I jumped through all these hoops today. I still don't have a delivery person or the keys to my van, which is the kind of issue that's obviously fatal to a delivery business.

I pull myself up and sit on the bed trying to think what to do. Unfortunately, I'm way past thinking anymore. I decide it might go better if I lay down. It certainly feels better.

For a second, I wonder if I can do the deliveries alone. I close my eyes and try to imagine myself navigating a rather large and unwieldy van through the mean streets of Manhattan.

I just can't see it. I do not know how to parallel park. I've never understood the magic of double-parking without getting screamed at or towed. I am completely unable to change lanes in crazy traffic on the absolute certainty that everyone else will just get the hell out of my way. I don't think I can punch through every green light convinced the pedestrians will make it to safety before my van slams into their unsuspecting bodies.

Kevin, however, makes this stuff look easy. I swallow my pride, pick up my phone and dial his number. Voice mail answers, of course.

"Look," I say. "I know you hate me because I'm shallow and stupid, but I'm really in a bind. I need someone, I don't care who, to meet me at the new kitchen tomorrow and help me with deliveries. If you, or maybe Duncan and Mark, would do that, I'd really appreciate it." I give him the address of the restaurant and then pause for a second. "And I'll pay double."

That should do the trick. Even if Kevin has written me off for good, Duncan and Mark always need money.

I close my eyes and fall into a fitful sleep. My pillow smells like cigarettes and bad perfume in spite of the new pillowcase I bought at Duane Reade. Also, I keep dreaming I'm standing on the sidewalk waiting for a delivery person to show up and the only person who does is my rabid ex-landlord.

This image brings me to the realization that driving a soup delivery van through rush-hour traffic might not be the scariest thing in the world.

CHAPTER 12:

Pink Elephants on Vicodin

- - - - - - -

APRIL 21 – 23, 2008

I awaken at four the next morning, before the alarm on my cell phone goes off. I'm so tired I'm afraid my wooden body will splinter if I stand up, but I drag myself out of bed anyway.

I dig through my muddy clothes in a vain effort to find something clean enough to wear. There's nothing, so I gingerly slink back into my Amish hooker outfit. I don't even care how ridiculous I look. All I can think about is whether my delivery people are going to show up.

I leave the hovel, go to an all-night grocery store and buy ingredients for cream of tomato and split pea, which are the easiest soups I can think to make, and then take a cab to the restaurant. Even with my half-working brain, I'm able to bypass the alarm thanks to Mac drumming the instructions into my head.

Once I'm in the kitchen, I flick on the lights and spend the next forty minutes getting the soups on the stove. While they simmer, I slice open boxes and start running the new crocks through the dishwasher. It's an industrial dishwasher that works much faster than Fig's, so I don't have any problems. I can't help but notice that the kitchen is not as clean as it was when I left it, though.

At seven o'clock, the soups are done. I take a break and walk out to the sidewalk on the off chance anyone is out there. If someone actually shows up, I can have the crocks filled in ten minutes. I'll give them some money and send them to Starbucks so they won't be mad at me for making them wait.

When I see the van pull around the corner with its headlights on, I know Soup in the City is saved.

I watch as Duncan and Mark get out of the van. Kevin isn't there, of course, and the atmosphere is decidedly break-up awkward.

"Do you guys want some coffee?" I ask. "I just have to fill the crocks."

"We're fine," Duncan says. "We'll just wait here."

I go back into the kitchen, fill the crocks and then stick my head out the front door and wave at Duncan and Mark. Pretty soon, they come into the kitchen pushing the rolling metal racks that came with the van. They load up the crocks without a word and leave.

"Bye," I say.

"Yeah," Duncan says. "We'll see you in a few hours."

After Duncan and Mark leave with the soup, I take thirty minutes to clean up the kitchen and bag up my cleaning supplies. Then I catch a cab back to the hovel, scrub the bathroom and take my first shower in three days.

I still have nothing to wear so I slither back into my dirty clothes and head out on a mission to find suitable clothing to wear to the bank. The ensemble has to be good because my deadline with the landlord is noon today, which means I have one shot to convince the bank to loan me a whole lot of money.

I finally find a souvenir shop that's open, but the best outfit I can come up with is an "I ♥ NY" T-shirt to wear with my prairie skirt. I'm doubtful this will impress the bank until it occurs to me that maybe people will think I'm one of the Olsen twins.

By the time I leave the souvenir shop, it's after nine. I call information and ask for the number of the main branch of my bank. I'm connected automatically at no additional charge, which is nice because at this point I'm in such a fog I can't even remember the bank manager's name so I have to ask for him by title.

"One moment, please."

I'm forced to listen to the theme from the Lone Ranger while I'm on hold. Then the woman comes back on the line. "I'm sorry. He's in a meeting right now. Would you like to leave a message?"

"No, thank you," I say. "I just want to make sure he's there at the bank."

"What did you need, ma'am?" She sounds suspicious, like I'm toting a machine gun and am poised to burst into the bank at any second.

"I just want to make sure he's there so we can sit down and discuss some things."

"Do you have an appointment?"

"I don't have time for an appointment. Can't you just tell me if he's there?"

"One moment, please." She puts me on hold again. In a few minutes, another woman comes on the line.

"This is Linda Shotz. May I help you?"

I might not remember the manager's name, but I'm almost positive Linda Shotz is the fraud woman who stripped me of my Coat and my final shreds of dignity. Evidently she's the person who steps in whenever some nutcase is in danger of harming the bank or its employees.

"No, thank you," I say. "I'd like to speak to the bank manager."

"He's not available right now. What did you need?"

The obvious answer is money, but I just hang up and decide to start over when I get to the bank.

Fortunately, now I know better than to pester anyone about the bank manager. I stand in line at the service desk and ask to speak to a loan officer.

"What kind of loan?" the woman asks.

"Fast," I say.

She looks at me. "Ma'am?"

"I'm in kind of a hurry. What kind of loan is quickest?"

"We offer expedited commercial loans to certain qualifying businesses," she says. "Would a business loan work?"

"It's worth a try."

She takes my name and I sit down and wait as instructed.

Fifteen minutes later, a tall man in a cheap gray suit walks up to me.

"Ms. St. George?" he asks, reading my name from a file. I stand up, shake his hand and follow him to his desk.

"So what can I do for you today?"

"I need to borrow some money."

"You're interested in a commercial loan?"

"Not necessarily," I say. "Just whatever I can get that's fast. I need the money by noon today." Once the words are out of my mouth, I realize this was exactly the wrong way to go, desperation being one of those less-admirable qualities in a borrower.

"Well, let's see," he says. "What's the purpose of the loan?"

"What I mean is I'd like the money today. It's to expand my business."

"And what business is that?"

I want to tell him it's the business of walking around with knee caps that don't have spikes driven through them. But instead I smile sweetly and say, "Soup. I have a homemade soup business called Soup in the City."

"Does the business have a checking account?"

"It's a sole proprietorship. All the cash receipts are deposited into my personal checking account here at the bank."

"This bank?"

I nod and he types some stuff into his computer. "Let's see," he says. "Your account has a balance of three thousand dollars. I also see a rather substantial personal loan in the amount of twenty-two thousand."

"Yes," I say. "If you look at the history, the loan was almost fifty thousand not too long ago. I've been paying down the balance as quickly as I can."

"And how much did you want to borrow?"

"Thirty thousand."

He nods thoughtfully. "Well, I can have you fill out an application. We'll review it and get back to you in a few weeks."

I smile again, but not so sweetly this time. "I'm sorry, but I don't have a few weeks. I really need the money now."

"Unfortunately, that's not the way it works, Ms. St. George. It takes some time for the bank to consider these things."

SOUP IN THE CITY

I exhale and try to speak calmly and slowly. "Yes," I say. "But that woman over there said you offer expedited loans to businesses. What about those?"

"Those loans are for businesses that have a solid history with us. All I can see for your business is some deposits of cash in the last few months."

"Yes, but you also have collateral. You're holding a sable coat valued at more than fifty thousand dollars. Can't I borrow against that?"

He shakes his head. "We never release collateral until a loan is paid in full."

"I'm not asking you to release it. I'm asking to borrow against its value again. You let me do it once before. Why is this such a big deal?"

"I don't know, Ms. St. George. You're the one who's in such a hurry."

"Okay." I take the title to the van out of my purse. "How about different collateral? I have a van I could borrow against."

"We'll definitely consider that on your application." He pulls an application out of his drawer and hands it to me. "Why don't you just sit over there and fill this out?"

I shake my head. "I just told you I don't have time to fill that out. What about a credit card? Can I get one of those right away?"

"Ms. St. George, this conversation is becoming unproductive. If you want a credit card, you can apply for one online." He hands me a card with the bank's web address printed on it.

I don't know what to do now, because money in two weeks is not going to help today. I get up, leave the bank and stop at the nearest Starbucks to regroup. I have two hours to come up with a whole bunch of money. Since this seems unlikely, I spend a few minutes planning my life on the lam and wondering how I'll manage the soup business from afar. Duncan and Mark could be like Charlie's Angels and I'll be the disembodied voice coming from the speaker phone.

Unfortunately, I feel ill-equipped to hide from someone when I don't even know how he found me in the first place. I didn't use a credit card for the hovel, so I doubt that was the connection. When I was at Fig's, nothing was in my name. In fact, the only thing Avery St. George has done recently is register the van and the address used for that was . . .

Fig's address.

Which means I'm the stupidest woman alive. The landlord could know everything about my whereabouts. Where I was staying. Where the van is parked. Where the restaurant is. Where I'm staying now. Maybe he can even track me through my cell phone.

If this is the case, there's no point trying to hide. I pick up the phone and call the landlord. He doesn't answer the first time so I have to dial him again, which feels a little like jumping back into shark-infested waters after seeing the fins and swimming like hell to get to the dock.

His voice is so low it almost sounds fake. But I'm obviously in no position to criticize.

"Uh, yes," I say. "This is Avery St. George. I got a message from you yesterday."

"You got the money?"

"How much is it exactly?"

"It's exactly a lot more than it should be," he says. "As of right now, it's thirty-two thousand."

"You still haven't rented the place?"

"Now how would that concern you?"

"You're required to mitigate your damages," I say. "I don't owe you any rent if someone else has been paying it."

"You signed a lease," he says. "You're obligated. End of discussion."

"The lease ended in March. How'd you get to thirty-two grand?"

He hesitates for a second. "Listen, you little bitch. I'm not going to split hairs with you. Consider it collection fees."

"Well, I don't have it," I say. "So you'll just have to put me on a payment plan."

"I'm not the Bank of America."

"No, but if I don't have it, I don't have it, and we both know something is better than nothing."

"I don't know about that," he says. "What I do know is I'm sick of chasing your fat ass all over the city."

The part about my fat ass stops me cold. I look down at my hips, which seem very slim to me. Suddenly, I'm quite certain this idiot has no idea what I look like, which would support the idea that all he has is my cell phone number from the van registration. And that's nothing to be afraid of.

I hang up the phone and go to the restaurant to settle up with the guys for last week's deliveries and try to find someone bony enough for Sheridan Chance to interview.

When I get back to the restaurant, it's after ten. Duncan and Mark are still unloading dirty crocks from the van, which is going to make Mac testy because I'm supposed to be out of the kitchen by now.

"How'd it go?" I ask.

"Tough," Duncan says, pulling the last metal rack of dirty crocks out of the van. "Mark can't drive for shit."

He hands me a bank bag with the money from the day's deliveries. I follow him into the restaurant. We unload and wash the crocks as quickly as we can with Mac fuming and slamming things around.

When we're finished, I motion for Duncan and Mark to follow me into the dining room.

"How about I buy you guys a burger while we settle up?" I point to the burger place across the street.

"Okay," Duncan says. We each push a metal rack out of the restaurant and load them into the van.

Five minutes later, we're sitting at the burger place ordering half-pound burgers with homemade fries and those huge milkshakes where they send out the leftovers in the metal mixing cup because it all won't fit into the glass.

While we wait for the food, I count out the money. I slide one stack back into the bank bag, pick up the other stack and put it on the table between Duncan and Mark.

"Well, anyway," I say. "Here it is. I can't pay this every time, but I appreciate you coming in on short notice."

I stop talking when the waitress arrives with the burgers. Duncan lifts the top bun off his burger and squeezes ketchup and mustard in a careful, crisscross design. Mark is already eating and taking great care not to look at me.

"So," I say. "I was hoping you guys would want to, you know, take over with the deliveries."

They don't speak. I'm not hungry but I don't know what else to do so I pick up my knife, saw my burger in half and start eating.

My chewing seems way too loud.

Duncan stacks some fries on his burger, replaces the lid and smashes it down with both hands. Then he sits back and wipes his hands on a napkin. "It's just that it's kind of awkward, you know? We've been friends with Kevin since grammar school."

I watch as Duncan picks up his burger and wolfs down a good chunk of it in one bite that's actually three bites without any chewing between them. I shove some fries in my mouth and chew. In spite of how shitty I feel, they taste great.

"So it would be better if you found someone else," Duncan says.

I keep my eyes on my plate and eat. The fries disappear at a calming, methodical pace.

"Don't be that way, Avery," Mark says. "We really don't want to take sides."

I look at him. "Sides seemed okay when I was paying double, though, didn't they?"

"Well, at least we showed up," Mark says.

"Well, that's certainly more than I can say for some people." I hope this gets back to Kevin. "Just give me the keys, then."

Mark slides the keys across the table.

I pull a fifty out of the bank bag and smash it down on the table. "This should cover lunch." I grab the keys and stand up. "Thanks. You guys have been great."

"Avery," Duncan says. "We're not leaving you high and dry. We'll stay on until you can find someone else."

I dismiss them with a wave of my hand as I turn to leave. "Don't do me any favors."

I'm out of the restaurant and halfway across the street when Duncan catches up to me and grabs me by the elbow. "Avery, at least let us take the van back to the garage . . ."

I whip around to look at him and am stunned and amazed when I'm blown off my feet straight into his chest. I can feel myself screaming, but I can't hear anything as we fly through the air and land near the sidewalk. I'm on top of Duncan, and he's flat on his back in the gutter with his head on the curb like a pillow. People are racing away and shouting and yelling, but I don't understand anything. The world is hot and black and orange and too toxic to breathe.

Mark is there, leaning over us and yelling in slow motion, but he disappears in a wave of heat. Then my face is smashed into the curb and all I can do is wrap my arms around Duncan's head so he doesn't disappear into the blackness, too.

Some time later, I open my eyes to a blinding overhead light. For a second, I panic, thinking I've awakened on the operating table. But when I look around I see it's just an ordinary hospital room.

I sit up to look for the button that calls the nurse, but I have to lie back down because when my head is upright it throbs like it's tightened in a vice. I think about yelling for a nurse, but my mouth is so gummed up I'm pretty sure something must have crawled in and died while I was out.

Fortunately, a nurse comes in before too long. She's wearing a rather voluminous and unflattering set of pink and blue pajamas. If this is her uniform, this hospital is one cruel place. I have to get out of here.

She smiles when she sees me. "Well, guess who's awake. How's your head?"

"Not good," I say. "You?"

She chuckles. "I'm fine, but then again, I didn't take a tire iron to the skull."

This image makes me nauseous and I have to fight to keep from throwing up. "Where's Duncan?"

The nurse walks over and hands me some pills and a small paper cup half-filled with water. "Who?"

"Duncan Schedler," I say. "His head hit the curb." I swallow the pills and give the cup back to her.

"He's your friend?"

I close my eyes. "He was there. And Mark Inglesby, too."

"Let me go check," she says. "I'll be right back."

A few minutes later, she sticks her head in the door. "Are you up to talking to the police just now?"

"About Duncan?"

"About the van that blew up. They're trying to figure out what happened."

I shake my head. "I think I'm going to be sick."

She runs over to me and shoves a bedpan in my face. "Here you go."

I lean over the shiny metal dish, but nothing comes out. "Sorry," I say. "I guess not." Then I lay back down.

"I'll just tell him to come back tomorrow," she says. She leaves for a second and returns with the investigator's business card.

"Is anyone else here?" I ask.

"Visitors, you mean?"

I nod.

"No, honey. There's no one else. Do you want me to call someone?"

I shake my head. "No," I say. "No, thank you. Where are my things?"

"Your purse is in that closet. Your clothes, they took as evidence."

"Can you hand me my purse?"

She opens the closet and brings me my buttery yellow bag, which is now scorched and charred and looks more like a charcoal briquette than a cupcake. I take my phone out of my bag and look at it. No missed calls.

"What will I wear home?"

"You're in no shape to go home. Tomorrow you can call someone to bring you something."

"There's no one to call." I put my phone back in my bag. The burned smell makes me sick so I ask her to take it away. Then I fall asleep and dream I'm on a flight to Beijing to protest the summer Olympics. I've just finished eating my shitty coach meal when the flight attendant comes by. She says there was a problem with my credit card, so I have to get off the plane now.

She keeps yelling at me to get off the plane, but we're over whatever ocean you cross when you fly to China so there's nothing I can do. I somehow sneak past her and escape to first class. Fig is there, taking the first few bites of one of those huge first-class sundaes, but he won't share it with me. Evidently it's against the rules for coach people and first-class people to eat off the same spoon.

When the flight attendant hunts me down, Fig takes his spoon out of the dish and gives her the sundae, which has suddenly grown to the size of a big tacky bowling trophy. He has to use both hands to lift it. She scurries away with it into the secret area behind the curtain that only flight attendants can enter. Fig looks up from his first-class seat and winks at me. "She'll leave us alone now." But all I can think about is how she's going to eat the whole thing and how much I hate her for it.

Then I wake up to find Fig sitting in the chair in the corner of my room gobbling down the last few bites of a banana split. I clear my throat and he stops eating and looks at me.

"Sorry," he says. "I brought this for you, but when you wouldn't wake up I figured I'd eat it before it melted."

"A likely story."

He stands up and brings me what's left of the ice cream, which isn't much. I wrinkle my nose and he scrapes the melted remains into a little pool and pours it into his mouth. Then he walks around the corner of the room and chucks the container in the garbage can under the sink. I can't see him, but I know there's a sink there because I can hear him washing his hands.

"So do you hate me now?" I ask.

He pops his head around the corner holding a couple paper towels in his wet hands. "I'm not going to bust on you in the hospital, Avery." He's drying his hands a little too carefully, like he's a surgeon when we both know he's not.

I don't say anything.

He disappears around the corner and returns without the paper towels. "Who do you think blew up your van?"

"It was blown up for sure?"

"Yeah," he says. "I went there and checked it out while you were asleep. There's nothing left but a burned-out chassis. And these were all over the pavement." He pulls some of my flyers out of his pocket and shows them to me. They're dirty and wrinkled but not scorched.

"Why didn't they burn?" I ask.

"They weren't in the van. Some guy named Mac was having a fit and tossing them around on the sidewalk while the police stormed through his restaurant looking for clues."

"They raided the restaurant?"

"I guess so," he says. "There's a bunch of police tape up. No one can go in there. They put him in cuffs and stuck him in a car until he settled down."

I imagine Mac flinging Soup in the City flyers around like a crazy man and the police pinning him to a car and cuffing him. "Why were you there?"

"It's all over the news, Avery. A Soup in the City delivery van blown to bits. It's getting a ton of coverage, probably because the announcers like saying Soup in the City over and over again. Anyway, I knew it was your business from your voicemail greeting."

"Oh."

"So who do you think did it?"

"I figured it was your mother."

"Huh," he says. "Not funny."

"Yet?" I ask.

He just looks at me and kind of smirks a little.

"Okay, sorry," I say. "I suppose you're in big trouble?"

"I was until I ran into Roberta Small," he says. "Maybe that'll help."

"Roberta Small?" The name is familiar, but I can't think who she is to save my life.

"She came to see you a little while ago," Fig says. He points to a bouquet on the windowsill. "She left those flowers. Now she's on her way to tell my mom how you single-handedly stocked her soup kitchen since January."

"You think that'll smooth things over?"

He shrugs. "We're all about feeding the hungry, you know."

For a second, I have a glimmer of hope that I may have done something right for a change. But then I look around at the hospital room and Fig's tense face and decide I must be delusional. "What about the co-op board? Are they kicking you out?"

"They don't really have proof of anything. It'll probably just blow over."

"I'm sorry," I say. "I guess I got a little carried away."

"Eh," Fig says. He lifts his hands and lets them fall on the bedrail with a thud. "What are you gonna do?"

"Well, anyway, I'm really sorry."

I wait for him to say, "No worries," which is what he always says when I've messed up and he's forgiven me, but he doesn't say anything else.

I pull at the neck of my hospital gown. "I hate to ask for a favor, but do you think you could get me something from the gift shop to wear home?"

He hesitates a second and then nods. "Okay, I'll be right back." He leaves and returns with a pink flamingo track suit and matching flip-flops, which is another very good sign that all is not forgiven.

"You have to get out of here now," I say.

"Okay," he says. "I'll just wait in the hall."

"No," I say. "You have to go. I am tainted. You can't be associated with me right now."

"Don't you think you're being a little dramatic?" But he takes a few steps towards the door as he says it.

"My van just blew up. So I'd say no. And you have to get out of here so I can clean up this mess once and for all, before it splashes all over everyone."

"Do you need money?" he asks weakly.

"Yes, but it's more than I feel comfortable borrowing."

"Oh, okay," he says. "Sure." He nods. I can see relief dripping over him like a fine mist on a hot day.

I unfold the pink sweatshirt and pull it on over my hospital gown. Then I tuck the pants under the covers and slide into them.

"Avery, can you just leave like this?"

"Seeing as how I have no insurance, I think it's the smartest thing I could do." I yank the hospital gown out from under my flamingo ensemble, ball it up and throw it on the end of the bed. "Anyway, I've got some things to take care of."

I rip the tags off my new pink flip-flops, thrust my feet into them and stand up. I'm a little wobbly at first, but I think I can make it work. I hold out my hands like I'm on a balance beam and practice walking in a straight line. "How did you find out I was here?"

"The police."

"Can you call them and find out where Duncan Schedler and Mark Inglesby were taken? They worked for me. I need to make sure they're okay."

"Done," he says. "You sure I can't do anything else?"

I stop practicing and look up. "I'm sure. Just stand by. I'll sort everything out and call you when I come up for air." I grab my bag out of the closet and give Fig a hug, which I fear comes off as a little inappropriate because I'm pretty dizzy and it feels good to hold onto something. Then I leave to go settle up my tab with the hospital.

The woman won't accept my payment without an address. "I'm homeless," I say. "There is no address."

"Well, if you're indigent you need to fill out some forms." She reaches behind her and starts shuffling through some vertical dividers.

"I'm not indigent," I say. "Just homeless."

She turns and looks at me. "What?"

"I can pay my bill but I have no address to give you."

"We have to have an address," she says.

"I just said there is no address. And at the risk of being obvious, I have to tell you that standing here arguing about this isn't helping my concussion at all."

She just stares at me, blinking like a cow at a new gate.

"Oh, for God's sake." I pull the rumpled loan application out of my purse and slowly read the bank's address while the hospital woman types it into her computer. "Send everything to Linda Shotz in care of the fraud department. She'll know how to find me."

"Fine," the woman says. "All I needed was an address." She takes my check, writes out a receipt and thrusts it at me. "I hope you feel better soon."

I take a cab to the hovel and pack my things with every intention of sneaking out and escaping to a new hovel no one knows about. But before I'm half-packed, I'm so dizzy and messed up I can't do anything but lie down and hope my head doesn't explode.

I go to sleep and dream Linda Shotz is strutting her stuff down a runway in The Coat. She looks surprisingly good, which makes me think I probably should have stayed at the hospital after all.

This suspicion is confirmed when I wake up the next morning. I can't get out of bed, because my head feels like a giant water balloon that's so full it will break if it's lifted. I wish I were one of those guys in the cop movies who can take multiple tire irons to the skull and still manage to do some pretty spiffy line dancing later that night.

But I'm not that resilient. If I had the energy to feel anything other than shitty at this point, I'd probably feel a little embarrassed at yesterday's overzealous, misguided insistence about how I was going to take charge of my life and clean up my messes. I couldn't even flee to a new dwelling as I intended. But I'm still alive and all knee caps are working so I feel pretty confident the landlord doesn't know about this place, which means the effort would have been unnecessary.

The other things I was planning to do, like call the clients to let them know Soup in the City was blown to bits, seem similarly unnecessary.

I'm sure they saw it on the news. I guess I could try to figure out how to get my business back on track. Maybe Mac will still let me in the door of his restaurant. If not, maybe I can find a new restaurant and rent a new van. But this effort also seems pointless because even if I could put the business back together, I'm clean out of delivery people.

At this moment, I hate Kevin McCall even more than I did before, which in my bruised and battered state of mind seems the perfect time to call him up and give him hell.

I reach for my phone. This takes a while because I have to contort myself in a way that keeps my spine, neck and head parallel to the floor at all times. Otherwise my brain will slosh out of my ears onto the carpet, which is already dirty enough.

Kevin answers right away, as if that's going to help.

"Avery?"

"Yes?"

"Where are you? I've been trying to call you but they said you checked out of the hospital. Are you okay?"

"I'm fine, but that's not what this call is about."

"Oh," he says. "What is it about?"

"I'm calling because I want you to know that what you did is total bullshit. That's what it's about."

"I had nothing to do with it. I swear."

"Nothing to do with what?"

"The van. I'd never do anything like that."

"I'm not talking about the van. I'm talking about you getting all pissed off about that guy answering the phone."

"Avery, I can't really get into it right now. I'm . . ."

"Now you listen to me, Kevin McCall. You will get into it because that was total crap. I don't own that apartment and you know I don't own it. In fact, you were speaking to the owner when you called. I don't even live there anymore, because now I'm in some fleabag *Hotel Rwanda*, and I can't check out because my brain has turned into a giant egg yolk."

I stop talking because pains are pulsing through my skull like a strobe light. Actually, it's more like a police siren because shrieking, piercing sounds are included for no extra charge. I relax my jaw and wait for the throbbing to subside. When it does, I realize Kevin McCall has not responded to my very reasonable accusations.

"Are you there?" I ask. More throbbing. Evidently the universe does not want me to rip into Kevin McCall just now.

"Avery, Duncan is going into surgery. I have to call you later."

Great. Now I'm even more of an asshole than I was two minutes ago. "Is he okay?" I'm grateful my tone comes off as much friendlier and less irritated than I really feel.

"His leg is broken and they're putting some pins in it. He should be fine once the cast comes off."

"What about his head?"

"Evidently yours took the brunt of it. Why aren't you in the hospital?"

"I don't have any insurance." I keep the part about being a sitting duck to myself.

"Yeah," he says. "Neither does Duncan." He's quiet for a second. "Look. I'm sorry I overreacted about the guy in the apartment. I'll call you later, okay?"

"Okay." I close my cell phone, reach for the hotel phone and dial the front desk. For the first time, I'm glad I couldn't afford the Four Seasons. If anyone in New York can get some really good drugs, it has to be the scary guy manning the hovel lobby.

"Front desk," he says.

"Hello," I say. "Do you think you could send up some painkillers?"

"What kind?"

"For my head. I got hit with a tire iron."

"You have cash?"

"Yes," I say. "How long?"

"Twenty minutes." He hangs up.

About a hundred years later, someone knocks on the door. I get out of bed and try to stand upright. It hurts too much, so I bend at the waist and sway across the room in my pink flamingo track suit. This effort is designed to keep my throbbing head as parallel to the floor as possible and has the happy byproduct of making me look like a drunken pink elephant.

I reach up and open the door. Charles Manson is standing there with a blister pack of Vicodin. I know I must look like something out of a David Lynch movie but he barely blinks.

"How much?" I ask.

"Fifty bucks."

I hand him a bill and take the blister pack in exchange.

"This stuff will mess you up," he says. "Whatever you do, don't stack it with Viagra."

"Okay," I say. "That's good advice."

I shut the door, swallow two pills and go back to bed.

Later that day, I'm feeling almost human so I drag myself out of bed and start digging through a rat's nest of paperwork looking for the insurance company's phone number. Perhaps a speedy settlement for the totaled van will hold the Unabomber landlord at bay for a little while.

Unfortunately, I can't concentrate because I'm still half-drugged and the damn phone won't stop ringing. Soup, soup, soup. That's all anyone can think about it. When can I get it and why not right now.

I ignore the calls as best I can, which becomes more difficult when the phone starts chiming with Kevin's ring. I'm pleased to find the stamina to ignore his first three calls. I don't succumb to temptation until the fourth. I don't feel too bad about this, though, because I'm in a weakened condition thanks to my recent encounter with a tire iron.

"Oh, good," he says. "I was starting to worry."

"Don't," I say. "I'm fine." I press my tiny phone against my shoulder with my huge, pounding head so my hands are free to continue sorting through papers.

"You don't sound fine."

"That's the thing about fine. You never really know how it sounds."

I take a second to wonder what the hell I meant by this. Kevin doesn't say anything.

"Anyway, what do you want?" I ask.

"I want to know where you are, what you're doing and why pieces of your van are scattered all over Madison Avenue."

I pick up another handful of papers and rip through them. "Kevin, I really don't have time for this. I have to call the insurance company and get the money for the van."

"You just got your head bashed in," he says. "Take a break for five minutes."

"I can't. I need the money right now to pay off . . . some debts."

"What debts?"

"Just some things from before. I really don't feel like talking about it."

"Well, you know I'll help you any way I can," he says. "What needs to be done?"

"By you? Nothing. I need someone I can rely on."

"Don't be ridiculous," he says. "You know you can rely on me."

"I knew that until I was limping along with no delivery people. Now I know nothing."

"Oh, please," he says. "Do you really think those two yahoos delivered all that soup?"

"Why wouldn't I?"

"Because Duncan is an actor and Mark aspires to be one as soon as he learns how to read. They picked me up as soon as the van was out of sight of the restaurant."

"That's not a very nice way to talk about your friends. And anyway, that's not what Duncan told me."

"Like I said, Avery. He's an actor."

By now, I've sorted through the last handful of papers but I've found nothing. This whole ridiculous conversation distracted me so much I skipped right over everything that may have had the insurance company's phone number on it. I throw the papers back to the pile in disgust. "Kevin, I don't know what you're looking for here, but I kind of have my hands full. Did it ever occur to you that not everything in this world is about you?" I exhale loudly and wait for a response.

When he speaks, his voice is ominously quiet. "That occurs to me every day, Avery. Maybe it's something you should try thinking about once in a while."

I sit up and grab the phone so I can speak directly into the mouthpiece. "What are you saying? That this is my fault?"

"Of course not," he says. "Nothing's ever your fault, is it?"

"What in any of this could possibly be my fault?" I'm so angry I'm shaking. I can't believe he could be this nasty after everything I've just been through.

"Let me ask you this, Avery. Do you have worker's comp insurance to cover Duncan's hospital bill?"

I snort through my nose like a bull. It would be just like Kevin McCall to use something like this against me. He is a sanctimonious asshole if I ever saw one.

"In fact," he says. "Did it ever occur to you to get anything like that in your whole self-centered life?"

The room starts spinning. "Leave me alone," I say. "You know I don't have it." My voice breaks and I start crying in great gasping sobs.

"Why not, Avery? Did you miss the appointment while you were out shopping for your Hamptons wardrobe?"

I look wildly around the hovel and try to think of something really mean to say. But nothing comes to me, and it doesn't matter anyway because I don't think I can speak through my tears. I close the phone and crumple to the floor in a soggy heap. I'm really upset, so I don't even bother to get up off the filthy carpet until one of the more brazen roaches crawls right in front of my swollen, stupid face.

I move to the relative safety of the bed and resume my sobbing position. Unfortunately, the crying doesn't come quite as freely this time, so I have to remind myself about how cruel Kevin was and how I can't believe he would talk to me that way after all I did for him and his friends. This activates the waterworks temporarily, but eventually it all seems just a tad too pathetic. I sit up and continue to cry in little hiccups for a few minutes, but even that subsides as the reality of what Kevin said seeps into my piteous consciousness.

I am self-centered. *Self-Centered.* I really had no idea, but it seems totally obvious now that he's pointed it out.

I never really did anything for Kevin and his friends. I just accepted their help when it was offered and paid them for delivery services rendered, which I would have had to do with anyone. I used Fig's apartment for an illegal soup business without any regard to the consequences he might suffer. Well, actually it was worse than that. I had some thought about the consequences, but I went ahead and did it anyway. And I thought again and again about how my administrative neglect of the business could cause some kind of trouble, but I never once got off my ass and did anything about it.

As Kevin so aptly pointed out, I went shopping instead. If that isn't self-centered, I don't know what is.

It's no wonder I'm a social pariah. And I have no one to blame but myself, which is a very bad feeling when you're lying in the gutter waiting to ooze down the drain with all the other sludge no one wants to think about.

I slide off the bed, sort through the papers and call the insurance company to let them know the van was totaled. When I get the check, I'll do the right thing and use the money to pay Duncan's medical bills.

Which means Landlord Bin Laden will still be riding me like a hard-driven camel. I pick up the papers of my failed business, shove them in a plastic grocery sack and throw the sack against the wall. It sticks briefly and then slides to the floor in a rustling little heap. From where it lands, I can see just a few letters of the red Gourmet Gallery logo.

"Go Gal," it says.

Obviously this is a happy little sign that's supposed to inspire me to dig deep and come up with a brilliant solution to all my problems, but I am in no mood for even the tiniest dose of saccharin-sweet cheerleading right now. I turn my back on the bag, fall asleep and dream I'm frantically chopping mountains of vegetables not suitable for display.

When I wake up in the early evening, I remain in bed for a few hours. But I can't sleep because I've slept all damn day. Also, the vegetable dream is sitting in my brain like a big, painful tumor. At this point it occurs to me that caffeine deprivation might be a major factor contributing to this headache problem.

It's almost ten p.m., but there's an all-night Starbucks not far from the hovel. I crawl out of bed, take a shower and get dressed in my pink flamingo track suit.

This ensemble seems somewhat reasonable until I hit the street, at which point it becomes clear that I look like a crazy person. I go back upstairs to change into my Olsen twins outfit, but when I get to the room I remember it's in police custody.

I'm standing in the doorway feeling like a big pink idiot when the "Go Gal" grocery bag catches my eye. Suddenly, just like in a movie, I am struck with a brilliant plan that will solve all my problems. I grab the bag and my computer, go back down to the street and hail a cab.

Starbucks is actually a little crowded. This initially surprises me but I guess it shouldn't. This is the city that never sleeps, after all. Everyone is dressed in jeans and black sweaters so my Pepto-Bismol ensemble seems more than a little out of place.

I ignore the stares and order a tall five-shot latte. Then I spread my papers out on the largest empty table, boot up my computer and get to work preparing financial statements, income projections and a shareholder's agreement for the soon-to-be incorporated business known as Soup in the City, Inc. The caffeine provides enough lubrication to get the project rolling. Once I get into it, I'm shocked to find it's actually kind of fun.

Six hours later, after much espresso and more water, I'm closing up my computer to go to Kinko's when The Tool slides into the seat across from me.

 226

His sleeves are rolled up, his tie is loose and he's more than a little bleary-eyed and boozy. He probably just came from some client thing at a strip club.

He taps his fingers on the table and looks me up and down. "What the hell are you wearing?"

I glance at my pink suit and then look back at him. His chicken lips are curled in the beginnings of a very mean smile. I cross my arms and say nothing.

"You want to get out of here?" he asks.

I look around the Starbucks, which is much emptier now, and down at my computer. "I have some things to do."

"That was an instruction," he says. "Not an invitation."

If he thinks he can order me to go home with him, he can think again. "Excuse me?"

He leans on his forearms, picks up my napkin and stares at it as he rips a long, thin piece off the edge. "I asked if you want to get out of here. Assuming you do, you'll shut up and listen for a second." He looks at me. "This week isn't going so well for you, is it?"

I shake my head.

He goes back to shredding strips off the napkin. I can't believe how many pieces he can take from it.

"Why'd you hang up the phone, Avery? Someone calls asking you for his money, you shouldn't hang up. That makes you look bad." He finishes shredding and crosses his arms. "Irresponsible, even."

"What do you care?"

He just stares at me. Veins bulge out of his neck like a monster and his eyes are way too tiny. I can't believe I ever was attracted to him.

"Did anyone mention a collector to you?"

"Yeah," I say. "I heard about that."

"So what do you want to do?"

I try to speak, but nothing comes out. I take a sip of water and clear my throat. "I'll make it right."

"When?"

"Well, you guys kind of crapped all over my income stream yesterday. Can you give me until Friday?"

"Friday at noon," he says. He stands and knocks on the table in front of me. "And we didn't have this conversation."

"Why?"

"Because it wasn't supposed to be a conversation." He swaggers out of the Starbucks like he's in his old NFL uniform, which I happen to know he still wears around his apartment once in a while.

I used to wear it, too, at least the jersey part of it, and I felt small and fragile and vulnerable. Kind of the way I do right now, except that tonight there's quite a bit more venom in the mix.

I wonder if it would feel good to bite back for once. And whether I have the teeth to get it done.

CHAPTER 13:

Hell Hath No Fury

- - - - - - -

APRIL 23 – 24, 2008

After my all-nighter at Starbucks and a quick stop at Kinko's, I return to the hovel to get ready for my day. Charles Manson whistles as I walk through the lobby.

He must be delirious. It's five in the morning and I'm dressed like a Beanie Baby, so I'm quite certain there's nothing to whistle about. But I smile at him anyway.

"How's your head?"

"Better," I say. "Thanks."

"Must be," he says. "Big night?"

"I was working."

"Oh, yeah," he says. "Right."

He must think I'm one of those prostitutes who have sex with stuffed animals. I think they call them plushies or softies or something. I press the button for the elevator and go up to my room.

I look at the unmade bed and wonder if I have time for some sleep. But it's already Wednesday, which gives me little more than forty-eight hours to put my plan into action.

I decide I can sleep when I'm dead.

I turn on the tap and wait for the tub to fill. This place is very stingy with the hot water so I have some time on my hands. Since I have nothing better to do, I spend the time twisting and pinning my hair into an up-do so elaborate I could hide a Volkswagen in it.

After a quick bath, I apply dramatic eye makeup and simple every-thing else and slip back into my pink track suit.

Then I go to breakfast and coffee. After way too much caffeine, I leave Starbucks, go to a pay phone and call the number on the investigator's business card.

"Tag," he says.

At first I'm confused, but then I look at the card. Tag must be short for his last name, which is Taglianetti. His first name is Benito. Benny Tag would be a good name for a character in a children's book.

"Good morning," I say. "This is Avery St. George. I owned the van that was blown up on Monday."

"Oh, yes," he says. "Thanks for calling."

I wait for him to say something else but he doesn't.

"Well, anyway," I say. "I'm calling because I know who blew it up."

"Who?"

"Why don't we discuss it in person? I could meet you at the Gap on Fifth Avenue across from St. Pats Cathedral at ten."

"How will I know you?"

"I'm wearing a pink flamingo track suit. You can't miss me." I hang up and take a cab to Gourmet Gallery.

I don't recognize any of the clerks when I get there. I walk through the store and find Joe in the back room. He's sitting at his desk pulling his hair out over incomplete time cards.

"Avery," he says. "What's the occasion?"

I plop my Kinko's bag on the desk and sit down in the chair across from him. "A business proposition."

He looks at me and blinks a few times.

"Don't worry," I say. I pull my freshly-printed documents out of the Kinko's bag and separate them by category. "It doesn't involve any time cards."

"What does it involve?" he asks.

"Soup," I say.

"Soup?"

"Yes." I spread the documents out on his desk. "Soup in the City."

The meeting with Joe runs a little long. By the time we've signed on the dotted line, I'm late meeting Detective Taglianetti at the Gap. I rush into the store, which is a ghost town at this early hour, and see him standing awkwardly near the registers. He's wearing a nice sport coat and looks more like an actor playing a cop than a real cop. He has a woman with him, whom he introduces as his partner Detective Henrietta Strug. She's short and sturdy and looks like she means business.

I point in the direction of the fitting rooms. "Can we meet in the dressing room? I just need to pick out some clothes."

They look at each other and back at me.

"I'll be right there." I quickly walk over to the women's clearance rack and select two pairs of jeans. On the way to the fitting room, I grab some white T-shirts and button downs.

I find the detectives just inside, standing around looking bewildered.

I pause at the door of a dressing room while a clerk unlocks it for me. "I'm sorry. I just ran out of clothes and I needed to get some." I look down at my bubble-gum outfit. "Obviously."

Then the clerk leaves and it's just me and the detectives.

Detective Strug pulls a notepad out of her jacket pocket. "So Tag says you have a suspect in Monday's bombing."

"That's right." I point into the open dressing room. "I'm just going to try some things on while we chat if you don't mind." I shut the door and slip out of my track suit.

"Not at all," Tag says. "Take your time."

Detective Strug makes a humph sound in her throat. "Do you mind telling us who it is?"

"I don't know," I say, flinging my pink clothes over the partition. "What kind of protection can you offer me?"

I slide into the first pair of jeans. They fit just fine, so I decide I'll wear them out of the store and take the other pair as well.

"What kind of protection do you need?" Tag asks.

I wrestle with a T-shirt for a second, but drop it in favor of a button-down when it becomes clear nothing is going over this huge hairdo of mine. "Probably a lot," I say, buttoning my shirt. "But I'm willing to wear a wire. Does that help?"

"Why don't we go to the station and talk about it?" Detective Strug asks. "This probably isn't the best place . . ."

I hear a tap on the door. "How are you doing in there?" It's the clerk who helped me get into the fitting room.

I open the door, rip the tags off the clothes I'm wearing and hand them to the clerk along with the other garments. "I'll take all this stuff. Let me give you some money."

"Are you an actress?" the clerk asks.

I nod and dig through my Birkin. "We're rehearsing for a special episode of Law and Order. Sorry for all the commotion."

"No problem," he says. He leaves with the money and the clothes.

I stand against the wall and cross my arms. "I really don't want to go to the station."

"Why?" Tag asks.

"I have no idea. I just don't. I guess it doesn't seem safe."

He smiles at me. "I think you've been watching too many movies."

Detective Strug looks at him and then at me and rolls her eyes at both of us.

Later that day, I'm sitting in the police station wondering why I put on such a wacky little show at the Gap. Clearly, there was no way we were going to organize a reasonable plan to take down the landlord and The Tool from a dressing room on Fifth Avenue. It's very involved, this plan, and requires many interviews, affidavits and running back and forth to someone called the Captain to get permission for this and that kind of wire tap.

The whole time, I'm sitting at Tag's desk sipping iced Starbucks and wondering if I'm a total nut job or just half-crazed from sleep deprivation and a pretty significant dent in my head.

Initially, the detectives insist on using The Tool's given name. But eventually they come around and start referring to him simply as The Tool, which obviously is my preference.

"So tell me again how The Tool threatened you," Tag says. This is about the fifth time.

"It's like I said. He instructed me to pay the landlord and referred to himself as The Collector."

"Do you want us to start calling him that now?" Detective Strug asks wryly.

"No," I say. "The Tool will do just fine." I look at Tag. "Does that seem like a threat?"

"Given the context, it certainly does," Tag says. "Do you think he's the one who physically planted the bombs?"

"How many times are you going to ask her that?" Detective Strug says. "She didn't know five minutes ago and I'm sure she doesn't know now. What is the matter with you?"

Tag sips his coffee and looks around dreamily. "I just can't believe The Tool was so stupid as to strong-arm her at Starbucks like that." He smacks his hand on his desk. "We're going to take this guy down, I tell you."

I have no idea why Tag is so fascinated with The Tool's minimally coercive efforts when it's clear the real problem is the dynamite-happy landlord. But whatever. Tag is passionate about his work, or at least certain aspects of it, and I guess that's all that matters for now.

"Now, Avery," Tag says. "You realize if there are other people involved in this organization, you're putting yourself on pretty dangerous ground, right?"

I nod. It occurs to me that the magnitude of what I'm about to do is what sent me over the edge this morning at the Gap. Maybe I'll get lucky and it'll all be over when the landlord and The Tool are arrested. If there are others involved, maybe they'll scurry like roaches under the harsh light of the law and leave me in peace. But in any case, I am prepared to leave the city for a while until everything blows over.

I spend that night under police protection at a Holiday Inn on Sixth Avenue, where I appreciate the cleanliness much more than the heightened security.

Late the next morning, Tag shows up at my door with a tray of Starbucks, a crew of soundmen and a stylist. The plan is to weave the recording equipment into my hair and to make it virtually undetectable in a razor-wire maze of hairpins.

Before we get started, I call The Tool.

"Hi," I say. "It's Avery."

"What're you doing?"

"Well, tomorrow's Friday." I'm nervous and want to keep babbling, but I force myself to shut up and wait for a response.

"You want to get together?"

"Sure." I count to three. "When?"

"Tonight?"

"Okay," I say. "Where?"

"I don't care. You pick."

"How about that Italian place on Ninth? The little one by the bakery."

"Okay," he says. "I'll meet you at eight."

"Okay, thanks." I hang up and look at Tag.

"Perfect," he says. "Now all you have to do is get him to talk. And keep his hands away from your head."

I sit down in a straight-backed chair and commence the tedious process of becoming bugged.

Later that day, I'm sitting alone in the hotel room wishing I could take a nap. But I can't because it would mess up the wires. And there's not really time for that anyway, because I have to call the Soup in the City clients and let them know we'll be back in business on Monday.

This includes Sheridan Chance, whom I've not spoken to since the day before the bombing. I feel a little bad about ignoring her, which is something I always do to avoid distasteful conversations. Of course, I have a pretty good excuse in that my business exploded and I was hospitalized. Still, I feel kind of sheepish because I'm sure she suffered some pretty frustrating days when she had photographers standing by and no idea where the hell I was.

Also, I know the truth, which is I could have called her even before pieces of the van were hurtling through the sky to let her know I didn't want to proceed with the article.

I put off the call to Sheridan until I have no more clients to call. I get up and walk around the hotel room a few times. Then I return to the bed and dial her number.

She answers right away. "So you're alive. The news said you were, but I didn't quite believe it."

"I'm sorry." I'm tempted to tell her it's been a crazy week or I got hit in the head with a tire iron, but that all seems like bullshit, even though it's true, because it's not relevant to this conversation. "I'm sorry I didn't get in touch with you earlier."

"Well, I'm sure you've had a lot going on," she says. "Do they know who did it?"

"I can't really talk about it because of the police investigation."

"Oh, of course," she says. "Well, anyway, I hope you're doing okay."

"I'm fine. And we'll resume deliveries on Monday."

"Great. So when can we get together with the clients?"

I hesitate for a second. "You still want to proceed with the article?"

"Absolutely," she says. "Now more than ever."

"Oh," I say. "Really?"

"You seem surprised." She seems irritated.

"Well, yeah. I guess I am. I didn't think a van blowing up would be interesting to your . . . readers." I'm glad I didn't use demographic as I initially intended. The word just sounds bitchy no matter how you say it.

"I'm going to play the angry competitor angle," she says. "I think it adds some spice, don't you?"

I'm silent.

"Unless, of course, there's evidence to the contrary," she says. "Obviously I'd never report anything that isn't true."

"I understand."

"So how's tomorrow morning work for you?"

I sigh. "You know, Sheridan. I was really flattered that you wanted to interview me. And I was excited about the article. But it's taken a direction that makes me a little uncomfortable and I'm sorry but I don't think I can find the clients you're looking for."

"Oh, don't worry, Avery. We're not looking for supermodels. Just two or three of the most attractive clients you have."

"Yes, well, that's the problem, actually." I take a deep breath and continue even though I feel like an idiot. "You see, this is the first thing in my life I've ever done that wasn't focused entirely on superficial appearances. It goes a lot deeper than that for me. And I just don't want to do anything that contradicts the fundamentals."

"The fundamentals of soup?"

I can tell she's making fun of me, but I don't care. "Yes. Weight loss is a happy by-product of soup, but it's not the primary objective. The whole idea is to achieve comfort, health and self-acceptance. The weight loss naturally follows from that. I don't want your readers to miss the message."

"Attractive clients can be as comfortable, healthy and self-accepting as unattractive ones," she says. "I really think you're reading too much into this."

"That may be the case, but the fact is there's nothing else to read. There's just page after page of women who look like skeletons and coat hangers. It's very seductive, and I spent years trying to starve myself into one, but it doesn't work and I just can't be involved in it."

She's quiet for a minute. "It sounds like you've made up your mind, then. Thanks for letting me know."

"Yes," I say. "Thank you. And again, I'm sorry for the inconvenience."

She hangs up.

I chuck my phone on the bed and watch it bounce. I feel kind of good but also stupid, like I'm standing on a crumbling principle and everyone is going to laugh at me when I fall on my ass.

But whatever. I certainly have bigger things to worry about today. I get up and go into the bathroom to put on my makeup for my debut performance with The Tool. I was planning to wear jeans, but at the last minute I decide the only thing that matches my huge hair is my jazz-singer dress.

I take the dress out of its plastic sheath and step into it. It fits like it was made for me.

Half-hour before the appointed rendezvous, I leave the Holiday Inn and walk to the Italian restaurant in a very precise route designed to allow the detectives to follow me every step of the way. They are driving an unmarked car that may as well have undercover police written all over it because it's a diarrhea-brown sedan no one but a detective would drive.

There also are a few other federal agent-types following me on foot. I don't turn around but I can feel them loitering behind me. I'm not walking very fast because I'm afraid that generating any wind would cause my big hair to come crashing down.

I feel kind of bad about setting up The Tool like this. Nothing he actually did to me would warrant being arrested, unless of course you count the things he threatened to do to me. But we have to get him so he'll roll over on the landlord, which is important because evidently the landlord is suspected of other, more important bombings, and you just can't have pieces of vans hurtling around like shrapnel in a place as crowded as Manhattan.

I have plenty of time to ponder this because the restaurant is quite a hike from the Holiday Inn. The cross-town blocks feel really long, like football fields. Or maybe even longer than that.

I'm carrying thirty-two thousand dollars in government-provided cash in my Birkin. I'm supposed to engage The Tool in conversation as long as I can, so the police can get as much information as they can, and then hand over the money at the end of dinner. At that point, I'll leave the restaurant and the police will come rushing in and arrest The Tool for various state and federal crimes.

This is obviously going to be the strangest date I ever had with The Tool. For the first time, I'm going to let the check sit on the table. I'm not going to look at it or even think about it. On second thought, if things go too long I might ask The Tool if he plans to buy dinner for once in his life. Or maybe I'll wonder aloud if he'd prefer for the FBI to pick up the check.

When I get there, the restaurant is about half-full. The Tool is sitting at a booth with his crooked fingers wrapped around the handle of a beer mug. He's had many fingers broken in his life, some so often they can't be set properly anymore.

The booth is not my first choice but I'm too nervous to ask him if we can sit by the window. I decide to make the best of it and slide into the seat across from him.

He takes a drink of beer and sets the mug on the table with a thud. "What's with the outfit?"

"I have something to do later. There won't be time to change."

"Like what? The Miss America pageant?"

"Uh, no," I say. "I'm actually working on something."

He looks at me skeptically and takes another drink. I look around for the waiter, hoping The Tool will drop the matter of my dress. "I think I'd like a glass of wine."

The Tool puts his hand in the air and the waiter comes over.

"What do you want?" The Tool asks.

"Chardonnay."

The waiter leaves. I smile at The Tool. "Thank you."

He nods and drinks more beer. I swirl the tip of my tongue around the roof of my mouth a few times so it has something to do besides chatter like an imbecile.

"So what are you working on?" he asks.

"What?"

"What are you working on that requires an evening gown?" He's enunciating like I'm hearing-impaired.

I take a drink of water and try to think of something. "It's open mike night at this club I go to. I'm trying to get a job as a jazz singer."

"You can't sing," he says. "I've heard you in the shower."

"Yeah? Well, Michael Jordan didn't make his high school basketball team, either."

As the words come out of my mouth, I envision the FBI agents in the van outside listening to this drivel. Their reactions are probably pretty similar to The Tool's, who is raising his eyebrows and looking at me like I've just sprouted horns.

"You're out of your mind." He empties his mug and sets it on the edge of the table. "Did you bring the money?"

"We're not having dinner?" I put on my best pout as the waiter sets my wine in front of me.

The Tool waves the waiter away and shakes his head. "I just want the money so I can get out of here. I'm tired."

"Too many collections?"

He laughs.

"Oh, come on," I say. "Why don't you have another beer? For old time's sake."

"Avery, just give me the money."

I click my tongue against my teeth while I think about this. "How do I know what you're going to do with it?"

"What?" he asks.

I take a drink of wine. "How do I know you won't just keep the money? Then I'll still owe the landlord and he'll just keep blowing up my vehicles. I'll just go into the office tomorrow and pay like I always did."

"You think that's how it works?"

"I don't know," I say. "How does it work?"

"I collect the money."

I chew on my lower lip for a second. "Nah," I say. "That's not going to work for me." I stand and pause by the table. "But it was good to see you. I hope we can do this again sometime."

"Sit down," he says.

"What?" My tone is very demure.

"I said sit your ass down."

Suddenly, the way he says ass seems a little too familiar.

"My fat ass?" I ask. This, of course, doesn't sound demure at all.

"What?"

I lean over the table and raise my eyebrows. "Do you want me to sit my fat ass down?"

He looks over and checks out my ass. "It doesn't look that fat to me. But sit down anyway. I mean it."

I hesitate for a second and then sit on the edge of the seat with my feet in the aisle. If the restaurant were really busy, someone would trip over me for sure. "I don't even know what we're fighting about. I have until noon tomorrow, so why can't I just drop off the money with the secretary like I always have?"

"And she'll give the landlord the money?"

I nod.

"Are you really that fucking dumb?"

"I must be," I say. "Because I can't even see what's dumb about that."

He covers his face with his hands and exhales. "I'm your landlord, you dipshit. Haven't you figured that out by now?"

I slide my feet under the table as I turn to stare at him. I feel like I'm getting in a car that's finally going somewhere. "You're my landlord?"

He rolls his eyes. "What did you think? I told you I could find you an apartment without a credit check or a broker's fee. I told you where to drop off the rent. When you kept pretending it was someone else, I played along thinking it was some kind of kinky game you were into."

"How would that be a kinky game?"

"I don't know," he says. "I always thought you were fucking nuts."

"I don't get this at all," I say, shaking my head. "The landlord has a different cell phone number."

He takes two cell phones out of his pocket and chucks them on the table.

"Oh," I say. "So I should give the money to you?"

He just stares at me, like this is too stupid a question to acknowledge, and taps his fingers.

"Well, then. Here you go." I hand him my purse.

He sets it on the seat between him and the wall, opens it and pulls out a brown paper sack. He peeks inside. "It's all there?"

"Yes," I say. "Do you think you can stop blowing up my stuff now?"

"I can do that."

I reach across the table and he hands me my now-empty Birkin.

"Okay," I say. "Pleasure doing business with you. Thanks for the wine." I stand and leave the restaurant feeling like Wonder Woman, Superwoman and Angelina Jolie all rolled into one. Detective Taglianetti holds the door open and smiles at me on my way out.

The sedan is waiting at the curb. I get in and go to the station with Detective Strug, where the police dismantle my up-do and remove all electronic devices.

When they're finished, my hair has amazing volume from all the hairspray plastered into the roots. I linger at the station for a while, but it quickly becomes apparent they have no further use for me.

"Is that it?" I ask Detective Strug.

"You're done." She takes a bite of a ham sandwich and wipes her mouth. "Just keep us informed of where you are in case this goes to trial." She takes another bite and looks down at her paperwork.

Thus dismissed, I am all dressed up with nowhere to go, so I decide to take myself out on reconnaissance in search of an open mike. The mission doesn't last long, however, because barhopping alone is just no fun.

Even for a superhero.

When I return to the hovel that night, Charles Manson is working. I'm beginning to think they never let him go home.

Perhaps, like me, he doesn't have one.

Tomorrow marks the last day of my seven-day rental here. The thought of coughing up another six hundred dollars to stay in the hovel another week is almost as bad as the thought of staying in the hovel another week.

Now that I've partnered up with Joe, I will get a salary from the store, which should help in securing a more suitable dwelling. But there's still the nasty problem of my credit rating. Also, the thought of starting all over, replacing the furniture I abandoned, is so daunting I can't think about it at all.

All I can think about is donuts. I wish I had the energy to go get some.

CHAPTER 14:

All Together Now

- - - - - - -

FRIDAY, APRIL 25, 2008 – THE END

The next morning, I'm awakened by my vibrating phone hopping across the night table near my head.

It's Detective Taglianetti. "I have something for you. Can you meet for breakfast?"

"What time is it?" I hope he's not bringing me flowers or anything like that. He seemed kind of flirty, and maybe I was, too, but that's just because I was nervous and caught up in the drama of it all. Now that our sting is over, I just want to try to get my regular life, whatever that is, back on track.

"Six a.m."

"Are you nuts?"

"Maybe," he says. "But I think you're really going to like this. Trust me."

I consider swearing at him, but it would take too much effort. We agree to meet at a diner near the hovel in thirty minutes.

I get up, splash some water on my face, brush my teeth and throw on my new jeans. When I get to the diner, Tag is waiting at a booth. Thankfully, there are no flowers in sight.

I slide into the seat across from him. "Do you always get up this early?"

"Nah," he says. "Mostly I just want to stay in bed with the covers over my face. Once in a while, though, this job is fun. Like today."

He slides a key across the table at me.

I eye it suspiciously. "What is it?"

"It's the key to the new lock on your apartment."

I look at him and then at the key and then back at him. "How did you get this?"

"The Tool has a warehouse in Queens. We searched it last night for explosives and other evidence."

"And you found this key?"

Tag smiles and nods. "He was cited for wrongful eviction, among other things. You can re-enter your apartment until such time as he manages to evict you properly. But I wouldn't worry about it. He's kind of tied up with other things right now."

I start to reach for the key but then let my hand fall back to my lap. "I'm not sure I want to go back there again."

"Don't be scared. The New York City Police Department would be pleased to escort you." He picks up his menu. "Let's eat. Then we'll go over there."

After a quick breakfast, we're on our way to my old place. When we get out of the car, the sun is shining and it's starting to feel warm outside.

I pause on the sidewalk. Tag holds the door open for me but I'm afraid to enter. "What if it's totally disgusting up there? I'm not sure I want to see it."

"Yes, you do." He puts his hand on my shoulder and nudges me through the threshold. The doorman nods and says, "Detective," as we pass through the lobby.

"You know him?" I ask.

Tag pushes the button for the elevator. "I stopped by earlier to check things out."

We get onto the elevator. "And it's fine?"

Tag nods. "He kind of messed up your things, clothes and stuff, but all the perishables were taken out, so it's not too bad in there. Most abandoned units I enter are a lot worse."

The elevator door opens and we walk down the hall. I turn the key in the deadbolt and open the door.

I walk into the apartment and stand in the living room. It's my apartment, all right, with all my things scattered exactly where I left them. I do not tell Tag this mess is actually mine. The place smells a little dusty but it's nothing a good cleaning won't fix.

I can't believe I'm back in.

"Well," Tag says. "I'll leave you to it."

I turn and look at him. "Thank you so much. This is unbelievable."

He pauses with his hand on the doorknob. "You know, as far as rent goes, it would be completely improper of me to advise you to ignore your contractual obligations. But I will say that you may have a right of offset against a potential civil claim you might decide to file against him."

I try not to smile but I can't help myself. "Are you a law student?"

He laughs. "I graduate next month."

"So you're saying, counselor, that I don't have to pay my rent?"

"I'd never say that. But if you didn't, I don't think he could do anything about it. I'm guessing you can probably stay as long as you like."

"Okay," I say. "I'll do that."

He bows and leaves the apartment.

I spend Friday and Saturday getting settled back into my old place. When I'm finished, the apartment is cleaner and better organized than it ever was.

My old clothes fit me now, although some feel on the verge of slightly too big. Best of all, at Starbucks on Sunday morning, I read in more than one reputable fashion magazine that shoulder pads are enjoying a bit of a comeback.

The only flaw in my happiness is my silent phone. Fig hasn't called and neither has Kevin. But I know I can't expect a happy ending after the way I acted.

Getting my castle back is fairy tale enough. I'll have to grovel for the rest of it, which doesn't bother me at all.

Very early Monday morning, I report for my first day at work as the managing partner of a newly formed joint venture between Gourmet Gallery, Inc. and Avery St. George, fly-by-night entrepreneur.

I get the kitchen staff started on the soup right away so we can resume deliveries immediately. We're also going to offer and sell the soup in the deli case for people who prefer to pick it up when they're in the store.

Joe will handle the administrative end of things, such as dealing with the staff, worrying about vans and other infrastructure issues, and the oh-so-important paperwork crap that I hate. I'm responsible to get the word out about Soup in the City and develop new business. Today this means I have to create some in-store promotional material so we can make existing customers aware of the Soup Diet. This probably will involve a banner that will hang above the deli counter and some kind of brochure or pamphlet that's more detailed than the flyer.

I take a second to make sure the delivery guys know Kevin's mom gets free soup. Then I sit down in the backroom with my laptop and start writing the brochure. After a few hours, it occurs to me I need a lot more room than a few pages to adequately explain everything I've learned in the last few months.

And this is how I come up with the idea for my next project, which is to write a book about how to shed ugly pounds and nasty credit card debt through liberal application of homemade soup.

I'm so excited about this I pick up the phone and call Fig before I remember he hates me.

When I hear the flat way he answers, though, it all comes crashing back.

"All right," I say. "I know you're pissed at me, and you have every right to be, but I have an idea." I tell him about the soup book and ask him if he'll help with the recipes. Fig loves cookbooks and his voice gets a little warmer as the conversation progresses.

The next time I call him, he answers with the cheery upturn at the end of his hello. Just like always.

Fig and I spend the next several weeks hammering out soup recipes in his fancy kitchen. Every night, I go back to my place and work on the other chapters. This is the hardest part of my day, because I find myself wondering if Kevin would like my apartment, or the soup we made that day, or what he would think about whatever it is I'm doing. I'm always tempted to call him and tell him what I'm up to because maybe he'd be proud of me and maybe he might like me again.

But for some reason, I don't think he wants to hear it so I never pick up the phone. I just keep plugging away on the book with Fig.

When we're finished, we present the manuscript and a business plan to Fig's mom and Aunt Candace. They like the idea, especially the part about how a portion of the proceeds will go to soup kitchens in the greater New York area, and agree to front the money for an initial print run of ten thousand copies.

We're on our way. All we need now is a great cover, and I know exactly where to get that. I traipse over to my favorite pool bar on Ninth Avenue to find my favorite pool player.

I peer through the window, spot him at the far table and enter the bar. I'm not sure exactly when he sees me, but when he finishes his shot he puts his cue down and comes over.

"Hey," he says. He puts his hands in his pockets and glances around. "What's up?"

Suddenly, it's clear to me that asking him to design my cover would be the exact wrong thing to do.

"You know," I say. "I was just wondering how you are and what you're up to."

He stares at me for a second. "You never asked me that before."

"I know," I say. "I get it." I bite my lip and nod a few times. "I want you to know I get it. And I'm glad to see you."

He smiles, and I can tell he's glad to see me, too.

ACKNOWLEDGMENTS

No book is born without incredible support from the innocent bystanders in the author's immediate vicinity. Accordingly, I extend my most sincere thanks to:

Anton Webre, the real-life Fig, whose constant reassurance gave me the confidence to quit the jobs that really needed quitting;

David Rothberg, the greatest S&P trader in the world, whose formidable talents keep my little boat afloat;

My sister Mindy Cardwell and my dear friends Rachel McDevitt, Sandy Biondo, Payge Hutchinson and Susan Chandler, who never complain when I serve homemade soup AGAIN and who can always be counted on to tell me exactly what's wrong with the manuscript;

Shira McKinlay and Alla Babikova, my hedge fund girlfriends, who never question the folly of my decision to continue this impoverished author thing, even if it means the end of shopping on Madison Avenue;

My mother Rita Hollingsworth, the best writer I know, who taught me the importance of words;

My father Ken Hollingsworth, who taught me to keep going even when it hurts;

Thad Osburn, my sweetheart, who is supportive in every way, right down to keeping my house from falling down around me.

Thanks also to Rodrigo Corral for designing a beautiful book I'm very proud to call my first.